GETTING ROUGH

C. L. Parker is a romance author who writes stories that sizzle. She's a small-town girl with big-city dreams and enough tenacity to see them come to fruition. Having been the outgoing sort for all her life – which translates to 'she just wouldn't shut the hell up' – it's no wonder Parker eventually turned to writing as a way to let her voice, and those of the people living inside her head, be heard. She loves hard, laughs until it hurts, and lives like there's no tomorrow. In her world, everything truly does happen for a reason.

Visit C. L. Parker online:

www.clparkerofficial.com
www.facebook.com/clparkerofficial
www.twitter.com/theclparker

BY C. L. PARKER

Monkey Business Trio

Playing Dirty
Getting Rough

GETTING
Rough

C. L. PARKER

piatkus

PIATKUS

First published in the US in 2016 by Bantam Books,
An imprint of Random House, a division of
Penguin Random House LLC, New York
First published in Great Britain in 2016 by Piatkus

1 3 5 7 9 10 8 6 4 2

A CIP catalogue record for this book
is available from the British Library.

ISBN 978-0-349-41045-6

Printed and bound in Great Britain by
Clays Ltd, St Ives plc

Papers used by Piatkus are from well-managed forests
and other responsible sources.

This book is dedicated to the good people of Stonington, Maine—specifically, Lance Bradshaw, Thomas Jones, and Kelly Kolysher. I hope I did you justice and that you will one day welcome me back into your warm embrace.

GETTING ROUGH

CHAPTER 1

Shaw

"Simi, where the fuck am I?" I growled into my cellphone.

"I don't know, asshole," would've been an acceptable comeback, given my level of rudeness, but my ever-professional virtual assistant kept her cool. "You're traveling south on Upper Falls Road."

You're, a contraction from a voice-recognition program. Wasn't technology nifty? Nifty, but not a whole lot of help. Left to figure it out on my own, I had to draw only slightly conceivable conclusions. The best I could tell, the flight I'd taken to Bangor, Maine, had somehow veered off course and into the Bermuda Triangle, which I was now convinced was a wormhole to an alternate universe where interstates hadn't yet been invented. That or all of this had been an elaborate scheme that my arch nemesis/part-time lover, Cassidy Whalen, had come up with in order to lure me away to a place where she could continue her torture routine and then eat my liver before dumping my body where no one could find it.

Truthfully, I'd be okay with the slightly creepy murder because being forced to endure that look of pity on her face every day for the foreseeable future was a fate worse than death.

I dropped my phone in the nook next to the gearshift, none too gently, thanks to my mounting frustration. I was exhausted, running on fumes after a ten-and-a-half-hour flight and nearing a two-hour drive. My stomach was gnawing at me from the inside, which I suspected was simply for the sole purpose of going in search of food on its own, since I'd placated it only with airplane peanuts.

Simi dinged, either to warn me to take it easier on her delicate structure or to issue a reminder to bust a right onto yet another state route on my journey through God's country. Thirty-six more miles on winding roads to the island that laid claim to a small fishing village called Stonington. Cassidy's stomping ground. What in the world was I thinking when I'd decided to hop that flight? Oh, right . . . I'd wanted to give her a piece of my mind. But right now, I wanted a piece of chicken to put in my belly.

Making a left into the parking lot of a gas station, I parked the compact rental car I'd been forced into when no other option had been available and got out. The cartoon chicken on the sign in the window shouldn't have made me salivate, but it did. Maybe I was on the verge of delirium because gas station chicken wasn't a smart decision. I'd pay for it later.

The kid behind the counter was patient as I decided between chicken chicken, chicken tenders, or chicken nuggets. As he gathered my tenders and potato wedges, I thought I'd double-check that Simi knew what she was talking about, though I might have used a hushed voice to make sure she couldn't hear me doing so. The last thing I needed was for her to get an attitude about me not trusting her. Women could be so testy. Even virtual women.

"Hey . . . Dale," I started, reading his nametag. "Is it normal for there to be a lot of back roads around here instead of interstates?"

Chicken Dale half-laughed. I guess he got that question a lot. "Yep. Where are you going?"

"Uh, Stonington," I said, taking my boxed meal.

He drew his head back like what I'd said was unusual. "Stonington?"

"Yeah. Why, am I going in the wrong direction? I knew it," I said, adding a curse under my breath.

"No, you're going in the right direction. It's just that no one goes to Stonington unless they're a local."

"Is that a bad thing?"

He laughed again. "Depends on who you ask."

"Great," I said with a sarcastic smile. "Thanks, man." I took my box, noticing the grease stains already soaking through. "I'm not going to die from eating this, am I?"

His shrug and expression said it could go either way. I'd make it, or I wouldn't. Oh, well. We all had to go sometime.

After paying for my heart attack in a box and bottled water, I got back on the road. At least what was supposed to pass for a road, anyway. The winding, unpainted pavement was bad enough, but the bumps along the way reminded me of being a kid in a shopping cart passing over a grooved sidewalk, the vibration from each notch making my *ahhhh* sound like a symphony of vocal acrobats. I might have even tried it out to prove a point, since there was no one else around to see me making an ass of myself. Until my phone rang, that is.

"Hello?" I cleared my throat, trying not to sound so much like a bullfrog was lodged in it. "Ben?"

"Yo, boss man!" came his far too exuberant response. "How's Maine?"

"So far, so shitty. What'd you find for me?"

"Well, there are only two places to choose from and one is

booked, if you can believe that, but I did score you a nice room at the Whalen House."

For some reason a massive migraine decided to strike like a lightning bolt from out of nowhere. "Wait. Did you just say Whalen?"

"Yep. And it's exactly what you think." I could hear the smile in his voice. "Lair of the ice queen, herself. Cassidy's parents own the joint. Per the four-and-a-half-star review, it's a quaint little bed-and-breakfast with a family atmosphere and all the amenities of home. You should fit right in."

I would've growled at him if I'd had the energy. "You're enjoying this, aren't you?"

"A little bit." At least *he* was honest with me. Unlike Cassidy.

"There's no other choice?"

"Nope."

"I'm firing you when I get back."

"Sure thing, boss. In the meantime, I'm pushing Denver's contract through to make everything real nice and legal."

Denver "Rocket Man" Rockford was where all of this had started. Cassidy Whalen and I had been in competition to represent the most coveted quarterback in the league and earn a slice of his pie, along with a partnership at Striker Sports Entertainment. I'd won. On a technicality. Denver had offered the contract to Cassidy first, but she'd turned it down and insisted he give it to me. All after she'd found out I wasn't the rich playboy I'd let everyone believe I was. If she hadn't been so goddamn nosy, so judgmental, so determined to pick me apart like I was a toad spread-eagle on a metal tray, I wouldn't be in a stupid tin can on a fucked-up road heading to a place no one else has ever even heard of.

I shoved my hand inside the greasy box, regretting it instantly when I found the scalding wedges, which must have been pulled from the vat of oil right as I'd walked into the gas station. "Son of a bitch!"

"Okay . . . I can hold it, if you want me to. But I've gotta ask. Are you actually changing your mind about scoring the biggest deal of your life?" I'd almost forgotten Ben was on the phone. Maybe I hadn't been far off the mark with the delirium thing.

"Is that even a real question? Of course not. I just burned myself," I said, sucking on the wounded finger.

"Funny, I didn't feel a thing. *Ba-dum-bum-ching!*" He was a hairsbreadth away from being replaced by Simi.

"Grow up, Ben," I said, taking charge and acting like a real boss. "Book the room, get the contract on Wade's desk, and get me on a flight out of here first thing tomorrow morning."

"You got it. But, uh," he hedged.

"Spit it out." I was quickly losing what little patience I had left.

"Just a heads-up, there's a nasty bit of weather forecasted for Maine over the next few days. Best be prepared for a longer stay, mate."

"Then you better make sure you get me out of here before it does because I have zero intention of sticking around any longer than I have to, so call me with the details once you've got them." With that, I hung up and tried to get my greasy grub on again.

Having zero intention of sticking around any longer than I had to was exactly right, but it wasn't like I had a reason to be here in the first place. Christ, what the fuck was I doing in friggin' Maine? See, Cassidy Whalen had this way about her that got into my head and made me act like a stark raving mad lunatic. Because of that woman, I'd done things I'd never do. Like seduce a co-worker in order to win a contract. Or at least, I'd tried to seduce her. It had backfired. Sort of. But at least I'd gotten my rocks off a time or two in the process, so consolation prize and all. Thing was, I didn't do second place well, and my consolation prize had skipped town and taken her delectable little pussy with her. I wasn't okay with that.

Shit. *Why* wasn't I okay with that? Over the years, I'd built up a wall to keep the crazy out, and bit by bit, she'd been chiseling away at it and making me *feel* things. I shivered, the horror of that thought prancing down my spine like a thousand tiny Cassidys doing their victory dances.

Don't get me wrong, the whole feeling things didn't mean I'd fallen in love with her or anything. No, the things she made me feel were the same emotions I'd left behind the night I'd watched a man get his head blown off right in front of my eyes. I'd been just a kid, but living in Detroit is a game of survival I'd been forced to learn early on. Feelings equaled weakness. And it wasn't like I had parents to shelter me from all that bullshit either. My folks couldn't give a shit whether I lived or died. Hell, they probably would have preferred I'd died because at least then maybe they could collect some sort of check on me.

With a frustrated growl, I shook the fucked-up situation with my parents out of my head because thoughts like those wouldn't further my goals in life. They were behind me. That life was behind me. I'd been moving forward since the day I became a man at the ripe old age of nine. Having no mother to coddle you after you'd just witnessed a brutal, bloody murder sort of put things in perspective. No one was going to take care of that little boy but the man he was meant to be. And the only way anyone could ever hurt me was if I gave them the ammunition to do so.

I'd worked hard to make my way in life. And I'd taken every opportunity I could to further my cause, but being handed a contract that had originally been offered to a fucking woman smarted. It was emasculating. Though I had no intention of backing down from the mother of all contracts, regardless of how I'd gotten it, the first thing I needed to do was reclaim my manhood. And at the moment, Cassidy Whalen was holding my balls in her purse. Once I got them back, I could put her and all the touchy-feely stuff behind me once and for all.

Deer Isle–Sedgwick Bridge loomed before me like a four-hundred-foot iron sentry that would either grant access to my destination or turn into a rolling and twisting amusement park ride to dump me into the waters of Eggemoggin Reach below. Obviously, the amusement would not be mine. But as luck would have it, I crossed without issue. The steel suspension cables even stayed in place, and I was fairly certain the ominous laughter I'd thought I'd heard had been only my imagination having playtime with the natural creeks and groans of metal on metal. Christ, I needed some sleep before the boulders scattered about the land-scape turned into rock people frolicking through blueberry fields.

Rock people did not exist. Just like the bumps in the road were not made by genetically altered super mole spies with ninja reflexes sent to keep track of me, and the sandbar supporting the causeway to Deer Isle would not turn into quicksand to suck me down to Middle Earth. But my phone *was* ringing.

"Shaw Matthews," I answered, grateful for the distraction. My sleep-deprived brain needed to save the neurons still firing some-where inside in order to help me keep my wits about me when I finally came face-to-face with the little piggy that had gone "wee, wee, wee," all the way home. I had a thing or two to say to her, and I was perilously close to forgetting both thing one and thing two.

"Hey, bro! Whatcha doing?" Chaz asked from the other end of the line.

"I can't be sure, but I think I'm driving through one of the seven gates to hell." Actually, I was fairly certain, but my sleep deprivation probably meant my judgment was questionable. "What's up, man?"

"Just wanted to give you a heads-up to tell you that you might want to keep your head down."

What Chaz had just said made perfect sense to me, which was proof positive that I had, in fact, crossed over into an alternate universe. "Do tell," I said, prepared for just about anything at this point.

"The girls and Quinn are catching a flight to Maine to be with Cassidy. It's supposed to be a surprise, so don't say anything to her or Demi's gonna put my nuts in a sling."

"Join the club," I said, still picturing my own boys in Cassidy's purse. I ignored his questioning response and instead opted to move the conversation along. "So why do I need to keep my head down?"

"Because they know you're already there."

Even so, it made no sense. Quinn had been the one to give me Cassidy's flight information in the first place, telling me to go after her. Only because he thought there was something romantic going on, which he was wrong about, but still, it had gotten me the information. Oh, shit. They'd probably figured out I was the cause of their bestie's quickie departure in the first place. Great. The last thing I needed was to have two pecking hens and a feminine-sympathizing cock to add to the little piggy I was already trying to hogtie and put back in the barn. What was I, Old fucking McDonald?

"All right, man. Thanks for the warning." I sighed. "With any luck, I'll be gone before they get here. I'm leaving first thing in the morning."

"What are you doing there, anyway?"

"I've been asking myself the same question."

"Well, that's answer enough, isn't it?"

"What? I don't follow."

"Dude, you jumped on a plane . . . Maine . . . girl . . ." His call had some serious breaks in the line.

I pulled back to look at my phone, showing only one wavering bar. I must have been driving through a dead zone, but I put the phone back to my ear. "Chaz? Hey, man, you there?"

The three beeps in my ear and "Call Failed" screen meant he wasn't. Oh, well. I'd call him back later because if the ocean on the horizon was any indication—and I was pretty sure the compact car I was driving wasn't going to Chitty Chitty Bang Bang into a boat—it looked like I'd reached my destination. Not that Simi had done her fucking job and told me so. *Pfft*, technology.

Popping over the hill and following the main road down to the small village nestled below, I couldn't help but be mesmerized by the simplicity of it all. It was like stepping onto the set of a fictional town in a movie or a book. I never knew places like this actually existed, but there it was.

The street corners were not home to Starbucks or McDonald's. There were no Walmarts or Targets. No shopping malls or gas stations. Not even a traffic light. Main Street was home to a handful of boutiques, one locally owned and operated diner, a convenience store, and a singular bank. But the hustle and bustle was concentrated at a dock, the hub of it all. A dock loaded down with just about every make and model of truck ever produced in the good ol' U. S. of A.

Just past the Opera House—"Wait. They have a fucking Opera House?" I asked myself incredulously—I made a left off School Street and onto West Main, where a giant, weathered sign in need of a fresh coat of paint told me I'd finally reached my destination. I parked on the side of the road, turned off the ignition, and unfolded myself out of the little windup-toy car. How clowns got so many of themselves into one during their circus act, I'd never understand.

Stepping out onto the sidewalk, I stretched and inhaled a deep breath of fresh air. Well, it wasn't so much fresh as it was fishy and sodium based, but it was natural all the same. My lungs must have been too used to the carbon footprints left behind by big-city living because the resulting cough attack had me scared shitless that I'd never breathe again. Once the spasm was over, I took a look around to be sure no one had seen me, and was struck dumb by the scenery.

Fishing boats moved in and out of the harbor, a flock of seagulls hot on their water trails. The sound of engines and horns, the call of the birds, and the stray shouts between fishermen as they passed one another was almost a lullaby compared to the harsh noise of the city. Islands of all sizes were scattered throughout the bay and beyond like a treasure map awaiting exploration. But most impressive was the horizon beyond. It was like a painter's canvas of blue skies the color of a baby's eyes, and streaks of sunlight penetrated marbled white clouds as if the fingers of a young god were playing with toy boats in a tepid bath.

Cassidy Whalen had been born inside a postcard and had stepped right out of it like a two-dimensional character brought to three-dimensional life. Rarely had I ever taken note of the splendor of such things. Maybe that was because I'd always been in a hurry, thanks to the fast pace of city life, but something about this backdrop forced me to stop and take notice. Chick-ish moment aside, I was in awe.

I took out my phone to call Ben to let him know I'd arrived and did a double take when I spotted the words NO SERVICE in the top corner where there should've been full bars.

Holding my cellphone in the air, I did a three-sixty. "No service? Is that even possible with today's technology?" I sighed in defeat and shoved my phone back into my pocket. Forget the postcard. I was in *The Twilight Zone*.

Looking around again, I shook my head at how easily I'd been duped. Like Cassidy, the small town was beautiful and nonthreatening, a succubus luring its prey with a false sense of security, and then *blammo!* You were under her spell with no choice but to submit to her will until she sucked the essence from your soul and then discarded your rotting corpse. Luckily for me, I'd figured it out way before it was too late, which was a miracle in and of itself considering my level of exhaustion.

Behind me, the Whalen House stood proud atop an incline that overlooked not just the harbor but the entire town. And I used the word "town" loosely. How fitting that it should be the place the great counselor, Cassidy Whalen, called home. Obviously, the high and mighty perch from which she passed judgment had been one she'd inherited at birth. I wouldn't be a bit surprised if I walked inside to find out her father was the town's judge, jury, and executioner.

If I'd been in my right mind, I would've turned around and made my way back to civilization. But again—thanks to the sleep deprivation—I'd traded out "right mind" for "one hallucination short of a padded cell" a long time ago. The one and only order of business at the moment was to make it inside and into a warm, comfortable bed to capitalize on some much-needed downtime for my brain. After that, I'd say my piece to the she-devil and then I'd make my hasty escape back to some normalcy in San Diego with my new and very lucrative partnership at Striker Sports Entertainment and an extraordinarily exceptional life.

Yep, everything I'd worked so hard for was just sitting there waiting for me to come live the dream. . . . As soon as I could get free of the nightmare.

CHAPTER 2

Cassidy

Life was a funny thing. All those inspirational sayings about how we are in control of our own destiny, that we have the right to choose which direction we take during our journey to the end, were a crock of manure.

Rarely had anyone born in my town ever left. If they did, they returned within a couple of years, max. The culture in Stonington was so unlike the culture anywhere else that the natives found it hard to exist outside of it. The rules were different; the way people thought was different. It was like being dropped in the middle of an ocean and being told to sink or swim. Without ever having the first swimming lesson.

I'd done it. I'd taken control of my own future, and I'd gotten out of Stonington, Maine. And not only had I learned how to swim, but I'd grown fins and gills. Yet this town had managed to suck me right back in anyway. I was not the master of my own destiny; I was a slave to my fate. I'd left behind everything I'd worked so hard for, only to return to a place I'd fought so hard to leave. Like an overprotective mother, Stonington had a way of grabbing ahold of its children, smothering them with her breasts, and refusing to let them go. I was simply the headstrong daughter determined to forge her own way.

The short trips I'd made home for visits in the past had been safe. Mostly because they were preplanned trips, with a definite date of departure that was nonnegotiable. This time that safe-guard wasn't in place. I had no idea how long I'd need to stay to see my ma and da through this crisis, but I was sure if Stonington had her way, I wouldn't be leaving anytime soon. It was a risk I had to take for my family. They were more important than any partnership or any client or any egotistical asshole with a giant chip on his shoulder who just happened to give cosmic orgasms.

It was an emergency phone call during the biggest moment of my life that had sent me dashing across the country in a hurry to get to my hospitalized mother. When Da had picked me up from the airport, he'd assured me she was fine, but warned that she looked much worse than she actually was. He'd been right. Ma looked like she'd gone through a twelve-round bout with the heavyweight boxing champion of the world and had come out on the losing end. The broken bones and concussion she'd sustained only further substantiated my analogy.

Despite the fact that I was sitting in a hospital—which always gave me the creeps—something felt off, unsettling. Every time I tried to pinpoint the cause of my uneasiness, Shaw Matthews's stupid face kept popping up in my mind, compounding my rest-lessness. Perhaps it was because there'd been no closure there. Not that it should matter. It wasn't like we were an item. Far from it. But I couldn't help the confusion over my inability to define the freaking relationship that I think I had with him in the first place. It was just sex, right? And if that was the case, why did I feel the need to check in with him? Explain to him that I'd landed safely, fill him in on how my mother was, and give him some sort of guesstimate as to when I might return. Because I was the blooming idiot who'd found herself back in Nowhere, USA, with little to no hope of ever escaping to civilization again.

"You all right, kiddo?" The gruff voice of my father suspended my internal ramblings and I glanced up to catch him studying me, concern furrowing his brow. My own gaze roamed over his familiar features and noted the many differences since my last visit. The old man's red hair was thinner and his beard was in need of a trim, but his barrel chest and potbelly were the same as always. Ma had been keeping him well fed, as usual. When I didn't answer, he looked at me with that weathered face. The squint to his eye had nothing to do with his curiosity and everything to do with his failing eyesight.

"I'm fine, Da. Just a little tired." On cue, a yawn snuck up on me and I stretched it out. "I see you're still not wearing your glasses."

"Bah," he scoffed, waving me off. "There's no place for those damn things on a lobster boat. Proved that when the last pair fell right off my face and into the ocean where they belong."

"Fell off, or got tossed off?" He wasn't fooling anyone.

Da shrugged. "What difference does it make? Somewhere out in the deep blue, a real-life Incredible Mr. Limpet is patrolling the ocean and keeping our country safe from enemy attack. You're welcome," he said with a wink.

I laughed because I couldn't help it. Leave it to my da to make accidentally on purpose losing his glasses a patriotic contribution. Duff Whalen was set in his ways and was fighting growing old with every breath in his body. It was one of the reasons he was still fishing when he should've been retired. He swore it kept him young and healthy. Truthfully, he probably had a point, though I'd never tell him that in front of Ma.

As if she could sense the conspiratorial thought—and she

probably could—Ma stirred in her sleep, her eyes opening just enough for me to see the caterpillar green of her irises. I might have inherited the ginger hair and short temper from my father, but Ma was the benefactor of my eyes and willfulness. A willfulness that had landed her butt in the hospital with a broken leg, a couple of cracked ribs, and some scrapes and bruises. Thank God it hadn't been worse.

"Hey, sleepyhead. You okay?" I asked, sitting up to brush a graying lock of hair from her face.

"Cassidy, you're here." Her smile was groggy, the prescribed painkillers forcing her to take a much-needed nap to help her body heal. It was a good thing, too, because otherwise Anna Whalen would've been out of that bed and walking the twenty-five miles back to Stonington to tend to her guests.

"You know, if you wanted to see me, you could've just called and asked me to come. You didn't have to go to this extreme."

Medicine-induced semicoma or not, it didn't stop her from quirking a sarcastic brow. "Didn't I?"

Here we go. I sighed. "Ma, don't start with the guilt trip, okay? You know how busy I am."

"Yes, I know. I really wish they hadn't called you in the first place. I'm fine. You should go back to California before you're missed. I wouldn't want my little accident to be the cause of some major catastrophe, like one of your fancy clients not having his favorite bottled water on the set of a commercial shoot for some athlete's foot something or other."

Jesus, she really knew how to lay it on thick, but I wasn't going to let her avoid a much-deserved interrogation by pointing out all my shortcomings as a daughter. "Oh, you're fine?" I challenged. "So you're in the hospital because . . . ?"

"Because you two are a bunch of overprotective hens who can't tell that these doctors are only trying to milk my insurance company out of more money than they've any right to. Can I go home now?"

I laughed with a shake of my head. "That would be a big, fat no."

"Well, why not?"

"Because you have an issue with your blood pressure, which you knew before you decided to go on a little adventure. Said issue is what caused the dizziness that led to the fall in the first place. And as a result, the doctors want to keep you here another night."

The information didn't sit well with my mother. Not that I'd expected it would. "I'm not staying here another night. I have guests to attend to." She started to pull the covers back as if she was going to get out of bed, but I stopped her.

"Oh, no you don't. Abby's taking care of them just fine without you there, and I'm going to relieve her in a bit. Right after I make the doc explain why the medication he gave you for your blood pressure hasn't been working."

Ma's gaze dropped to the covers and she occupied her hands by smoothing out nonexistent wrinkles in the sheets. If I hadn't already sensed her guilt, Da's reaction would've been a dead giveaway. He could always read her like a book.

"Damn stubborn woman. You haven't been taking your medicine, have you?" He threw his hands into the air as if he already knew the answer.

My mother shrugged. "Not as often as I should."

"Why not?" I asked.

She looked ashamed, an apologetic glance at my father preceding her words. "Because we can't afford all the medication we have to take between us and still be able to keep the bed-and-breakfast running."

"Oh my God. Are you kidding me right now?" I asked, flabbergasted. Turning toward my father, I asked, "Did you know anything about this?"

His face drew up in disgust. "Hell no! Do you think I would've let that happen if I did?"

It hadn't been my intention to insult my father, but I had. "I'm sorry. Of course I know you wouldn't." I whipped my head around and focused my attention where it belonged. "Ma, why didn't you say something?"

"Because I didn't want anyone to know. It's my fault. This stupid recession has affected the tourism in Stonington and we need to keep the house open because it's not just a source of income; it's the roof over our own heads. So I cut some corners. I figured if I took my medicine every other day, it wouldn't matter so much and I could stretch out the prescriptions until things got better."

"Oh, you figured that, did ya?" Da grumbled from his chair. His face was flushed, the top of his ears a ripe tomato red, and I worried that his own blood pressure was peaking at a dangerous level.

"Should I ask if you've been taking your medicine, too, Da?"

My father brushed off the question with a casual wave of his hand, ignoring me and staring down his wife instead. "You also figured you'd climb up on the ladder, didn't ya? Look where that landed ya."

Ma huffed. "Well, someone had to clean out the gutters."

"And I told you I'd do it when I got home, woman." Da's face was beginning to tinge red with his insistence.

"Mmhmm . . . Just like you fixed the antenna? People aren't going to want to stay at a bed-and-breakfast that can't even offer them good reception on the television set."

"Why can't you just admit that you climbed up there because you wanted to be able to watch your stories? That's exactly the reason you wouldn't wait. Damn near killed yourself over it."

I closed my eyes, knowing what Da said was true, but hoping it wasn't. "Ma, please tell me that's not why you did it." Not that she needed to. She was obsessed with her soap operas. Stonington was one giant, real-life soap opera of its own, sans the cameras, lighting, and sound equipment. And I wouldn't put it past some of its residents to have some, if not all, of that setup to keep tabs on their neighbors.

Ma turned toward me, and the bruise to her cheek made me cringe. If anything had happened to her . . .

With a sigh of concession she said, "Well, you know . . . two birds, one stone and all."

"Ah, jeez, Ma. I can't believe you!"

My exasperated chastisement was cut off when a new voice joined the conversation from the door to the room. "What's that saying about the pot calling the kettle black?"

I knew that voice. It was the sort of deep and gravelly with a smoky undertone that couldn't be faked or replicated, and its calm strength had given me comfort when I'd most needed it throughout my life. I closed my eyes to gather my wits about me before I opened them again and turned toward the sound.

He stood in the doorway, leaning against the jamb with his hands tucked into the front pockets of a pair of faded jeans that knew his body better than he knew it himself. His legs were crossed at the ankles, scuffed logger boots showing the wear and tear of a job that had defined his life. A navy blue button-down was left open to reveal the black T-shirt he wore beneath, clinging to pecs developed by years of lobstering, not time spent in the gym. And the crinkles at the corners of his eyes were etched there by nearly three decades of sun exposure and genuine smiles.

"Casey . . ." The last syllable of his name sounded like the air being let out of a tire, only the tire was my lungs, and I was completely breathless. My heart raced, punching at my already-constricted chest like it wanted desperately to break free and run into his arms.

Casey's left cheek lifted with the corner of his mouth for a lopsided grin, which he topped off with a wink that made my breath catch. "Where you been all my life, darlin'?"

Jesus, there was something about Casey Michaels that always made me go weak in the knees and get all girly. It was an involuntary reaction no other man had ever been able to evoke from me. I didn't hate it, but I couldn't say I liked it, either. It was fine, maybe even cute when we were kids, but as a grown woman, I preferred to feel like I had at least a modicum of control over my own body's reaction to a person's presence.

If the way my feet sent me flying across the room and into his arms before my thoughts could fully process what was happening was any indication, it was clear that control was something I lacked.

Casey caught me—because he always would—and I buried my face in his neck, breathing him in. That familiar aroma of salty air, motor oil, and hard work was a combination that couldn't be bottled, but would always be home. I was safe, though I was confused as to why knowing that was such a relief. What did I need safety from?

The question I asked him was muffled thanks to the tight hold I still had on him and my refusal to let go for fear he'd disappear if I did.

Casey laughed and nudged me back a little. "I have no idea what you just said, but my answer is yes, darlin'. It'll always be yes."

"You will? You'll have my babies?" My voice was laced with a fake hopefulness that Casey would undoubtedly understand, because he got me like no one else ever would.

My oldest and dearest friend, who just happened to also be the man of my dreams whom I'd chosen to leave behind in favor of a career, looked away with a wince. "Damn, it's gonna hurt when

I try to push them out," he said, almost contemplatively, before he turned back to me, his mind made up. "But you're worth it."

We both laughed, as did Ma and Da.

"Seeing you two together and still acting silly is making me feel so much better already," Ma said, sitting up.

I narrowed my eyes suspiciously. "Nice try, old woman."

Ma gasped. "Casey, don't let her be so mean to her mother," she said, pouting.

Casey threw his hands up into the air as he crossed the room to her. "You know she's just going to do the opposite of what I say, Anna. I figured that out our freshman year when I tried to talk her out of trying out for the football team. She was too hardheaded to listen."

Leaning down, he kissed Ma on the cheek as she said, "Not hardheaded enough. She got knocked unconscious during the first practice. Served her right for not acting like a lady. I blame you, Duff," she said, pointing at her husband. "Always rough-housing her and treating her like the son you never had."

"What did you want me to do about it, woman? She liked football better than dolls and tea parties. And that was just fine by me. Look at her now. My girl is representing the best of the best, and can get me any autograph I want." Da gave me a nod of his head as if to say he was proud of me. I knew he was. Neither of my parents ever missed an opportunity to tell me so.

I groaned, tired of being in the spotlight. "Enough about that. What are you doing here, Casey?"

"You're my favorite girl, Cass. Where else would I be?"

Every girl in town wanted Casey Michaels, and I was his favorite. That kind of untouchable status tended to make a girl feel special. But we were no longer together, so I didn't want to send mixed signals.

"Ah, that's sweet, but you could've seen me in town when

they release Ma in a couple of days." Because of that whole "not wanting to send mixed signals" thing, I couldn't tell him that I was glad he was there then and now. There was something to be said for knowing your safe harbor was within reach when a chaotic ocean was tossing around your insides like a boat headed for a rocky shore. *Thank you very much, Shaw Matthews.*

Da jumped in, pulling me back to the business at hand. "You're not staying here another night. The boy's here to take you home."

"To San Diego?" I was confused, and pretty sure I hadn't purchased a round-trip ticket. I'd been prepared for the worst case, so had everyone else, but Ma was a tough cookie. Still, she'd be out of commission for quite some time and I'd need to stick around to help out for a while.

"You can only have one home, and San Diego ain't it, kiddo." Da strained to get up, the chair creaking right along with his own aging bones. "Stonington is. Always has been, always will be.

"I'm perfectly capable of staying here and taking care of my wife, but my patience is too thin to be waiting on a bunch of strangers hand and foot and cleaning up after them. So you go do that, and I'll bring her home when she's able. Or when they kick us out because she's nagging too much."

"Duff Whalen!" Ma scolded him.

"See? It's already started," he said.

I didn't feel right about leaving Ma in such a vulnerable state, but I knew Abby would need the relief. It was my duty as the daughter to step in and take control until Ma was back on her feet, and I wouldn't let them down. Besides, it wouldn't do a bit of good to argue with the old man. Truthfully, I was too exhausted to anyway.

Casey took my chin between his fingers and stooped to eye level. "You look tired," he said, still able to read my mind as if our brains had been connected by cables. And then he gave me a conspiratorial smile that said he knew I was in need of rescue even though I'd been back only a short time. "Come on, let's get you out of here."

I returned his smile. Because he was my knight in shining armor. Because he always put others before himself. Because he was *my* Casey. Because he wasn't Shaw Matthews.

The short forty-minute drive to Stonington seemed like twice that. Maybe it was because with each mile that brought us closer, the further we seemed to warp back in time. For me anyway. Stonington was my past. Casey Michaels was my past. Yet there he sat to my left, a vacant distance between us, like someone else was occupying the space and keeping us apart. My own emotions started to warp through time as well, those timeworn but familiar feelings and habits threatening to resurface. The old Cassidy would've reached across the space that separated us to take his hand. She probably would've even scooted across the seat to snuggle into his side and drape his arm across her shoulders. It would've been easy to do. As easy as breathing and just as natural. Sort of like slipping back into a favorite pair of faded jeans and an oversized sweatshirt after a long and stressful day. And God was I ever tempted to do it.

But I wasn't that Cassidy anymore. The Cassidy I'd become felt the tension in the air, and it was so uncomfortable that it was almost claustrophobic, as if I was sharing a confined space with a stranger. How was that possible when this stranger knew me better than anyone else ever would?

Casey and I had grown up with each other. Our parents were the best of friends. They had done everything together. *We* had done everything together. From childhood playmates that laughed, cried, and fought—not only for but also because of each other—to teenage lovers who explored everything else together. He knew my most intimate secrets and I knew his darkest fears. Our lives were more intertwined than the knotted roots of a century-old oak tree, and the bond every bit as strong.

A prickling of awareness danced across my skin. I knew he was staring at me, but for some reason I was paralyzed at the neck, unable to do anything but look straight ahead. Maybe it was a defense mechanism, a trick of the brain for my own good; one meant to keep me grounded and looking forward instead of back. After all, Casey was Stonington's secret weapon.

"So, are you going to tell me what's wrong, or do I need to tickle it out of you?" Casey reached across the space I'd been unable to breach to lightly poke me in the ribs.

I flinched with a playful giggle, more for his benefit than mine. It was just like my childhood boyfriend to use silly antics to lighten the mood and defuse what was quickly shaping up to be an awkward situation.

"Stop." I smiled and batted his hand away. "What do you mean what's wrong? Isn't it obvious? Ma's in the hospital."

"And?"

"And I'm worried about her."

"Bullshit," was his simple response.

"What, bullshit?"

"You saw for yourself that she's fine."

"She hasn't been taking her medicine. It bothers me that they haven't had the money for it and didn't ask me for help."

"Cass, have you really been gone so long that you've forgotten how proud islanders can be? Come on, darlin', you're one of us, and probably the most stubborn. What would you have done if you were your ma?"

While it was true he had a point, it didn't mean I had to like it. "I would've tried to figure it out on my own, too, I guess."

"Oh, I know you would have," he said with a confident grin, and then the grin fell as his brows furrowed and he looked at me, then the road, and back to me again. "Something else is wrong. What's going on in that beautiful mind of yours?"

I shook my head. "Nothing."

For some reason, the question immediately brought back the memory of Shaw's face the last time I'd seen him. Which was in an empty apartment he'd kept for pretenses only. I'd confronted him on his secret life, a life I'd made it my business to expose only to end up feeling terrible for having reopened a wound he'd tried to keep closed. For all his posturing, he had been nothing more than a fraud. He'd made everyone believe he was something he wasn't: a self-made man with enough money to show off, unprecedented influence, and a celebrity list of friends and clients that made him nearly as famous as they were.

In reality, Shaw Matthews was an underprivileged kid who'd been forced to survive the unsympathetic streets of Seven Mile in the heart of Motor City, USA. And he'd never known the love of a parent. It was sad and pathetic, through no fault of his own. And I'd passed judgment on him, assuming things I'd had no right to assume. I didn't know anything about the man I had shared my body with—repeatedly—but never my heart. And while I was busy fucking him on almost every available surface, my parents had been enduring a financial struggle I'd known nothing about.

Oh, how the self-righteous will fall.

"Stop being so hard on yourself," Casey said, again reading my thoughts. Which had me wondering how much he could see. If he knew about all the things I'd done to Shaw, all the things I'd let Shaw do to me, it would break his heart.

I tilted my head and looked at him, trying to see if I could get a read on whether or not he was involved with anyone. But Casey was a master of disguise, quick with a distraction if he thought someone was trying to figure out something about him that he wasn't ready to let him or her know. His go-to diversion for me was yet another one of his famous winks, the one that made all the island girls swoon. That and his sexy smile were a lethal combination to any human with a vagina. Maybe it wasn't just humans.

"Is that the smile you use to make all those she-lobsters throw themselves into your traps?" It had been a running theory among the locals that Casey's success at lobstering was due to his flirtatious nature with crustaceans of the female variety.

Casey's head fell back with a hearty laugh. "You're back in town for all of a day, and you're already making jokes, huh? What's the matter? You jealous?"

"Not in the least. You might want to watch out for that crusher claw, though. Pretty sure it would be murder on the genitals. Unless you're into that sort of thing."

We both got a good chuckle out of that, and it felt damn good. Normal. For the first time since I'd landed, I was carefree again. That was my Casey. He was the only person who'd ever been able to successfully pull off the "simmer down, miss" with me. And he made it look so easy when even I knew it wasn't.

"Maybe you should take one back to California, sneak into your boy's, Shaw's, place when he's sleeping, and slip it under the covers with him. With any luck, he sleeps in the nude. That'll teach him to mess with you, huh?"

And just like that, my happy bubble burst—right in my face—leaving me feeling sticky and uncomfortable. No matter how I tried to block that man from my thoughts, I couldn't escape. Even Casey, whom I considered my safe haven, was speaking his name and causing all sorts of doubts to rise to the surface. What was he doing in my absence? *Who* was he doing? Probably a couple of beach babes with collagen-filled lips, hot pink fingernails, and bleach-blond hair on a yacht he spent a year's salary on just so he'd look good to anyone who might be watching. The pompous, superficial bastard.

"Damn, darlin'. What did he do to you?"

I turned back around to find Casey staring at my white-knuckled fists balled up in my lap. Embarrassed by my reaction, I released the hold and placed my palms down on the seat instead.

"I'm sorry. It's nothing."

"That didn't look like nothing to me."

"Shaw got the partnership," I admitted. It wasn't the full truth, but close enough for me not to feel guilty. "I guess I'm a little resentful of it."

"Oh, shit. I'm sorry to hear that. I know how much you wanted it."

Yeah, I'd wanted it pretty bad. According to Shaw, I'd wanted it bad enough to sleep my way to the top. Though that wasn't at all what had happened, nor was it ever my intention to do so. I had done something much worse. I'd slept with Shaw. Multiple times. And whether I wanted to admit it or not, I'd started to care about him. Maybe a little too much.

God, how could I be so stupid?

I must have said that last part out loud because Casey reached over and took my hand, sending jolts of warmth to my very core. "You're the smartest person I know, Cass. Whatever happened, I'm sure it wasn't anything you could see coming or you would've cut it off at the pass. You're crafty like that."

I couldn't bring myself to tell him the truth, that Denver Rockford had chosen me to be his agent and that I'd won the partnership, but couldn't accept the win because of the call for me to come back to Stonington. Even though it wasn't something within Casey's control, I knew he would still count it as a failure on his part. He always had and always would feel responsible for me.

I rested my head against the cold glass of the window. God, I was tired.

"There's more. Talk to me, babe."

My head bobbed back and forth with the bumps in the road. "It's just . . . It doesn't matter anymore."

"I hate to break it to you, darlin', but it sure sounds like it does."

We started the descent into downtown Stonington and nostalgia took over. Nostalgia and claustrophobia. "No, it doesn't. Shaw Matthews is no longer an issue in my life. I have more important things to worry about, like getting Ma better so I can just go home."

"Same ol' Cassidy. Always running away." Casey gave a lighthearted laugh, but I felt the weight of his comment.

"I didn't run away," I mumbled, because I really didn't want to have the same conversation we'd already had, like, a million times.

Sensing my mood, Casey suddenly changed the subject. Thank God. "So we have a celebrity in town," he told me with a giant starstruck grin. I'd never pegged Casey Thomas for a fan girl.

A snort of "yeah right" escaped me. "Funny. Celebrities vacation in places like Aspen or Bora Bora, not Maine."

"They do when they're an author looking to get away to finish a book that just happens to revolve around a sexy lobster fisherman looking for love," he said with a waggle of his eyebrows.

"Oh, yeah? Well, she's definitely in the wrong place for that," I said, and laughed.

"Hey!" Casey chastised, only slightly offended. "I can be sexy." He flexed his pecs Dwayne "The Rock" Johnson style, and all I could do was shake my head and laugh again.

That was my Casey. God, I'd missed him.

CHAPTER 3

Shaw

Sleepapalooza had been one of those events during which I was so out of it that I'd never recall the time I'd lost. Though I was sure my very long trip cross-country had been the true culprit, the amazingly comfortable bed I'd found myself in when I awoke surely hadn't helped matters. Neither had the soft sounds of boat whistles, waves, and bird cries from just outside the picture window in my room. A room I hadn't even had the chance to check out before I'd fallen face-first into bed . . . how many hours ago?

I managed a stretch across the distance to the bedside table to turn the alarm clock toward me. Shit. 10:00 A.M. I'd been out for more than twelve hours. My arm dropped like deadweight and I closed my eyes again, wanting nothing more than to double that time, but I knew I had a flight to catch and one hell of a drive before I'd make it back to the airport, and none of that was happening before I had a chance to face off with a certain Cassidy Whalen.

Hauling myself out of bed with a groan and a stretch, I made my way across the room, feet dragging and all, to take my cellphone off the charger and check my messages. Damn, but I'd forgotten the zero cell service shit. Luckily, Wi-Fi at least enabled me to get an iMessage to Ben for my flight information, which he should've already sent to me, I was sure to point out. After pressing the send button, I hit the shower.

When my phone dinged, I abandoned my watery haven and crossed the room, stark naked and dripping wet, only to find a screenshot message from Ben with the flight information he'd sent exactly as he should have. Only, for some reason it'd never made its way to me. And I'd already missed my flight. I was a giant ass for getting in his face when I should've known better. So I shot him a very rare apology and told him to hold off on making other arrangements until I had a better idea of when I could make it to the airport. I hadn't had my say with Cassidy, and I wasn't about to leave until I did. I just had to find her first.

By the time I was fresh, pressed, and dressed, I felt halfway human again. I even had a little pep in my step with the realization that the element of surprise was on my side. Cassidy had no clue I was here, in her town, right under the same roof where she'd grown up. I had to admit it made my dick hard, which just meant I was looking forward to seeing her that much more.

The aroma of fresh-baked cookies wafted up the stairs as I started my descent, teasing my stomach into a whimpering sort of growl. Tendrils of sugar-laced air were like fingers with a come-hither curl leading the way to their origin. The wooden steps creaked under my weight, which I was pretty sure was the only thing covering the roar of hunger coming from some place inside me.

At the bottom of the steps, I made a left into a large kitchen, bright and cheerful with its whitewashed everything and over-sized windows framed by curtains of blue and yellow flowers. The countertops were a country blue, the same color as the stools that circled the island bar in the center of the room. A short, plump woman was busy transferring chocolate chip patties from a cookie sheet to a cooling rack as she hummed a cheerful tune in a soft voice. Something about the scene made me pause to soak it up, wishing with all my might that I'd had this stranger for a mother instead of the alcoholic who'd given birth to me and then left me to fend for myself.

"Oh, I didn't realize anyone was standing there," the woman said, wiping her hands on the apron fastened around her waist. Her dark blond hair was only barely contained in a messy bun at the nape of her neck, a few unruly locks having made their escape to frame her soft, round face. When she batted one away from her eyes, a streak of flour marked her wrinkled skin like war paint on a Native American.

"Not sure if you remember the introduction from last night, but I'm Abby. I'm running things around here for the time being. And you must be starving." She put a hand on her hip and leaned against the counter. "Normally, I'd ring your room to give you a last call for breakfast, but I didn't want to take a chance on waking you. You just seemed so tired when you checked in."

"Did I?" I knew how delirious I'd been so I wasn't sure why I'd asked.

"Well, I hadn't even made it out the door after showing you to your room before you were face-first and snoring, so I'd say yes." She laughed, taking my arm to usher me over to one of the stools at the island. "Sit. I'll make you something to eat. Would you like eggs and bacon or a turkey sandwich?"

I smiled up at her, but I was the one who'd been charmed. "Whichever one gets me a cookie for dessert."

"Turkey sandwich it is then," she said, and then shuffled over to the refrigerator, pulling a few contents from within. Over at the stove, she pulled out a skillet, and busied herself with whatever else she was doing. "You never said if you're here for business or pleasure or how long you'll be staying."

It sounded like a question, one she expected me to answer. But how much should I say? If she was Cassidy's mother, would she warn my target of my presence before I could get to her?

"I'm, uh . . . I'm actually here to handle a personal matter before it can affect me professionally." It was the truth, though it could've been the other way around as well. "Hopefully, I'll be checking out today." And to be sure I could, I picked up my cellphone, prepared to call Cassidy and find out where she was.

"Oh, honey, if you're trying to communicate with someone off the island, you best do it the old-fashioned way." Abby waved to the rotary phone on the wall.

Seriously? Those things still worked?

"The town had a Wi-Fi connection installed last year, but it's still sketchy at best, and you can forget about cell service unless you go up to the top of the hill. There's a phone in your room, though. You'll need a calling card to make long-distance calls, which you can get down at the store."

They still make calling cards? I no longer thought I was in an alternate universe or *The Twilight Zone*. I was now convinced I'd somehow traveled back in time; only, the silver DeLorean was a little white Yaris.

A plate slid in front of me holding a buttery toasted sandwich cut in half to expose a mound of turkey and bacon with cheese oozing from the center. A pile of chips and two dill pickle spears took up the rest of the plate. When I'd asked for a turkey sandwich, I'd assumed it would be a cold cut on white bread with a slab of pasteurized cheese and a thin layer of mayo. What I got was a culinary masterpiece, every red-blooded American man's fantasy. My taste buds started pushing and shoving toward the front of my mouth, salivating for the first smack of flavor. Using both hands, I picked up one half, careful to avoid the burn of melted cheese, and took a bite.

"Have mercy . . ." I moaned around the decadent sensation making love to my tongue.

Abby giggled, and it was damn adorable, too. I wondered if she'd adopt me, or if, at the very least, I could adopt her. She brought me a glass of ice water before going over to the stove and sink to start the cleanup process.

I was more concerned about the sandwich than the water and I took another giant bite, as though someone might try to take it from me if I didn't eat it in a hurry. It would be a mistake they'd never make again. "You have a lovely home."

Abby gave me a look, most likely because the words I'd said had been fighting for room with the food in my mouth. Yep, she was definitely somebody's mom. "Do you want to try that again?"

I swallowed before I made the same mistake. "Sorry. I said you have a lovely home."

She smiled in approval and then went back to her cleaning, happy to be doing so, from what I could tell. "Oh, it's not mine. It's Anna's. I'm just helping out."

"Anna? Anna Whalen?"

"Yep, just like the sign says." She rinsed the skillet she'd washed by hand and put it in the drainer. "My Thomas and I have known Anna and Duff for all our lives. Everyone knows everyone around here, in fact, but the four of us . . ." She paused before continuing, "The *six* of us couldn't be any closer to family if we shared the same blood."

"Six? I'm usually pretty good in math, but I only counted four names. What am I missing?"

"Oh, I meant our children."

"Ah. One of those children wouldn't happen to be Cassidy Whalen, would it?"

She turned to face me, eyebrows reaching for the sky. "You know our Cassidy?"

"I do. She's actually the reason I'm here." When she looked confused, I clarified, "We work together."

"I see. So you're from San Diego, are ya?"

"Well, I live and work there, yes." I finished off the sandwich and pushed the plate away, which Abby replaced with a saucer that held three cookies. "You wouldn't happen to know where she is, would you? We have some unfinished business I really need to get wrapped up before I leave."

The sound of a Hemi engine started up the driveway, getting louder the closer it got to the house until it came to a stop and cut off just outside the back door.

Abby undid her apron and hung it from a hook on the wall. "Ask and you shall receive," she said with an infectious smile. Just then the door off the mudroom opened and the object of my obsessive and impromptu mini vacation popped inside.

"Abby!" Cassidy squealed, and then practically skipped through the room to hug my kind hostess without noticing, or maybe not caring, that anyone else was present.

Her back was to me, which meant I got a great glimpse of her ass in a pair of black leggings. I wasn't used to seeing her attire so relaxed, but I would for damn sure be on Team Leggings from then on. Long ginger hair swung from a ponytail that I also hadn't been used to seeing, and an oversized sweater was another added surprise. She was damn sexy and my cock was impossibly hard. Forget yelling at her. I wanted to fuck her until she could no longer walk. And I would. Just as soon as I could get her alone.

"Ah, Cass, you're too skinny," Abby said, taking a step back to confirm with her eyes what she felt with her arms. "It's all that Californian, so-called healthy-eating-lifestyle crap. Tofu and veggie shakes are not food. Not to worry, I'll fatten you up in no time."

"Abbs, you keep making those famous chocolate chip cookies I smell and my ass will spread from the aroma alone."

And that was my cue. "Huh, and here I thought it was the leggings."

Cassidy nearly jumped out of her skin at the sound of my voice. When she turned to see me sitting there with a shit-eating grin on my face, she yelped a "Holy crap!" and then grabbed her chest as if by doing so she might be able to keep her heart from making a run for cover. It was cute how she stumbled backward and would have fallen if it hadn't been for Abby's quick save.

I allowed her a moment to recuperate, which was pretty human of me, and more than she deserved. Especially since she got the added bonus of Abby doting on her all the while to be sure she was okay. Meanwhile, I ate my cookie and did that thing with my eyes that usually had women naked in two point three seconds.

Apparently, Cassidy was immune, but I blamed myself. It was hard to feel sexy when you were in fight-or-flight mode. Unless that was the sort of thing you got off on. I knew some women like that.

When Cassidy finally found her voice again, it was too composed. "What the hell are you doing here, Matthews?"

I was equally calm. After all, I no longer had anything to hide, but it seemed Miss Shifty Eyes did. "Oh, I think you know very well what I'm doing here. I, however, can't say the same about you."

Cassidy made a whole bunch of sounds that were either syllables out of order or words that weren't fully formed. None of it made sense, but judging by the expression on her face, maybe that was because she was just as confused as her vocabulary seemed to be.

That, or the cat had her tongue. Seeing her get all squirmy like that made me wish it'd had mine. I'd make sure my wish was granted soon enough, but as long as the roles were reversed, I saw no reason I couldn't have a little bit of fun with it.

"Is something the matter between you two?" Abby was in mama

bear mode, ready to defend her cub, though I honestly didn't know if it would be Cassidy's rescue she would come to or mine.

"No, we're fine," Cassidy lied, and then she plastered on a fake smile. "Shaw and I work together. I'm surprised to see him here . . . *in my home* . . . *unannounced,* though." Clearly, she didn't expect to see me here, but that was the point, so boo on her for stating the obvious.

"I'm surprised to see you here, too . . . *not* in San Diego . . . *unannounced,*" I mocked her. "*Why* are you not in San Diego?"

"My boss, my friends, and my clients know why I'm not there. As far as I knew, they were the only ones I owed an explanation. Why do you care?"

"We have unfinished business. Or did you conveniently forget?"

"I said all I'd wanted to say. There's nothing unfinished about it."

"Isn't there?" I countered. "Maybe we should go somewhere a little more private to discuss the matter."

Cassidy looked from Abby back to me before answering. She looked more nervous than any innocent person should. She was definitely hiding something. "I can't. I'm here to relieve Abby, so you should probably go back to San Diego, *crazy stalker man,*" she said through a forced smile.

Abby waved her off, completely ignoring the "crazy stalker man" comment. "Nonsense. I'm right where I want to be. Besides, what else am I going to do besides sit around and worry myself to death? At least here I feel like I'm doing something productive," she said then grabbed the plate in front of me, but I snatched the last cookie before she could take it away, which earned me an approving smile and a pinch of my cheek. I really liked Abby. Maybe I could fit her into my suitcase and steal her away.

"Besides, it's been a while since you've been home. You probably need some time to get familiar with where everything is again."

Ouch. If the pained expression on Cassidy's face was anything to go by, I'd say that innocent statement had cut pretty deep. My little round hostess seemed much too kind to have done it on purpose, so I guessed this was one of those times when the simple truth had hurt like a son of a bitch. There was definitely a story there, and even though I was curious, I shouldn't have been. It would be best for me to handle my business and get the hell out of there. After I fucked Cassidy for one last time, that is.

And then the mudroom door opened again and this man that drew a vague recollection in my mind strolled in and sidled up next to Cassidy like he was staking a claim. If I hadn't already known this island was chock-full of lobster fishermen, I'd swear the bow in this guy's legs was put there by years of riding horses on a stud farm. Not that I was saying he was good-looking enough to be a stud himself. On the contrary, he looked like he'd just mastered the upright movement on the human evolutionary timeline. His face was covered in three-day-old stubble and he looked sturdy as hell, so it was quite possible that he was the missing link. The way his brow furrowed over his eyes when he looked at me only added credence to my theory, but it still wasn't enough. If I could just get him to carry a giant club and grunt out a few words like "me make fire," I'd be on my way to the Smithsonian with my discovery.

And then suddenly there was a pregnant pause in the room, one that was long enough for things to start shifting around with a primal realization. We'd somehow gone from a prehistoric jungle to the plains of some hot-as-fuck wilderness. Maybe it was instinct that had me on high alert, something ingrained in the very fiber of my makeup that made me steel up my stance, like a predator about to face off with another predator of equal strength. Cassidy stood between us like a zebra in the grasslands, frozen in place. Something in my gut told me shit was about to change.

"Are those my cookies?" the new guy grunted.

Well, he didn't so much grunt as growl the words, but I wasn't far off the mark. Jesus, had he eaten gravel for lunch?

Abby smiled up at the guy. I'll admit, it made me a little jealous. "And this would be my little cookie monster." Up on the tips of her toes, she pulled at his collar until he stooped so she could kiss him on the cheek. A cheek she then patted a little too hard, but it seemed he was used to it. "You have to share your cookies with the guests, Casey. Don't be stingy."

Whoa, wait. Casey? I'd heard that name before. Worse, I'd *seen* that name before. In permanent ink. Right above the lovely ass cheek of the woman I'd recently been fucking.

Said woman squeezed her eyes shut like she wished she could rewind time and carve those two little syllables out of the script before hitting the live button again. Oh, I was going to have too much fun with this. But first impressions were lasting impressions, so I had a little alpha work to finish first. And the one thing that spelled alpha, even more than brute strength, was confidence.

I crossed the kitchen like I commanded it, the infamous Casey giving me the once-over all the while until we were standing toe-to-toe. And then I took one more step forward, breaching the invisible barrier to his personal space just to see if he would take one back. He did not. Instead, he squared his shoulders and leaned in. The thickness in the air that separated us arched with opposing energies of testosterone, our inner lions giving silent roars to test which had the stuff it took to be king. With his chest puffed and shoulders flared like a cobra's hood, he stood his ground and looked me in the eye. I was impressed, though not intimidated.

The offering of my handshake before he had the chance was the first victory in what I was sure would be a pissing match for the ages. The grip as he shook my hand was his silent acceptance of the challenge that now lay at his feet.

"Casey, was it?" We all knew I'd just heard his name, but not acknowledging it was like dismissing its importance. Hence the smirk on his scruffy face.

"Yeah. Casey." He released the shake, crossing his arms and leaning against the wall, an act that said he wasn't threatened by a surprise attack. Nice maneuver on his part. I wondered if he knew I'd been fucking his girlfriend. "And you are?"

I had my answer. Obviously not.

"I'm the man eating your cookies." To prove my point, I finished off the one I'd been savoring right in front of him, and then dusted the crumbs from my hands.

"He," Cassidy interrupted, "was just leaving."

I didn't even spare a look in her direction. Not necessarily to be rude, but because to take my eyes off the man before me would be a point in his favor. "You know . . . I think I've changed my mind. I could do with a bit of fresh sea air in my lungs."

Casey nodded. "Sea air is very therapeutic. Might even put some hair on your chest."

Touché.

"Actually, I find most women like a man to be nice and smooth. *Every*where." My meaning was well caught.

"Not Stonington women," he said with a wink.

I chuckled because I simply couldn't help myself. "You sure about that?" I asked with a quick glance toward Cassidy and back.

That confident smile dropped just as quickly, and the muscles in his body tensed. Bingo! It was like a double bonus-point score for me in the testosterone-driven game we'd decided to play. Someone probably should've told him how competitive I could be.

"Casey Michaels, I'll have no more talk about grooming habits in this kitchen," Abby said in a stern, motherly tone that made both of us stand a little straighter. "Cassidy, you go on upstairs and make up the bed in our guest's room. We're still running a business here, ya know. Then I want you to get yourself some rest before suppertime."

"No!" Cassidy said loud enough to cause every head in the room to snap in her direction. She shifted her weight from one hip to the other, attempting to look casual. "I mean, Shaw doesn't really want to stay here. He has so much work to do to get Denver signed to a team and ready for training."

"I'm sure it's nothing I can't handle from here." Backing out of Casey's compromised space, I came to a stop at her side. I'd planned to permanently attach myself there to make her as uncomfortable as I possibly could for the duration of my stay. That, and I felt like being a cock-block for Missing Link Casey. I could be a real dick sometimes.

My eyes were pinned on Casey as I threw my arm over Cassidy's shoulders, staking a wee bit of a claim of my own. Cassidy shrugged me off, but I put it right back because, yeah, she was mine and maybe Casey wasn't the only one who needed to know that. "Besides, this seems like so much more fun," I told her, and then I leaned closer to her ear. "All work and no play makes Shaw a very dull boy."

She tried to shrug me off again, but I flexed, not allowing the deadweight to drop. Of course Cassidy wasn't okay with that, so she grabbed my hand and shoved my arm off. But she didn't release her hold once the task had been accomplished. Instead, she gave Abby and Casey a tight smile and said, "Will you please excuse us? We have some business to discuss so Shaw can be on his way." And then she dragged me from the kitchen.

I laughed at her because it was damn cute how aggravated she was, huffing and puffing and towing me through the foyer to the stairs. "What's your rush, Cassie? I already told you I'm sticking around for a bit."

"No, you're not. And, *Cassie*? Really?" she asked, though she didn't stop pulling me up the steps, a task I didn't make particularly easy on her.

I leaned back, not giving her all of my weight but still enough resistance to give her a good workout. "Oh, is that not what they call you? Cassie and Casey just sounded like it would be a thing." Even though her back was to me, I still did the air quotes with my free hand. "A thing like the two of you are a thing, right?"

She stopped and turned on me. Only then did I realize we'd somehow made it to the top of the staircase despite my attempt to be a major pain in her ass. Cassidy was breathing hard from the effort, but she hadn't broken a sweat. Christ, I wanted nothing more than to see her sweating and breathing hard for an entirely different reason. Plus, there was still the matter of those damn leggings and a pussy that needed tending.

When she looked from right to left, I swear I could read her mind. She had no idea which room was mine, and I was all too happy to show her. With swift movement, I pulled her against my chest and looked down at her. She was looking back, that heavy-breathing thing still fucking with my guttered brain and making my cock want to join it there. The way she looked up at me, that bit of desperateness in her eyes. Well now, that was the Cassidy I'd come to know when she and I were alone. She needed me just as much as I needed her. And maybe . . . just maybe she wanted to be claimed.

My hands went to her ass, which felt even more amazing than it looked in those damn leggings, and farther still to her thighs where I grabbed on and hoisted her up so she could wrap her legs around my hips. And then it was on. Lips met lips, fingers found purchase in hair, and Cassidy was sucking on my tongue. Jesus fucking Christ, where the hell was my room?

CHAPTER 4

Cassidy

He smelled like Shaw and tasted like Casey, thanks to Abby's cookies. I found myself burrowing deeper into the crook of his neck, desperate for more of the delicious aroma emitting from his body like some addictive form of untried confectionery. My fingers latched on to the strands of his hair and I didn't want to let go, despite the conflicting emotions oscillating through me at this new, yet disturbing, concept.

I should have stopped, but my legs only tightened further around his waist as Shaw propelled us down the hall to an unknown destination. And I realized it didn't matter where he was going as long as I got to go along with him. He was everything familiar. And I really needed familiar right then.

My God, but his cock was a raging bulge pressed to the core of me. One that couldn't and wouldn't be ignored. And all I could think about was how badly I wanted to taste the salty hint of his flesh, feel the heavy weight of him on my tongue, and lick him from root to tip.

I'd already begun to plot out how I was going to make that happen when Shaw crossed the threshold to a room—his room, I assumed—and kicked the door shut with the heel of his shoe. And then my back was slammed against the wall.

"What the—"

My protest was cut off when his hand covered my mouth. Shaw brought his face inches from mine and I could do nothing but lose myself inside the blue heat of his eyes.

"Shut up." His words were clipped and edgy, but the pulse of his arousal continued to demonstrate how turned on he was. And my mouth watered at the thought of taking his length and sucking him. Hard.

When I made no attempt to struggle out of his tight hold, his fingers squeezed my cheeks before relaxing back against my face.

"Good girl," he murmured.

Without lessening his grip, Shaw leaned forward and nuzzled the side of my neck. The softness of his lips moved across my skin and my eyelids drifted closed. I was trapped—entangled by my own lust and his overwhelming presence. Until his teeth clamped down on the sensitive flesh of my neck. It infuriated me, both because I liked it and because he knew it. Not only that, but his hand over my mouth was preventing me from being able to put his cock there.

Besides, this was my house, dammit, and everyone knew the house ruled. If it was a fight he wanted, it was a fight he was going to get. So I grabbed a good handful of his hair while prying his hand away. Finally my mouth was free, though the snarl to Shaw's lip meant he wasn't happy about it and likely wouldn't allow it to go on for long. My mission was only half complete, as I still needed to get his cock in my mouth, so I had to act fast.

I fisted another handful of hair to keep him in place, while releasing the hold my legs had around his waist so I could drop to the floor. Shaw wasn't having it. He kept me pinned to the wall with his body, a sexy yet annoying smirk on his face even as he continued to pull against the hold I had on his hair. At any moment, I expected him to break free, with or without his mane intact.

"Let me go," I ordered, bucking against him and kicking my legs back and forth to jar myself loose.

"Say please."

I narrowed my eyes at him. "No."

"Then we're going to do this my way."

"Do what?"

With a quick move that caught me off guard, Shaw released me to the floor, catching me with one arm around my waist until I was firmly planted on my feet. And then he pinned me again. "Whatever I want to do."

There was a wicked gleam to his eye and something told me I'd just played right into his hands. Well, we'd see about that.

"We're not doing anything until you tell me what you're doing here." I wasn't sure my words carried very much weight, what with them sounding all breathy and just plain flimsy. Though his lips and teeth had returned to my neck, so I passed the blame for my mousiness on to them. Not only that, but Shaw was moving lower and lower, his mouth closing around the nipple he'd managed to find even though he couldn't see it through the sweater . . . and cami . . . and bra. But he didn't stop there. No, he took the position I'd wanted. I would've hated him for it if it hadn't been for the added perk I knew would be mine.

"That makes zero sense, seeing as I'm already doing it. Why haven't you ever worn these things before?" Shaw was on his knees before me, studying my leggings. I could feel each warm exhale of breath on my center when he nuzzled the tight space between my thighs with his nose.

I closed my eyes, trying to concentrate, and then I asked the question again, "What are you doing here, Matthews?"

The undeniably hot, wet stroke of his tongue when he licked me through those stupid, beautiful leggings was my undoing. My knees buckled from the sensation, but Shaw was there to pin me back in place. Working me with his full mouth, he buried his head and moved back and forth with each deep sweep of his tongue until his teeth scraped my clit, sending a jolt of "something wicked this way comes" through me. The description wasn't far off the mark; the orgasm already building was definitely evil in nature.

Breathe, Cassidy, breathe.

Shaw pulled back then—only slightly—giving me a reprieve I was sure was more for his benefit than mine. He didn't even look at me, but he did finally answer, "Tasting you. What are *you* doing here?"

He didn't wait for an answer, which was just as well. I had lost all ability to form a coherent thought, much less the ability to string words together and make a logical response. Instead, I drowned in sensation as his strong, capable hands moved across my hips and then over my thighs before circling around my back. There, he cupped my backside, kneading my bottom and molding my flesh under his large palms like a piece of malleable clay.

When I felt his fingers seize and curl under the waistband of my pants, all the air rushed out of my lungs. I glanced down my body as every nerve ending went on high alert. Shaw, on his knees, was a sight to behold. As he began to lower my pants, the tendons in his arms were taut with the rigid control he always kept in check but hovered just below the surface. You could practically feel his strained urgency pulsate between us with a life force of its own.

His movements were maddeningly slow, deliberate even as he stopped short of pulling the thin scrap of material over my hips.

I grabbed the stupid leggings to give them a shove, but Shaw flexed against my hold, not allowing me any control. Damn him.

His jaw ticked and nostrils flared, though I wasn't really sure what he had to be so mad about. He was the one causing the delay. Maybe the control he'd refused me was only barely contained within himself.

"Not until you answer the question." He nuzzled me again, making it impossible for me to think clearly.

"Um, I can't remember what it was."

"Then I'll ask it again."

I tried to focus, I really did, but the soft kiss along the seam of those godforsaken leggings wasn't helping matters.

Shaw released a heavy breath. "You ran." His fingertips pressed into my flesh with his tightened grip. "Why?"

With each rise and fall of my chest, my nipples became increasingly sensitive. It was as if the oversized sweater I'd thrown on that morning had turned into some erotic sex apparatus. Jeez, had someone slipped me some ecstasy when I wasn't looking? "I did not run. What would I have to run from?"

He yanked my pants down. Just enough to bare my pussy, and then he came to an abrupt halt. "Me." With that one clipped word, Shaw clutched the rolled leggings at my thighs and pulled me toward him. His hot mouth zeroed in on my clit—tongue, lips, and teeth working together to make me forget everything I'd ever learned since birth with the exception of that feeling of intense pleasure given to a woman only by a man.

Just as quickly as he'd begun, he stopped again. Good God, but my girly bits were getting whiplash. What little part of my brain that wasn't obsessing about getting his cock in my mouth was now calculating the stealthlike maneuvers needed in order to knock him to the floor so I could ride his face.

"Continue," he demanded. "And make it quick."

I peeled my hands from the wall and pushed my fingers through his gorgeous bedhead of hair. I might have even nudged him a bit to encourage a continuation of his previous action. "I wasn't running from you. I wasn't running from anything. I was running to something."

"Casey?" he asked. His voice dripped with little green monster ooze. Maybe it was sick and twisted, but his jealousy turned me on even more. Surely he had to see the proof of that right in front of his face.

"No, not Casey. My mother had an accident. I had to come home. My family needed me."

"Maybe they weren't the only ones."

At least I think that was what I'd heard him say. His voice was muffled by the fact that his face was buried between my thighs again, which I wasn't complaining about, but still. Wedging my hand between my nether region and his forehead, I pushed, forcing him to stop what he was doing. "What did you just say?"

Shaw tilted his head up, rubbing against my hand like a cat taking the stroking it deserved. And then his soft kiss brushed my palm.

"Touch yourself." It was an order and a request.

"That's not what you said," I told him even as my fingers dipped between my folds.

With hooded eyes and parted mouth, he watched. And then his tongue made an appearance to wet his lips. My fingers swirled around my clit, the pleasure intensified with the knowledge that Shaw was held hostage by my explicit movements. My breath stuttered. He wasn't content to simply watch, though. Hooking an arm around one thigh, he pushed a thumb inside my pussy from behind. My head fell back with the sensation of finally being filled, my moan barely stifled by the bite to the inside of my cheek. I wanted to ride the euphoria as far as it would take me, but Shaw—as always—had other plans.

The warm, wet, velvety glide of his tongue as it met my core shot me straight into oblivion. My fingers, his tongue . . . they might as well have been skipping along in a meadow filled with daisies while holding hands. That was my happy place.

My other hand found the back of his head and I urged him even closer while his thick thumb worked me from behind. Biting down on my lip, I closed my eyes and let the dual sensations take the lead. I didn't give a crap why Shaw was there. I was just glad he was and that he was giving me what was shaping up to be one hell of an orgasm.

I wanted to part my legs to give him more room, but those stupid leggings had me restrained. Something I'm sure had been Shaw's intention all along. I was trapped, but there was no place else I'd rather be in that moment. My orgasm continued to rise and I'd begun to ride his face and his thumb . . . desperate to help even though my own manipulations had stopped in favor of feeling his. And then his finger entered my ass.

I came. Hard. My teeth clenched with a barely contained moan. How the hell I had the presence of mind about me to be careful of not being too loud, I'd never know, but thank God I did. Shaw did not, however. His moan of approval had thankfully been muted, though not intentionally. The sound barrier presented by my thighs and vagina had everything to do with that. And the vibrations from that moan had only one place to go. Directly to my clit. I came again, pushing my hips toward his face, pulling his head closer, and somehow managing to rock back and forth on his thumb and finger still inside me.

The heat from the boiling inferno within me had broken free, coloring my skin a light pink and causing a thin sheen of sweat to take up residence in order to cool my body back down. The pulse of my orgasm battled with the rhythm of my heartbeat, making the euphoric cadence radiating through me go straight to my head. I was dizzy, filled with a bliss I knew would be short-lived, but you better believe I was going to ride it out for as long as I could.

Then it occurred to me . . . the one thing I'd wanted, even more than my own orgasm, was Shaw's cock in my mouth. Once again, he'd somehow managed to get his way and deny mine.

So I refused to bask in the afterglow. Jesus, that sucked, but not as much as it would suck for Shaw's ego. He'd no doubt be disappointed by my mediocre response and it would wipe the arrogant smirk right off his too-handsome face.

I wanted his cock. And I was going to have it.

Resolved, I placed the sole of my boot on his shoulder and extended my leg with deliberate ease. His thumb and forefinger slid from my body and I fought the urge to put them back where they belonged.

Shaw rocked back on his haunches, a confused expression on his face as he tilted his head to the side, quizzically.

"Stand up." The order was quiet, methodical.

The corner of Shaw's mouth lifted before he rose to his feet and crossed his arms over his chest. He raised a single eyebrow, waiting to be dazzled.

Pushing off the wall, I pulled up my pants, the proverbial Closed for Business sign dangling from my navel, and stepped to him. Reaching up to cup the back of his neck, I pulled him down to me, kissing him deeply and tasting myself on his lips. It was my tongue that took the lead, coaxing his to play along even as I massaged his cock through his pants to do the same. Shaw's breath was heavy through his nose, his body a willing participant to what I wanted.

His hand covered mine and squeezed, encouraging me to stroke him harder. His cock was thick, firm, and pulsed inside my grip. With a quick maneuver of my feet, I turned us so that he was now the one with his back to the wall. Amusement washed over his face and he chuckled. I may have controlled his body and held his cock in my hand, but there wasn't a doubt in my mind that Shaw had allowed this. It didn't matter.

Dropping to my knees, I made quick work of his belt and freed his erection from the confines of his pants. I grinned in satisfaction when the object of my obsession finally sprang free. I'd just prepared to suck him off when Shaw cupped his cock and pulled it to the side. Away from me.

"No," he said when I peered up at him with a furrowed brow.

"What do you mean, no?"

"No is a pretty basic concept. What is it that you don't understand about it?" The corner of his lip caught between his teeth and he pushed a lock of hair that had fallen from my ponytail behind my ear. What was that look he was giving me? And, God, he was rubbing himself.

"Let me get this straight. . . . I want your cock inside my mouth, and you're denying yourself the pleasure?"

"You just said it yourself. You're the one who wants it. So who is it that I'm actually denying?" He stroked my hair, reverently, and that simple touch of affection startled me. I didn't know whether to press closer or back away.

But his cock was right there in front of me, so I went for it. Shaw was faster, pinning my head to his thigh so that my cheek was against his skin. Undeterred, I made another attempt, and again, Shaw refused to let me have what I wanted, even pulling farther away.

I went for the next best thing.

With little effort, I was able to lean forward and sample the treat before me. Shaw's balls tightened under my tongue and I gave them a long, exaggerated lick.

Shaw's hands were like the fingers of God forcing the Red Sea to part as his cock went in one direction and my head went in the other.

"Ah-ah-ah," he admonished. I was dripping wet between my legs again. Why was this so sexy to me?

"Look at me," he said, and I did as directed, though I still couldn't move my head.

"Do you remember earlier when I told you to say please and you refused?"

He was right. But I wanted him . . . *it* . . . and apparently I wasn't above swallowing my pride to get what I wanted.

I hated the desperation that leaked into my voice. "Please?"

"Please, what?"

Christ, he was going for the kill. "Can I please have your cock in my mouth?"

He quirked his head. "I don't know, *can* you?"

You've got to be kidding me. "*May* I please have your cock in my mouth?"

He was stroking himself, a wicked tease before my eyes, like a fat kid eating the whole damn Christmas turkey in front of a hungry man. "Yeah? You want it?"

I licked my lips in anticipation. "More than anything."

"Then have it." Holding his cock, Shaw aimed it toward my mouth while simultaneously controlling my head to put me in position to receive his gift. As eager as I was to take him into my mouth, he held me close to his thigh, still controlling every minute detail as if this was for my pleasure, not his. Maybe it was.

"Open," he said with a pat to my cheek.

My lips parted and Shaw finally pushed into my mouth. Though not all the way, thanks to the grip he still held on the base of his cock. I was sort of grateful for that. Shaw wasn't abnormally long, but his girth was enough to stretch the corners of my mouth. And he was freaking delicious.

"There you go," he groaned. "That's what you wanted, isn't it?"

My lids shuttered closed and I couldn't suppress the low moan around his flesh.

Yes. Mine.

With greedy sucks, I took him to the back of my throat and worked his erection hard. Saliva pooled and coated his flesh as I moved my tongue over every ridge and contour.

"Slow down." Shaw fisted my ponytail and pulled me back until only the tip of his cock remained. I whimpered, afraid he was going to put a stop to my fun, but then he eased back inside, still gripping my hair.

"That's better." He controlled the glide and pace, despite the rising urgency flooding every cell in my body.

With each push and pull, the ache between my legs worsened. I needed to come again. I clawed at his thighs, cementing my knees to the floor. With his tight grip in my hair, the controlled thrust and retreat of his hips, there was no doubt who prevailed. I was along for the ride and that was fine by me. We both had what we'd been after.

I wanted to see his face, so I looked up at him only to find his head had just started the backward descent to rest against the wall behind him. The view was magnificent. The tendons in his neck were taut, the veins in his forearm were thick with blood, and the grip he still had around the base of his cock seemed almost painful. With his fingertips pressed into the base of my skull, he maintained the rhythmic pace best suited to his liking. It was clear to see . . .

Shaw was in ecstasy.

I continued to maul his thighs, my short nails scraping his skin, but I was pretty sure he liked that, too. His cock was delicious, that bit of precum foretelling his impending release. I could hear Shaw's breaths, his light hisses, and soft moans. God he was going to come. He was going to come hard. His muscles tensed underneath my touch and the lazy, yet controlled thrusts grew erratic. I recognized all the signs and I was ready for it. In fact, I'd never been more focused in my life.

His cock thickened, the veiny network just below the smooth skin growing with the intensity of each stroke of my mouth. His grip on my hair tightened, and he held me in place, looking down at me with eyes that dared me to move. He was ready. So ready.

The soft rap at the door might as well have been blasted through concert speakers, so loud in the quiet space of the room charged with so much unspent energy.

"Cassidy? Are you in there?" came Casey's voice through the door.

I yanked myself out of Shaw's hold, his still-rigid cock falling free of my mouth. With the back of my hand, I wiped my mouth and scrambled to my feet.

"Fuck!" Shaw cursed under his breath.

"Cassidy?" Casey asked again.

I squeezed my eyes shut, hoping Casey hadn't heard Shaw. *We aren't together. Casey is not my boyfriend,* I kept repeating to myself over and over inside a subconscious riddled with guilt. So why did I feel like I'd just been caught cheating? My heart raced in my chest, my skin on fire. Though I couldn't quite pinpoint if my body's reaction was due to the very hot exchange that had just happened with Shaw or the panic over having been caught in the act.

"Um, I'll be out in just a minute. Is everything okay?" Even I could hear the shaky timbre of my voice.

"Yeah, your pop's on the phone for you," he called back. "You weren't in your room, so I thought maybe you were here. Is everything okay in *there*?"

"Everything is just peachy," Shaw said, grimacing as he tucked his hard cock back into his jeans.

"No offense, but I was asking Cassidy, not you."

"I'm sorry, she couldn't answer because she had my cock in her mouth," Shaw whispered and then flipped him the bird, though Casey obviously couldn't see it.

I rolled my eyes at his immaturity and gave his chest a slap. "I'm fine, Casey. I'll be right down."

"Might want to hurry. Your ma's okay, but you know how impatient your pop can be," he warned.

Which wasn't entirely true. My da was about as patient as a man could be, but he absolutely detested talking on the phone. He much preferred to be face-to-face with a person because he said most of the conversation happened in the body language.

Giving myself a quick once-over in the mirror to be sure nothing looked out of place, I turned to Shaw. "We're not finished," I told him.

"Obviously not," he said, motioning toward the awkward bulge in his jeans. "Though I'd say *you* got finished well enough."

I grinned because, yeah, I did. And maybe I even delighted a bit in his uncomfortable predicament. "I meant with the conversation. As far as the other, maybe next time," I said with a wink.

"Well, that's just great," he grumbled.

I couldn't help the smug feeling I had when I left the room, knowing he was still standing there staring after me with his hands on his hips and a raging hard-on in his pants.

There would definitely be a next time, though I couldn't quite pinpoint the moment when a "maybe" had become a sure thing.

CHAPTER 5

Cassidy

Shaw Matthews was in my house. And I had no idea why or how he even knew where I'd gone. But I had a pretty good idea of where to start to find the answers he'd refused to give.

The call from Da that had interrupted the pornolike oral trade-off between us had been like a glass of cold water being thrown in my face. Though I was pretty sure it hadn't had quite the same effect on Shaw. His cock had still been furiously engorged, desperate for a release when I'd left him, which sort of made me a happy camper. Served him right for playing keep-away like a mean kid on the playground.

Da had called only to give me the update from Ma's doctor. Her blood pressure had improved dramatically and he'd be releasing her in the morning with plenty of medication to get her through. I'd see to it that the pharmacy had my credit card on file to process both of their prescriptions each month after this because knowing they were killing themselves, literally, while trying to afford their medicine when I was sitting on more than enough money to help out was not okay with me.

Ma's release was great news, even though she'd be wheelchair-bound until the cast on her leg came off and I'd have to stick around to help out. But how was I going to explain Shaw's presence to my parents—or worse, to Casey—when I didn't know why he was there myself? There were only two people who'd known where I'd gone, and only one of those would've been brazen enough to spill the beans to Shaw. So I got comfortable in the sitting room and pulled out my laptop, cueing up the Skype application and dialing the culprit's phone number.

Quinn answered by the second ring as if he'd been waiting for a call he had no way of knowing would come. "Cassidy? Oh, um . . . hey, you!" My roommate was still in bed, which wasn't odd since it was ten o'clock in San Diego on a Saturday morning. What was odd, however, was that he was bright-eyed and bushy-tailed, every hair in place and maybe even a little sexy with all those blood-red silk sheets and white satin pillows surrounding him like he'd been preparing for a half-naked boudoir photo shoot. I almost felt intrusive. Shame oozed from his nonexistent pores as if he was hiding something.

Naturally, I was suspicious. "Quiiinnn . . . What did you do?"

"Huh? Nothing! I swear!" He might as well have spilled his entire guts with that reaction. It probably would've been easier if he'd gone ahead and pled guilty, throwing himself upon the mercy of the court.

But due diligence was a must. "Right. So do you want to tell me how it is that Shaw Matthews knew where to find me?" I asked, giving my roommate the opportunity to confess his sin.

Relief washed over his features. "Oh, that." Quinn sat up and pushed his shoulders back, the "deer in headlights" look replaced by something a little more holier-than-thou. "I did what I had to do. I will not apologize. You're welcome."

"I'm welcome? For what? Shaw Matthews is in my house!"

Quinn shushed me. "Hold on. I think I just heard something," he said, cocking his head to the side to have a better listen. He nearly came out of his skin when the door to his bedroom burst open. There was a flurry of confusion then as the screenshot bounced around, the sound of a sheet covering the microphone muffling the multiple voices.

"Quinn? Are you okay?" I asked, concerned that I was about to witness the murder of my best friend.

"Are you still in bed? Wakey, wakey, sleepyhead!"

"Christ almighty," Quinn grumbled. "Hello, naked gay man under the sheets. How did you two pervs get in?"

Finally, the screen settled back into place and the sheet half covering it was ripped off to reveal a very jovial Demi and Sasha now sandwiching Quinn. They'd done their best to popcorn him and all his perfectly laid pillows out of bed, which he didn't look too happy about.

Demi held a silver key inches from his face. "You gave us a spare, duh."

Quinn groaned and plopped back onto his pillow. "Leave that shit on the counter when you see yourselves out, Creepy McCreepersons."

"Nope," Demi said, popping the *P*. "Not until you're out of the woods."

He wasn't the only one lost in the woods. "What's going on?"

Quinn rolled his eyes. "I'm on suicide watch, didn't you know?"

Sasha waved him off. "He's not on suicide watch. We simply want to be sure he doesn't get too lonely." She shifted around to get more comfortable, fluffing the pillow when she suddenly stopped and pulled her hand away. A pair of black fuzzy handcuffs dangled from her index finger while she examined it. "What's this?"

"Stop being nosy," Quinn said, yanking them away and tucking them back under his pillow. Ignoring Demi's and Sasha's laugh, he attempted to change the subject. "Cassidy, how's your mom?"

"Well, you know. . . . She looks like she fell from a ladder, but she's going to be okay. My ma's a scrappy little thing. She's not going to let a couple of broken bones, some scrapes and bruises keep her down for long. I was scared to death, of course, but the good news is that the doc is going to let her come home tomorrow."

Quinn sighed. "Oh, thank goodness. The girls and I were going to come out, but my stupid boss wouldn't let me off work, the heifer. She said I've taken off too much lately, which is all because of Daddy." His expression soured. "I hate him. I hate his very existence, the fat bastard."

Daddy wasn't fat, but he *was* Quinn's most recent ex-lover. A very rich, very married, very hot ex-lover who didn't like the ultimatum Quinn had given him to come out of the closet or lose him for good. Daddy had chosen to stay with his wife instead, shattering Quinn's heart to smithereens. Quinn had gotten even by shattering the bathroom mirror in the penthouse apartment Daddy had bought for him and then taken away. Plus he'd carved "He's gay" into the wall, essentially forcing him out of the closet. Unless he did the patchwork himself, contractors were going to know the truth. And a truth like that, about someone with as much money and stature as Daddy had, was bound to get leaked.

"Sorry, Cass, but we couldn't leave him," Demi said with a squint of her eyes as if it pained her to say the words. "Of course if you think you might need us, we can always split up and one of us could come there."

"Don't be silly. There's nothing for you to do here. I'll mind the bed-and-breakfast for Ma until she's back up on her feet and then I'll be home in no time. I hope. Meanwhile, I want to talk about those handcuffs," I said, grinning at Quinn.

"You know what they say," Demi started. "The best way to get over a man is to move on to the next. Quinn is all about forward progression." She shouldered him playfully. "But just like Daddy, his new flavor is top secret, too."

"Oohh," I said with a waggle of my brows. "Any clues on the identity of this secret lover?"

Quinn huffed. "Y'all want to talk secret lovers? Fine, let's talk secret lovers."

He was a little too quick to agree, looking at me as if I'd set something in motion that couldn't and wouldn't be stopped. I realized I found myself precariously standing in the middle of a trap before I had the opportunity to see the metaphorical net suspended overhead.

With a quirk of an eyebrow, Quinn yanked on the rope. "Miss Sassy Cassie, do you want to tell them or should I?"

He couldn't have meant what I thought he meant. "Tell them what?"

"Oh, so you're going to try to play stupid? Okay, let's see. . . . How should I say this?" Quinn cleared his throat. *"Shaw and Cassidy, sitting in a tree. K-i-s-s-i-n-g,"* he sang.

Nooooo! "Oh, God." Those were the only two words I could get out of my mouth.

Demi gasped, loudly. "Shaw?"

"Shaw Matthews?" Sasha asked. Which was silly because how many other Shaws did we know?

"Fuck me," I said, managing to find two more words.

Quinn laughed. "Oh, I'm sure he did, girl."

My cheeks flamed red, that feeling of being caught in the act resurfacing yet again. "How did you know?"

Quinn laughed some more. So much that he could manage only one syllable, but that one syllable said plenty. "Shaw."

"He told you?" I was outraged, ready to cut off his balls for cutting my legs out from under me.

My roommate got his laughter under control and sighed

heavily. "Not really. I *might* have suggested I already knew. And he *might* have assumed you'd told me. So I *might* have let him."

"You tricked him?" I ran my hands over my face. "Oh, my God, Quinn, you're such an asshole. That was so underhanded and devious!"

"And brilliant," Demi tacked on, high-fiving him.

Sasha gave me a cheeky grin. "And really not anything we didn't already know."

"You did not know." It sounded more like a question than a statement of fact. Did they know? How could they have when we'd been so careful? Actually, I hadn't thought we were trying to be careful so much as I'd thought no one was paying attention. Or maybe I simply hadn't been thinking at all in lieu of letting my vagina make all the decisions for me, consequences be damned.

Sasha dipped her chin and smacked her lips sarcastically. "We have eyes to see the little looks you two give each other."

"And ears to eavesdrop on not-so-private conversations," Demi said, cupping her own as if to prove her point.

Quinn got überclose to the webcam, making his lips appear superbig. "And mouths to gossip with each other and compare notes," he said before backing away again.

I was sure I must have looked like a codfish with its mouth agape. "Seriously? You need help. All three of you. And I need a restraining order because you're all a bunch of stalkers."

"Speaking of stalkers," Demi said, pointing and looking over my shoulder.

Sasha's smile was bright as the sun. "Hi, Shaw!" she said with a cheerful wave.

I turned to see him standing there, every bit as creepy as my intrusive friends, apparently listening in on my—what did Demi call it?—*not-so-private* conversation. Jesus, did no one respect personal boundaries anymore?

Shaw

My scalp was sore as shit and my balls were aching and in desperate need of a release. So I'd gone in search of Cassidy with every intention of getting my caveman on and throwing her over my shoulder to take her back upstairs so she could finish the job she'd begun before we were quite rudely interrupted.

Adjusting the still raging hard-on in my jeans, I groaned. Each step down the stairs looked awkward as hell. And every bit as painful as it actually was. You'd think the sound of another man's voice would have been enough to put the deflate on my chubby little buddy, but Cassidy's performance had been quite impressive. So impressive, I found it nearly impossible to erase from my mind the pleading look in her eyes as she'd begged for my cock in her mouth.

"Goddammit," I groaned as the visual sent a renewed sense of urgency to my cock. Maybe the only way to make him simmer down would be to punch him in the head until he was unconscious.

Casey passed by at the bottom of the staircase as he headed toward the kitchen and glanced up at me. I straightened to my full height, the issue in my pants automatically disappearing when the testosterone-driven need to appear more threatening took the driver's seat. My opponent pretty much matched me in height, so standing on the stairs would be my only chance to look down on him, which had alpha dog written all over it. Baring my canines might have been overkill, so I put that back into my bag of tricks.

I smirked, the sort of smirk that said, "I just had my cock in your girl's mouth." No, Cassidy hadn't admitted he was her boyfriend, but she didn't have to. Anyone could tell those two had a thing. Whether that was in the past or still a present issue I'd yet to figure out, but what I did know was that I was hell-bent on making sure it wouldn't be a future one.

Busting a right when I reached the first floor, I shouldered my metaphorical club for the time being and followed the sound of Cassidy's voice. Beyond the all-wood foyer and old-world check-in desk, I traversed the length of the hall to find her sitting on an olive green couch in a den that had been closed off to the rest of the house. If I had to guess, and I did, I'd say this was a space dedicated to the Whalen family's personal use. Though thanks to the sliding wooden door that she'd left cracked, I could hear the entire conversation she was having with her friends.

Well, our friends. I might have been closer to Landon and Chaz, but we were all tangled, what with Landon and Sasha being an item, finally, and Chaz and Demi having that sort of thing going on where they both liked each other but neither of them were doing anything about it.

It was a revealing conversation, with two very valuable nuggets of information being exposed. First, the jig was up on the affair we'd been having. Our friends now knew we'd been fucking. And, for whatever reason, I wasn't mad about it. There was no question in my mind that we were going to keep doing what we were doing, so it was inevitable that those closest to us would find out about it sooner rather than later. I was okay with that. And I had no idea why that didn't cause me to panic.

I also didn't panic when Demi and Sasha ratted me out.

Cassidy slammed her laptop closed, abruptly disconnecting the Skype call with the rat finks and Quinn without so much as a goodbye. It was just as good a time as any to broach the second nugget.

Pushing the cracked door open, I stepped inside and closed it back behind me. "Your mom hurt herself? That's why you left San Diego?"

Cassidy stood, busying herself with connecting her laptop to charge. "I told you that before. You thought I was lying?"

She was calm. A little too calm. I'd figured there'd be a lot of yelling and mud slinging between us when this conversation finally happened, but I didn't feel like doing any of that. Maybe it was because the energy it would take to do it was percolating in my pants with all the unresolved sexual tension still arcing between us. Unresolved for me, at least. Jesus, she really needed to stop bending over furniture right in front of me.

"I thought you were running away from me." She should run away from me. And maybe wear a chastity belt or something.

She stopped and turned toward me. "You said that before, too, and I told you I wasn't. You, however, never answered any of my questions. Why are you here, Shaw?"

The caveman imagery popped into my head again, the weight of that proverbial club on my shoulder begging me to knock her unconscious so I could steal her away. I'd gone in search of her to put an end to the raging boner in my pants, which was what had led me to the spot I now occupied. But I don't think that was what she meant.

"Denver told me he'd offered you the contract first, but you turned it down and told him to give it to me instead."

Cassidy shrugged. "So?"

My jaw ticked as I recalled my annoyance, and I wanted to punish her all over again. Not verbally. Not physically. Sexually. "So you'd just found out about my past. It looked like—"

I saw the proverbial lightbulb illuminate behind her eyes. "Like I was giving it to you?"

I wanted to give it to her. "Right."

She put her hand on my chest to stop my forward momentum, which I hadn't even been aware of. But she didn't push me away. No, she raised that self-righteous chin and placed her hands on those curvy hips, so that her sweater tightened at the shoulders and accentuated her breasts. Her voice was low, sensual. "You should've known better."

She was right.

"I'm too competitive to give anything away unless it will benefit me and my end goal. I'd won that contract fair and square and earned the right to rub it in your face, and would have if my family hadn't needed me back here."

Oh, she'd rubbed something in my face, all right. Or rather, I'd rubbed my face in something. The problem was that I'd been left unsatisfied. The denim cage imprisoning my engorged cock was only barely containing it.

"Some things are more important than a partnership. Even a partnership I'd worked so hard for. But that still doesn't explain why you're here." Cassidy's sweet breath was inches from my face.

She wanted an explanation? Fine, I'd give it to her. "I went through a lot to make sure nobody ever found out where I'd come from because I didn't want anyone to pity me. I never took a handout, never asked for help, never depended on anyone to take care of me because I was determined to make my own way. And I was proud that I'd been able to do so. When it looked like you were making me your charity case, it was like you were tearing down everything *I'd* worked so hard for with one blow. I was pissed."

"So you flew three thousand miles to tell me off?" That smart mouth of hers had been the puppeteer to my cock since the first day I'd met her. The effect was magnified times infinity now that I'd had her, and even more so in that instant because I'd been left unsatisfied moments earlier. Christ, everything that made me a man ached to be inside her.

"Yeah, I guess I did." Hearing myself saying it out loud like that really made me sound like an idiot.

"Wow." She took my hand, toying with my fingers in a way that was sensual and maybe a little too intimate, but I liked it. "That's dedication to the cause."

"I'm nothing if not dedicated." It was the truth, though I don't think either one of us was buying the excuse in this situation.

We were both silent then. The entire journey here, I'd thought of how this confrontation of sorts was going to go, and this was not it. Yelling, name-calling, bulging forehead veins, accusations, lots of swearing, and maybe even flying objects had been the expectation. But here we were, close yet not close enough, voices even, heads cool, and tempers calm. I didn't want to tear her limb from limb. I wanted those limbs wrapped around me while I moved inside her.

"So do it." Her fingers were now playing with the hair at the nape of my neck, making me even more insane. And hard.

I closed my eyes. Just for a second to catch up with the conversation we were apparently still having. "Do what?"

Cassidy leaned closer, whispering in my ear, "Tell me off."

Her breath on my neck, I could feel the tingly goosebumps rising to the surface to hijack my flesh. That tingling sensation traveled the nervous system superhighway to find a permanent residence inside my too-tight jeans, shacking up with my balls and cock as roommates. Goddammit, the woman was too close, too fuckable.

Once again, I hadn't realized I'd been positioning myself, positioning her. Cassidy's back was pressed to yet another wall. Or was it a bookcase? Maybe it was the corner of a wall and bookcase. Either way, my hands on each side of her would make damn sure she wouldn't escape, not that she was trying to. When Cassidy's grip tightened on the front of my shirt and her soft lips brushed my neck, it dawned on me that maybe the whole setup hadn't been me at all; it had been her.

"I'd rather get you off," I said, inhaling the soft scent of her hair. Jesus, the pulse of my cock was as thick as the anticipation in the air.

Her teeth tugged at my earlobe in time with the tug of her fingers on my hair. "You did that already. Twice."

I grinned because yeah, she was obviously good to go again. "Third time's a charm."

I pushed my knee between hers, forcing her legs to part so my confined cock could make contact with the warmth of her center. Fuck me, but I could feel her all the way through my fucking jeans. By some cosmic chance, we'd somehow found ourselves back in the same position as earlier. Maybe this time the universe would see fit to allow a happy ending for me.

"We can't. Not here." Cassidy arched her back, rubbing herself on me. She didn't mean a fucking word of what she'd said, and that was just fine by me.

"Why? Are you afraid your boyfriend will catch us?"

Her hands went to my ass, kneading me and pulling me closer. "He's not my boyfriend."

"Someone should probably tell him that."

Before she could say anything more, I kissed her. I didn't want to talk about Lobster Casey. I didn't want to talk about Quinn, Sasha, Demi, Denver, or that fucking contract. I didn't want to talk at all. It was my turn to get a little come action, but I saw no reason why I couldn't get Cassidy off again while I was at it. Yeah, I was that fucking generous.

The forward roll of my hips lifted her up to ride my thighs while my mouth got busy at her neck. The metal of my zipper against my cock was like making out with a washboard, but it was a good sort of pain when it brought her that much pleasure. Cassidy held on, her fingers digging into my shoulders, her hips moving in time with mine as she used me for her own gratification.

Her heavy breathing was at my ear, a small moan like a plea she was trying desperately to keep quiet. I palmed her thighs, moving my hands higher to the cheeks of her ass to bring her closer. The new angle must have been much more preferable because Cassidy's undulation became so wild that I had to brace one hand on the wall behind her to steady us both.

My mouth latched on to her neck and I sucked at her skin. Cassidy yanked away, denying me the mark I'd attempted, which only made me want it more. It was stupid. I knew it was, but I'd seen the way her little boyfriend looked at her. He still wanted her, but she was mine. And to prove it, I was going to make her come so hard she screamed, right under the very same roof where he was doing who the fuck cared what as long as he heard her.

"Shaw . . ." Her whisper was followed by a moan. "I'm going to—"

"I know," I told her. "I want to hear you."

She kissed me, her hips pressing forward and with even more purpose. I met her grind with an urgency of my own, needing her to get off so I could finally let the ache in my loins go. I didn't give a damn about the chafing, I didn't care who might walk in, I didn't even mind the fact that we were both still wearing all of our clothes and this was going to be a very messy situation by the time we were done. I just wanted to fucking come already.

Cassidy's moan started low, but she was still kissing me, and I'd meant it when I'd said I wanted to hear her. So I pulled back from the kiss, nearly jizzing all over myself when I saw the look on her face. Her eyes were closed, bottom lip caught between her teeth, brow smoothed as her head fell back and she continued to ride me. And then the grip that she had on my shoulders tightened to a painful sting when she pulled me to her, burying her face against my neck and ear as she came so hard I could feel the wetness seep through her leggings and the thick material of my jeans.

The best sight in the entire world was that of a woman achieving orgasm because I'd fucking done that for her. And then Cassidy slowly opened those shamrock greens to look at me and made me rethink all of that. It wasn't any woman. It was this woman.

Fuck.

"Your turn," she said with a mischievous, albeit very satisfied, smile.

"Goddamn right, it is," I told her.

Planting my feet, I pinned her to the corner between the wall and bookcase, and then tilted her body at an angle that was favorable for my stroke. A stroke that would hopefully be less mosh-and-slam and more bump-and-grind on my highly sensitive man parts.

Oh, my God, but she felt so good. I was all ready to shoot my load before she started kissing my neck, but then she did that little suckle thing and I thought for a second she might actually be trying to mark me, which made my fucking dick even harder because, yeah, someone was going to notice that. With any luck, that someone would be Lobster Casey, and he'd have to put two and two together, inevitably figuring out that me plus Cassidy equaled he'd never be fucking her again.

But then Cassidy moved to a different spot. Maybe she hadn't been trying to mark me at all. I, however, was still trying to get off. I could feel the percolation down deep in my boys, building and building. A couple more strokes was all it would take to . . .

The sound of the door sliding open was like a sadistic dominatrix grabbing my shit to put the halt on my release.

"Hey, Cass . . ." came a voice that belonged to neither Cassidy nor myself.

Why, universe? Why do you hate me? I mentally shouted to the cosmos.

Cassidy's buck and shove was enough to make me drop her to her feet and back away just in time for Casey to step into the room. He pulled up short when he saw that she wasn't alone. The once-over he gave me, coupled with that ticking jaw was proof enough that he knew what was up. No doubt our flushed cheeks and heavy breathing were dead giveaways.

A victorious grin tugged at the corner of my mouth even though I really wanted to slam his face into the wall for cock-blocking me yet again. Damn. Did the man have built-in radar to detect when a dude was about to get off on his girl or what?

A very flustered Cassidy attempted to cover the bust with a forced smile and too sweet greeting. "Hey! What's up, Case?"

Cock-block Casey wasn't fooled. I prepared myself for the brawl I knew was about to ensue, almost welcoming it because yeah, I wanted the chance to get a shot or two in as well. But I was surprised when he turned his daggered glare away from me, and instead looked at the unoccupied space to his left.

"Mom wanted me to tell you it's time to get dinner started." It was as if he couldn't bear to look at Cassidy when he spoke to her. "She's in the kitchen." With that, he turned and walked out.

"Shit," Cassidy mumbled under her breath.

I'd rarely heard her curse. She only ever did so when she was pissed at me, and even then, I'd really been pushing her buttons. Clearly, this was an issue for her. Feeling the painful throb of my still-disgruntled cock, it was an issue for me as well. Though for a different reason, I was sure.

Cassidy fixed her clothes and made to walk past me without a word. That just wasn't okay, so I grabbed her by the elbow to stop her in her tracks.

"You're just going to leave me like this again?"

She glanced down at the very obvious bulge in my jeans and smiled. This time, the smile was genuine. So was the enormous hard-on that caused it. I wondered if Casey had seen it as well. But then again, how could he have missed it? I did a mental fist pump because even though my shit was backed up and causing me a great deal of discomfort, the points just kept adding up in my favor.

With a sympathetic frown she said, "I'm sorry, but if I don't get in that kitchen, she's just going to come looking for me. And the wrath of Abby is something neither one of us wants to incur. Believe you me, she might look sweet and innocent, and she is for the most part, but if you get her upset, you better look out. They don't call her Hurricane Abby for no reason." She laughed and the sound was fucking beautiful. Since when had that happened?

"We still have things to discuss."

She shrugged and then shook her head. "Not really. I mean, what more is there to say? You came here to bitch at me over an incorrect assumption you'd made. So I suppose now that you know the truth, you'll want to get back to San Diego so you can bask in your win. Right?"

I knew the answer to her question in an instant. And it was a shocker for me. Maybe there had been more than one reason I'd followed her to Stonington.

"Wrong. I'm not going anywhere yet." Seeing Cassidy's Skype conversation had given me an angle to work with that I hadn't considered amid the no-cell-service debacle. I could conduct business just as well from here as I could from my desk at Striker Sports Entertainment.

Cassidy tilted her head to the side to regard me as if I were a complex portrait hanging in a historical museum. "Why not?"

That question was one I wasn't sure I had the answer to yet. Things were a jumbled-up mess in my head and I needed time to sort them out. If I told Cassidy that, she'd just push until something stupid and even more confusing got blurted out, so I gave her an answer she'd expect to hear from the Shaw Matthews she knew.

"I've gotten you off three times already today. You owe me. Fair is fair."

She laughed again, completely at my expense, so I decided to have a little fun with what I imagined to be the Stonington man mentality. Dropping my voice an octave, I said, "Go make me some dinner, woman," and then I gave her a smack on the ass to send her on her way.

As she left the room, Cassidy looked at me like I was cracked. I probably was. In my defense, I'd very recently scored the most sought-after quarterback in the nation as a client, traveled diagonally across an entire country, suffered through an extreme bout of sleep deprivation, and then went unconscious for way longer than was probably healthy only to wake up to two—count them, *two*—highly erotic encounters with a woman I loved to hate that had left me less than satisfied. My balls felt like they were trying to castrate themselves, and the zipper on my jeans had rubbed my dick raw. Yeah, I was probably teetering on the edge of insanity.

And now I was sending my little woman off to make me dinner. *My* little woman? "They're going to send the padded wagon after you, Matthews," I said to myself as I attempted to shake the crazy from my noggin. But my brain was like a dog with a bone on that one. Maybe I should consider shock therapy.

Nah, I knew what the problem was. I just needed to get off. Everything would right itself after that. Looking down at my crotch, it occurred to me that the only way that was likely to happen was if I took the matter into my own hands. I raised the one that would do the deed and gave it a wink. "Take the crazy away, baby. Daddy needs some perspective."

CHAPTER 6

Shaw

Jacking off was a no go. And not because I hadn't put forth my best effort. It was because even though I wanted and needed to come more than any fucking thing, somehow Denver Rockford's face kept popping up in place of Cassidy's. The flaccid mess that followed had nothing to do with the fact that he was gay, and everything to do with the fact that my warped imagination was picturing him pacing and not so patiently urging me to hurry up and get my rocks off so I could handle his business.

Damn. I threw in the towel, literally slinging the one I'd recruited to play wide receiver back into the cabinet with the other benchwarmers. My balls were at center, keyed up and ready to rocket one off for the game-winning touchdown, but my cocky quarterback's arm had gone limp.

The hard-on might have been gone, but the blue-ball syndrome wasn't. I closed my eyes, trying to cope with the annoyance and succeeding only in making it worse. Maybe if I got my mind off things, if I concentrated on keeping the contract that had started all this nonsense in the first place, it would go away.

Tucking my pathetic dick back into my pants, I zipped up, splashed some cold water onto my face, and pulled out my laptop.

Thanks to the time difference, Ben would still be in the office, but even if he wasn't, I knew he'd check his emails. So I shot one off, telling him I'd be extending my stay in Stonington for a while longer, and that he needed to be sure he had Skype downloaded to his computer at the office and on his cell. I also told him to get in touch with Denver to ask him to do the same, so I could contact him.

Within moments of hitting the send button, I got a call. Ben might have been a smart-ass, but he was a professional smart-ass and he always went above and beyond when it came to handling business.

My greeting was met with a "Hey, boss man! You're looking . . . constipated." Like I said, smart-ass. "You need me to send a poo care package?"

"Fuck off, Ben." The line separating our professional and personal relationship might have been blurred, but it worked for us. "Catch me up on everything."

Ben did exactly that, going through messages I might have missed thanks to the zero-cell-service thing, and taking notes on issues I needed him to handle. He confirmed he'd gotten a message through to my star client, Denver, and he'd be ready for my call.

It wasn't really that we had a lot to do at the moment since the attorneys were still drawing up contracts, but superstar athletes like Denver were used to getting a lot of attention from their agent. I wasn't going to fail him on that. Ben also told me that Denver had already relocated back home with his parents in Colorado and was ready to start training as soon as the ink was dry on the final draft of his multimillion-dollar deal. All great news. His enthusiasm for the game was the very thing that had propelled his success and kept it going. That and his superhuman arm. They didn't call him the "Rocket Man" for nothing.

Cassidy had already done most of the negotiating with Colorado on Denver's behalf before he'd even made a decision on which of us he'd pick for his agent. The cut of that was going to be hefty and would be deposited into my bank account, but for the first time in my life, I knew I'd break her off a sizable chunk of it. Like I'd told her: fair was fair. I'd been handed Denver's contract and I'd been in talks with Colorado regarding finalizing it, but I hadn't really earned the big score. Despite what I knew that Cassidy thought of me, I wasn't about taking something that didn't rightfully belong to me.

The partnership with Striker, however, was another story. It was mine, fair and square. Monty Prather had groomed me for it before he'd retired, and Wade Price knew I was the man for the job even though he'd been rooting for his protégé, Cassidy, to take the win. Wade and I had a great deal of respect for each other, so the new partnership would be a seamless transition. The big announcement to the rest of the company would wait for my return from my "well-deserved vacation," according to Wade.

My Skype call with Ben had just been coming to a close when he asked about Cassidy.

"How is the ice queen?"

I was surprised by my reaction. Not so much the way my cock sprang back to attention at the mention of her name, but because I wanted to jump to her defense in a way I never had before. "*Cassidy* is okay." She might have been the ice queen in sunny California, but in frigid Maine all of that seemed to melt away.

It occurred to me that Ben had never asked for the reason I was here with her in the first place, so I asked him why that was.

He looked guilty as hell. "Promise you won't fire me?"

"What good would it do me? Every time I do, you just keep showing back up on my doorstep like a flea-infested cat," I told him. "Out with it."

"The truth is, when you first came to the San Diego office, Ally and I bet on when you and Cassidy would finally hook up. I won." Ben got a big cheesy grin on his face.

Having come from Detroit, not much shocked me. This? This did. I didn't even know where to start with my questions.

"What makes you think we hooked up?"

"Dude, you chased her across the country," he said as if that was all the explanation needed. When it was clear that it wasn't, he continued. "The only reason a man does that is if he's pussy-whipped."

I should've hung up on him right then and there, or at least told him to pack up his desk and mean it this time. But I didn't. "And the two of you thought we'd hook up because?"

"Because you can't stand each other," he said matter-of-factly. "Like Ally says, there's a very thin line between love and hate."

I nearly choked on my own saliva. Love was definitely not the issue. Lust, yes, per my newly engorged cock, but *not* love.

"Ben"—my voice was even, all business—"if there's even a hint of a rumor that Cassidy and I are hooking up, she'll get fired. For real. Technically, I'm her boss now. Do you understand what I'm saying?"

My assistant was straight as an arrow then, the big picture crystal clear. Whether his suspicion was right or not, didn't matter. Cassidy hadn't done anything wrong, and I'd be damned before I'd let her go down in flames over something we'd both consented to. Even if I was the one who'd seduced her. Well, it was iffy on who'd seduced whom in the beginning. I'd say it was a dead-even draw, either way.

"No worries," Ben reassured me. "Ally and I won't breathe a word about it."

I believed him. Ally and Ben were so loyal, they'd put their own jobs on the line to save Cassidy's and mine.

I supposed I should stop fucking Cassidy now that our positions on the totem pole had changed, but feeling the heavy bastard of a cock on my thigh again, I knew I wouldn't. Good God, the ache in my balls was a persistent annoyance. Dinner would be ready soon, and no way was I willing to suffer through it with this thing hijacking my every thought. So I hung up with Ben to try to take care of the issue yet again.

Before I could even get the zipper undone, my hand was down my jeans and gripping my cock. A moan I hadn't meant to set free was the precursor to the jack fest that ensued after that. There was no lotion or acceptable lube nearby, so I had to rely on the bit of precum that seeped from the fat head to prep my chafed cock for the punishing strokes that followed.

I didn't have to search my mind for a subject to focus on while getting myself off because the memory of Cassidy's lips wrapped around my cock was already queued up, and that was more than enough. For safety measures, I cupped my balls, gently working them while I watched my cock in my fisted hand sliding up and down its rigid thickness.

I was hypersensitive, the chafe from earlier making my manipulations uncomfortable, but I could deal with that much better than I could with that persistent ache creeping its way up my sac. It was as fierce as an imprisoned monstrosity hungry for raw meat, but with any luck, ejaculation would curb its appetite.

The veins of my cock were thick with blood, the head tinged red by the maddening sweep of my thumb over its angry ridge. Thin, soft skin was stretched taut over a shaft that had never been harder, and the heart in my chest played a fast-paced cadence to match the tempo of my strokes. I could feel it building, my release. The breath in my lungs was shallow, as if with each quick inhale and exhale it would push my orgasm closer to the brink. Maybe it could.

With rapt fascination, I watched, pulling my shirt up and tucking it under my chin to prepare for the sticky mess to come. And it would at any moment, thank God.

Squeezing my cock, I pumped harder, coaxing the cure to what was shaping up to be a whole lot of frustration. It was right there. Right . . .

I jumped at the sound of a loud bang on the door.

"You've gotta be *fucking* kidding me," I growled when my release receded back from wherever the hell it came from.

"Ay, yo! Dinner's ready!" came Cock-block Casey's voice through the door.

I was going to murder him. In cold blood. With my bare hands.

"You hear me, man?" He was a persistent fucker.

"Yeah, yeah. I'll be down in a minute," I called back, mentally calculating the length of rope I'd need to tie him off to the bumper of my tiny rental car and drag him down the street.

"Better hurry. Mom doesn't like it when you're late to dinner."

"She's not my mother," I reminded him.

"Doesn't matter. She's mine."

It was an indirect threat, and I couldn't help but wonder if he was talking about Abby or Cassidy.

Dinnertime was obviously a big deal in the Whalen House. The dining room table was large enough to accommodate twelve, but was set for six. A crisp, white table linen was spread over the length and not a single crease marred its perfect plane.

Fried chicken, white gravy, mashed potatoes, fried corn, green beans, and biscuits looked to be on the menu. My stomach growled at the sight of it, battling with the achy throb farther below for attention. I damn sure couldn't jack off at the table, so I settled for getting my fat-boy grub on to satiate at least one need.

Platters and bowls of food started to make their way around the table as we served ourselves. Well, most of us did, anyway. Abby was attending to the old man at the head, so I guessed him to be her husband. He looked to be at least a decade older than her—maybe midsixties—a spitting image of Casey with some years etched into his wrinkles, a whole lot of wisdom behind those eyes, and the result from a little more time at the dinner table wrapped around his midsection.

"Everything looks delicious, Abby," I told her as I chose the empty seat my hostess had pointed out between Cassidy and the man I hadn't yet met. Casey was next to his mother, directly across from Cassidy, and there was another setting next to him that hadn't yet been occupied.

Abby stabbed a piece of fried chicken breast with a fork and put it on the plate of the man beside her. "Thank you, I hope you like it."

"If it's anything like the sandwich you made for me earlier, I'm sure I will."

"Let me guess," the man interrupted. "You had the Abby melt?"

I had no idea what an Abby melt was, but if it was anything like the manna I'd eaten for lunch, a more appropriate name would be something like the monkey spank or toasted orgasm.

"Grilled turkey, bacon, and cheese sandwich?" I asked.

"Yep! That's the Abby." He laughed as the sandwich's namesake plopped down a dollop of mashed potatoes in front of him. "Best sandwich in town."

"He's a little biased," Abby said, passing the potatoes to Casey and picking up the gravy. "Of course he has to be if he wants to keep eating," she said, laughing. "This is my Thomas. Thomas, meet Shaw Matthews."

"Shaw Matthews?" Casey asked. I was a little surprised no one had given him that information yet. When I nodded, he continued. "Cassidy's told me a lot about you."

"Has she?" Putting the napkin in my lap, I shot him a disingenuous smile. "Huh. Well, I wish I could say the same."

Cassidy kicked me under the table, but I'd grown so used to it after all the board meetings we'd attended together that I didn't even need shin guards.

"And this," Abby said, looking up at the straggler that had just entered the room, "is Mia Morgan."

Casey put the bowl of potatoes down and jumped up to pull out the seat next to his. Mia was short, with dark eyes and long brown hair, cute in an understated girl-next-door sort of way. Though the way she was gawking at Cassidy had girl-on-girl action written all over it.

Cassidy gave her a welcoming smile, something warm and friendly. Something I'd never really seen from her before. At least not toward me. "Hi, I'm—"

"I know who you are. You're Cassidy," Mia finished for her. Then she dipped her head and nervously took the offered chair as if she'd just realized how stalker-ish she'd sounded.

When Cassidy looked taken aback, Casey jumped in. "Yep. That"—he paused—"is my Cassidy." He regarded Cassidy in a way that felt almost intrusive to witness, like he was swept up in some moment the rest of us hadn't been meant to see.

A squirming Cassidy felt the weight of that moment and looked down at her lap, clearing her throat. It was enough to jar Casey from whatever fantasy he'd been playing out in his mind and bring him back to the present.

"I'm sorry I'm late, Abby. I sort of got swept up in a scene I had to get out or risk losing altogether." Mia waved her hand in the air as if it was a silly excuse.

"It's okay, dear. We've just started, anyway." Abby turned toward Cassidy and me. "Mia's a romance author. She came to Stonington to do some research on a book she's writing."

Cassidy nodded. "Casey told me there was a celebrity in town. He just didn't tell me you were staying with us." She gave him a disapproving scowl then returned her attention to the newcomer. "I can think of a thousand more romantic settings. What's so special about Stonington?"

Cassidy was a well-known agent who was surrounded by world-famous athletes on a near daily basis, so she wasn't about to be awestruck in the presence of this woman.

"Well, for one, it's absolutely breathtaking," the author began with a dreamy air about her. "And for two, my hero is a lobster-man."

When Mia looked at Casey and blushed, the polite smile Cassidy wore dropped and then reappeared again, the same but different somehow. "Oh. I didn't realize lobstering was considered a particularly romantic vocation."

"Well"—Mia shrugged—"there are women here. Most of whom stay, so there must be something about a lobsterman that draws them in."

"There is. Money," Cassidy said, quite bluntly. She pinched off a piece of biscuit and popped it into her mouth.

"Hey now!" Abby said, insulted.

Cassidy dropped the biscuit back onto her plate. "Sorry, Abbs, but you know it's true." She picked up her fork and pushed the green beans around on her plate. "So what kind of research are you doing, Mia?"

"I'm just getting the layout of the town, but mostly I wanted to interview a lobsterman. Since I write fiction, I can take some creative liberties, but I like what I write to be as close to reality as I can get it. Makes it so much easier to put the reader in the moment if I can make them feel what I feel, see what I see, et cetera. You know?"

"Not really, but maybe that's because as a law graduate, I tend to deal with fact over fiction." Ouch. Cassidy let that hang in the air, looking for all the world like the ice queen I'd known her to be in San Diego. "So who are you interviewing?"

"Me," Casey said, coming to Mia's rescue.

Cassidy snickered. "Since when do you like putting your life under a microscope?"

"Since someone cared enough to ask about it." Casey cocked his head to the side and met her with a challenging brow.

That shut her up. Guilt radiated from Cassidy's body next to me, and her attention went to the potatoes on her plate.

Mia started explaining as if she was trying to get Casey out of trouble. "When I booked the room here, I asked Anna if she knew of any fishermen who might agree to talk to me. She's the one who volunteered Casey to do the job."

"She did, did she?" Cassidy's smart mouth rallied. I knew it would. She was never one to back down from an argument, even if it was one that no one else in the room knew she was having. I knew though. She and I had gone around and around like that for years now. No doubt, her mother would know, too, once she returned.

Casey might as well have reached across the table with a stick to poke the hibernating bear when he said, "Since I had so much free time on my hands, I figured why not?"

If those potatoes hadn't already been mashed, they would have been well on their way to it in the manner in which Cassidy was stabbing them. Something weird was happening. Cassidy was acting like a wife who'd just caught her cheating husband red-handed. And Casey? I couldn't tell if he was parading his mistress around or begging forgiveness for his infidelity.

I figured it out when I caught an exchange I probably wasn't supposed to see. While Mia was busy talking about the setup of the story behind Casey's character in her book, Casey was eyeing Cassidy, and then those eyes slid to me before cutting back to her as if to say, *You aren't so innocent yourself.*

Part of me wanted to high-five him. Part of me wanted to defend her. But the biggest part of me wanted to pull her into my lap and tell him that he didn't need to worry about what she was doing because she was my business now. Which was an asinine thought, of course.

Mia finished up the rough outline of her story and Cassidy looked stunned. "Wow, so you're pretty much writing Casey's biography, huh? Which means *my* biography."

"Most of what he's talked about is you, yes. You've been a very important part of his life, maybe even the center of it. But I would never think it to be okay to put you on display. Either of you. I apologize if it came across that way. It's mostly how he thinks about things, the way he thinks about you, the outlandish adventures the two of you have had that I'd love to play off of. If that's okay, I mean."

Cassidy softened. "Yeah, we've had some really great times. Huh, Case?"

"God, yeah."

There was a moment of reflection behind her eyes and then she grinned wide and bright. "Hey, do you remember that time when we first went out on the boat?"

"It was your first time, not mine," Casey corrected her. "But yeah. How could I forget? You were such a brat. Always were."

Cassidy rolled her eyes. "Whatever. You deserved what you got and so much more."

"Oh, really?" Mia lit up like a golden ticket winner for Willy Wonka's chocolate factory. "Casey getting what he deserves? That sounds like a fun story. Do tell."

Cassidy chuckled when Casey groaned. "You just told her all the highlights of the mighty, mighty Casey Michaels's life, huh?"

He gave her a "well, duh" look. "She's writing a romance story. Why would I tell her something that makes me look like anything less than the hero?"

Mia shouldered him. "Because it makes you a flawed human being like the rest of us. And because perfect imperfection is real and sexy."

Thomas guffawed. "I don't know about sexy, but I'll tell you the story, if he won't."

Casey sighed in defeat before waving toward his father. "Go ahead. You tell it better than anyone else, anyway."

"Bet your ass I do," Thomas said, settling in. "Around here, fathers take their sons out on the boat to teach them about lobstering at a pretty early age. The first time I took Casey out was right around the time he first started to walk. Wanted him to get his sea legs along with his land legs."

"Cassidy always threw a fit about it," Abby added. "She was such a tomboy. Never was into the girly things. It drove Anna crazy. Whatever Casey did, she wanted to do, too."

"Because she wanted to be like me," Casey said and laughed.

"Ha! You wish! It was because I was competitive and had to prove I could do whatever you could do, and better."

Cassidy and I had butted heads more often than not, but I'd always respected and admired her competitive nature. Damn, thinking back on it, it had probably even been a huge turn-on for me. That and her ass. And maybe even her smart mouth. Those thoughts did absolutely nothing good for the bastard of a cock lying thick and hard on my thigh, or for the uncomfortable throbbing of the pent-up frustration needing a release, still.

"Anyway," Thomas continued his story, "I did that every now and then until he turned twelve, I guess, and that was the first summer he was going to start working. Well, Cassidy had had enough of being told she couldn't go, so one morning, she snuck out of the house and onto the boat before any of the rest of us. We were way offshore before she decided to come out of her hiding spot, and by then, it was more of a hassle to take her back than to let her stay. Plus, we thought maybe it would teach her a lesson and she'd stop wanting to be such a pain in the ass."

"It didn't," she said with a cheeky grin.

"So there we were, pulling in a trawl, when Casey pulled a shedder from a trap and decided it would be funny to throw it on Cassidy to prove how much of a girl she really was." Thomas sat back, rubbing his very full belly. "He proved it, all right. That shedder—"

Though I was sure it made me look stupid, I had to ask, "I'm sorry, what's a shedder?"

Mia answered, "It's a lobster that has shed its shell and doesn't have the hard one yet." When Cassidy looked at her, impressed, Mia blushed. "Casey's been teaching me a lot, I guess."

Casey threw his arm over the back of her chair and grinned wide and proud. "And you've been a very attentive student. It's been nice to have someone take an interest in the things I love."

"Anyway," Thomas said, getting the topic back on track. "That shedder got its pincher claw on Cassidy's—" He stopped, seemingly looking for the word.

"My boob," Cassidy said with a roll of her eyes. She crossed her arms over her chest as if to hide them, but there was nothing doing with a rack like that.

"Yeah, that," Thomas said with a cough.

Casey laughed, and even I had to admit it was pretty funny.

"Laugh all you want, lobster boy," Cassidy told him, setting that damn determined chin of hers. "I got even."

"She sure did." Now Thomas was laughing. "Cassidy punched him square in the jaw and knocked him overboard."

I knew that punch. In fact, the memory of it sent a residual jolt of pain through my newly healed eye and I winced. Cassidy had given me a right hook when I'd insinuated that she'd sleep with anyone to get to the top. Of course I knew then that it wasn't true, but she'd been taking nonphysical jabs at my personal life prior to my untoward comment, so I'd felt the need to get even. Childishly. Whatever. She should've minded her own damn business. Now, it seemed she was the one under the microscope.

Thomas and Casey's laughter at Cassidy's expense was so loud I wouldn't have been surprised if the neighbors heard them. Mia and Abby were slow to join them, but join them they did, like they'd caught a serious case of the tickle bunnies. A pouting Cassidy and I seemed to be the only ones immune. Though that might not have been true for me if the little swimmers housed in my nut sack hadn't been revolting with pitchforks and torches.

Once the moment passed and everyone seemed to simmer down again, Casey took a deep breath and wiped the corner of his eye. "It was the first time I ever noticed she had breasts. And I've been in love with them ever since."

"Casey!" Abby yelped, appalled.

"Not Cassidy's, Mom. Breasts in general," he tried to cover, realizing too late that he was only making matters worse. "I mean . . ."

"You'd best stop before you dig that hole any deeper, boy," Thomas told him in true fatherly fashion.

"Just don't try that on me when we go out tomorrow," Mia said, elbowing Casey in the ribs.

Casey jumped, giving her a playful wink. "No worries, babe. When you're with Casey Michaels, you're in good hands. I'll never let anything happen to you."

Cassidy sat up a little straighter. "You're taking her out on the boat? I thought that was a no-chick zone?"

"I'm making a special exception for Mia."

"Oh. So I guess that means I'll have time to show you around town tomorrow after all, Shaw." Cassidy smiled at me like we were the best of friends and this was a normal thing.

It wasn't, and I was lost. "I'm sorry, what?"

"You asked me to give you a tour and I told you I'd have to pitch in around here, but since Mia's our only other guest and she's going to be busy with Casey tomorrow, I can devote my full attention to you, now."

Yeah, she'd totally just made that up, but I got it. She was trying to make Casey jealous and she was using me to do so. It wasn't cool. Not because it was mean to do that to him—I could give a shit about that—but because she was fucking with me. Plus, I wasn't going to be a pawn that she used to make her boyfriend want her more than some other chick. Fuck that.

Cassidy leaned closer to me, putting her hand on my knee and moving it up the inside of my thigh. My fucking cock went ape-shit crazy, and I knew if it were at all possible, the damn thing would've gotten down on its knees and begged her to touch it. You'd think that would be hot, but when my boys were as blue as they were and we were sitting in a roomful of people—which pretty much made it impossible to do anything about the shit storm she was stirring up in my pants—it wasn't good.

I swatted her hand away, still trying to be inconspicuous, since the last thing I wanted was to draw Abby's attention to my predicament. But then to make matters worse, my refusal of her advances only made Cassidy curious, and she looked down at my lap to see the issue for herself. I might have even angled myself toward her and put my hand over the damn thing to make sure it was really defined for her. Hopefully, that would be warning enough. Then again, she was Cassidy fucking Whalen, the woman who seemed to thrive on making my life a living nightmare.

Shit. She smirked with a devious glint in her eye. I knew my onetime adversary slash part-time lover well enough to recognize that look. She saw two birds and one stone, and she was going for the kill.

Her hand was back on my thigh again, the pressure she applied a stark indication that she would not be moved. All the while, she continued to chat with the others at the table, a conversation I couldn't concentrate on, or much less give a fuck about, because she was massaging my leg. Each move of her body as she was supposedly lost in conversation was only an excuse to reposition said hand higher and higher until her knuckle was grazing the head of my cock.

I held my breath, mentally willing myself not to come. Football stats, wicker furniture, clowns in full costume—none of them did the trick. Because now her hand was on top of my dick, slowly moving in a wave from fingertip to wrist. I tried to elbow her, but my attempt only caused her to grip me fully so that she held on. Goddamn, but the woman was a sadistic succubus.

Tilting her head to look at me, she bit her lip in time with the stroke of my cock through my jeans. It was all over. My orgasm boiled to the surface, but I squeezed my eyes shut, might versus nature in a battle of determination. I was losing. I was losing so bad. And I was going to come.

"Shaw, are you okay?"

I jumped at the sound of Abby's voice, hitting the table in my surprise and only barely saving myself the embarrassment of being a complete and total pervert in her presence. But at least Cassidy's hand was back in her own lap.

Jesus fucking Christ!

The pain that had been playing havoc on my nuts shot straight up into my lower abdomen and it was taking everything in me not to let it show on my face. Something hot and wet was running onto my thigh, but I didn't have to wonder what that something was. For all my effort against coming, it hadn't stopped a little bit of semen from oozing out. You'd think something like that would provide at least a smidgen of relief, but nope. It only made matters worse.

Like getting kicked in the balls, that sickening feeling in the pit of my stomach forced me to really concentrate on not hurling all over the dinner table. Making a run for the nearest bathroom wasn't going to happen because even though I'd jizzed in my pants, it wasn't enough and I was still rock hard. The wet spot on my jeans coupled with a very obvious boner was definitely not something I wanted anyone else to see. I was fucked, only not actually.

"Shaw?" Abby asked again.

"Oopsie, looks like you've made a mess. . . ." Cassidy's sing-song was a taunt that only added insult to injury. Oh, she was going to pay for this one dearly.

It wasn't until then that I noticed I'd bumped the table and knocked the gravy bowl over, the creamy white substance spilling all over the table. Damn, but that sort of mockery just couldn't be planned.

"Yeah, I'm fine. Sorry. I'll clean that up." I started to grab the napkin from my lap, but thought better of it. It might come in handy if I had no other choice than to vacate my spot.

"Don't you worry about a thing, hon," Abby said, getting up. "It's time to clear the table and do the cleanup anyway. My boys are early risers." She gave me that motherly smile again and it made me feel like shit because of what had just gone down right under her button nose.

Everyone started getting up from the table then, but I still couldn't move. I'd wait for the room to empty, and then I'd make my escape. Only to wait some more. Patiently.

An early bedtime meant there was a light at the end of the very narrow tunnel that I'd been trapped in for an entire fucking day. Cassidy got up to help Abby, leaning over me to grab my plate and silverware. I was sure it was for the sole purpose of putting her tits in my face, but I used the opportunity to exact a little revenge of my own and give her fair warning.

"As soon as the lights go out, you're mine," I whispered. And then I let my lips accidentally graze the nipple strategically placed before them.

Cassidy went rigid, the flesh on her exposed skin pebbling in an instant. The sound of the silverware clattering on the china was a dead giveaway to her shaking hands. Yeah, she knew what was coming. Or rather, who. She also knew who wouldn't be.

CHAPTER 7

Cassidy

It was late by the time Abby and I finished cleaning up after dinner. Well, late by Stonington standards, anyway. Besides the fact that daylight hours were shorter this far up north, fishermen were always early to bed, early to rise. Most of whom were up and at 'em before the light of the sun kissed the horizon.

Thomas had headed home right after dinner, while Casey stuck around to see that Abby had an escort. Now that I was home, there was no reason for either of them to spend the night. Shaw and Mia had been turned in for quite some time.

Mia. I didn't really know what to make of her yet, but she sure seemed to know an awful lot about Casey. Strange. Casey had always been more reserved with the facts of his life, with everyone except me, of course. Now he was pouring his guts out to this Mia Morgan chick as if . . . as if she were me. I didn't like it. Especially since some of that outpouring included details of my life as well. Probably most of it, in fact.

Turning off the light to the kitchen, I made a mental note to grill him on exactly how much she knew. The house was dark, except for the pale moonlight spilling in through the windows. It didn't matter. Nothing about the furniture arrangement ever changed, so I could walk it blindfolded if I had to. Climbing the stairs, instinct guided my footfalls around the steps I knew had a creak, which I knew how to avoid.

Hearing the rustling of my clothes as I made my way to my room, I was suddenly aware of how eerily quiet everything was. Not only the house, but all of Stonington. There were no boat whistles, no voices of fishermen calling to one another, no bird-calls, or sloshes of water against the pier with the tide. The hush was as if God himself had commanded silence out of respect for the fishermen. Fitting for a town that treated their main economic source like it was a religion.

At the top of the stairs, I hesitated, sensing a presence I couldn't see. The fine hairs on the back of my neck rose to attention, and I knew I was being watched. All of the doors were closed except for my bedroom, though it was so far down the hall that the moonlight coming from inside was no help on the landing. Maybe my mind was playing tricks on me, but I could've sworn I heard someone breathing.

I didn't need the banister as a guide, but I kept it on my right because doing so meant there could be no surprise attack on that side. As I turned the corner, I heard a creak and I let out a surprised gasp.

A dark figure stepped from the shadows, but before I could make a run for it, I was wrapped up in a pair of strong arms and denied the ability to identify my attacker. I went stiff, natural instinct commanding a flood of adrenaline to surge through my blood. But this adrenaline rush was rooted in excitement born of fear. Fear I felt even though I knew this man. His scent, the rhythm of his heart as it pounded against my back, his energy in the air . . . they were all familiar, welcomed.

Shaw's lips were at my ear, his warm breath on the exposed

flesh of my neck. "Mm, look what I found prowling around in the night."

I grinned even though he couldn't see my face, since I knew what this was about. Relaxing into his hold, I arched my back and teased the hard cock pressed to my backside with the roll of my hips. "What's the matter, something keeping you *up?*"

The short huff of laughter was menacing, and even more so was his voice when he said, "You're about to get fucked. My way. Right now. It won't be easy. It won't be slow. And you will get absolutely no enjoyment out of it." His teeth caught my earlobe. "Still think this is funny?"

No, I didn't. I believed everything he said. But he was wrong about one thing. I would enjoy it. Very much.

With an abrupt shove forward, he commanded me to walk. Though he didn't tell me where to go, I knew where I would take him. Shaw Matthews was in my hometown, in my house, and I would have him in my bed. Or rather, he would have me.

I didn't turn to look over my shoulder as I went toward my room because I didn't need to. He would follow and he didn't need any light to see me. No doubt, my body's pheromones were leaving a trail he'd be able to track as if we were animals in the wild at the height of mating season.

As soon as I stepped into my bedroom, I turned, coming chest to chest with him. The picture window allowed a flood of moonlight to infiltrate the darkness, so I could see every minute detail of his face. Shaw's eyes were dilated, his jaw ticking and nostrils slightly flared even as the muscles in his body coiled in preparation for his attack. One flinch was all it would take to set him off. A wicked grin lifted the corner of my mouth. God, I wanted to set him off. So my lips parted to exhale the breath I'd been holding.

Shaw pounced, his lips crashing to mine and his strong, capable hands crushing my hips to his. There was a frenzy of activity then, both of us working to get me undressed.

Grabbing my sweater with both hands, I yanked it over my head, and that was where I stopped. Shaw already had my pants down to my ankles, impatiently waiting for me to kick my shoes off so he could finish the job. I did, only then feeling the kiss of cool air on my naked ass. I guessed the panties were wrapped up in the leggings. My bra wasn't even a factor, apparently, because before I could tend to it, Shaw had lifted me up and laid me across my bed, occupying the place between my thighs.

His mouth was on me then, furiously kissing my mouth, neck, jaw, and shoulders while he unfastened his pants. I tried to help him with the shirt, but he was so focused on his pants that the shirt didn't seem to matter.

Desperate. Shaw's movements were so hurried and desperate and I knew exactly why. He wasn't going to chance another interruption. I sort of felt sorry for him. He'd been denied his release while being more than generous with mine. It wasn't fair. So I gave in, offering myself up to him like a sacrificial lamb to do with as he wanted.

And he did.

Without a word, without even a precursory stroke of his finger to be sure I was ready, Shaw entered me. My back arched to his sudden presence. Although I'd had him inside me before, he was very well endowed and no preparation made for an uncomfortable stretch.

Shaw moaned, the sound of pleasure and relief making me swell with pride because I'd done that for him. He didn't pause, didn't wait for me to acclimate to his penetration, didn't stop to make sure I was okay, and that was just fine by me. His face was buried in the crook of my neck as he grabbed my thighs at the knees and spread me wide for him. Pinned in place by his hold and his body, I could do nothing but endure his wild thrusts. They were deep, hard, and for his enjoyment alone.

Shaw wasn't normally a selfish lover. He'd always made sure I'd been well taken care of, but it was so clear that in this instance, he was putting his own needs before mine. There was something wholly erotic about knowing you were being used for someone else's pleasure. Something that had an orgasm edging closer and closer. But it would not come to fruition.

There was nothing more than three carnal grunts that preceded his quick withdrawal. Shaw's fisted hand was working up and down over his length so savagely that I couldn't fathom the pleasure it brought him, but then hot semen spilled onto my abdomen in stuttered spurts. I touched myself while watching him because it was sexy and I was still so close to having my own orgasm.

Shaw grabbed my hand and pinned me to the bed. "I don't think so," he growled. "Twice you left me less than satisfied. And then you decided to toy with me at the dinner table, with others in the room because you knew I could do nothing about it."

His free hand went to my pussy, his fingertips lightly massaging my clit just enough to make me squirm under his manipulations. More. I needed more pressure, more movement, more of anything. Shaw gave me more taunts.

"You caused me a great deal of discomfort . . . a great deal of frustration." He watched his own fingers work me, seemingly fascinated by my body's reaction to his touch. And I certainly reacted, not that it did me any good. With an arch to my back, I rolled my hips, seeking more friction. I was denied.

"Did you think I wouldn't get even?" His voice was menacing. "I could, you know. I could leave you. I should leave you."

I closed my eyes, knowing he might while willing him not to. It would be what I deserved, after all.

"But unlike some people, I would never be that cruel." Shaw plunged a finger deep inside me, burying it to the knuckle. I clenched my fists and bit back the moan in my throat because that was all I could do. And then he started doing this thing with his finger inside me, teasing my G-spot with his thick length. God, the man should've been a pianist.

It occurred to me that this could quite possibly be a trap, some cruel form of torture like the night he edged me over and over again on my balcony before letting me come. But eventually he had let me come. Maybe he would do so again. Either way, the things he was doing to my body could not be ignored. I reveled in it, soaked up every minute stroke and let it drive me to the brink.

"Not yet," he whispered.

Before I could register what was going on, Shaw was gone and so was his hold. He grabbed the back of my knees and pulled me to the edge of the bed, flipping me and forcing me to bend over, face-first until my cheek was kissing the mattress. Holding me by the neck, his fingers stroked the wet folds of my pussy from front to back and then retracing the path again.

"So pretty," he said. I could still see him from the twisted angle of my neck, but he wasn't looking at me. At least not my face. No, Shaw's attention was focused down below. My arousal was heightened by his fascination, and I could feel myself moisten even more as if my girly bits were preparing to put on a show for him.

He dipped his finger into the wetness, collecting it before moving to circle my anus. Some part of me wanted him to take it, even though I knew it would hurt like hell. But that wasn't his intention. Again, his finger was inside me, flicking back and forth as if beckoning my orgasm. He'd have it soon. Especially if he kept the pressure of his thumb on my anus like that.

Apparently dissatisfied by the position, Shaw dropped to his knees behind me and added another finger, thrusting them in and out of me at a pace that matched the maddening pace of his cock just moments before. I gripped the duvet under me, biting my lip and wishing for all the world that I'd been able to sink my teeth into his flesh as the heel of his hand smacked at my clit with each knuckle-deep plunge. The depth of each stroke hit that special spot inside me, and I could do nothing but clench and wait for the orgasm building to spill forth. Faster and harder he fucked me with his fingers, his soft lips kissing the cheeks of my ass while his other hand spread me wide for him. I could feel the stretch on my anus, a delicious tease that only amplified the other marvels playing havoc on my senses. And then the hot, wet sensation of his mouth on that forbidden entrance pushed me over the edge.

It happened. The dam cracked and the force of my orgasm broke free, the warmth of it trickling down my thigh as it gushed forth. My body tensed and my teeth clenched as my abdomen contracted and I let it go. I'd never come with such intensity, such ferocity.

"Fuck. There's my good girl," Shaw growled, and then he nipped at my ass.

His fingers retreated, but continued a gentle stroke of my tender flesh as if soothing a wild animal after a tantrum. My body could take no more and I finally collapsed. I couldn't move, couldn't speak, and could barely breathe. My eyelids felt heavy and my mind fuzzy as an orgasm-induced coma crept up my paralyzed body and hovered on the edge of my consciousness. It was only a matter of time before I went lights out, but I did manage to register Shaw's movement at the end of the bed and the blanket I kept there being pulled over my naked body.

"You're welcome. Sleep tight," he whispered before I felt his lips on my cheek and then I drifted off to sleep.

_____

The next morning, I rolled over and reached my arms overhead, pointing my toes for a delicious stretch that I capped off with a curl back into myself to snuggle my cuddle-buddy pillow from the night before. It was a beautiful morning, and I knew it before I even cracked an eye open. So I did them both at the same time, sighing with a huge grin when I saw the stunning sunrise coloring the skyline with vibrant oranges, pinks, and blues.

I remembered that sunrise. I'd woken up to it every single morning for years that spanned my earliest memory to the day I left Stonington for college. But it seemed different somehow. For the first time in a really long time, I felt . . . refreshed, maybe even a little rejuvenated.

Kicking the covers off to start the day, I had a sudden shock of awareness when the chill of the room kissed my naked flesh. Well, I was still wearing my bra, it seemed, but everything else was scattered about the floor. A smile stretched my cheeks when all the memories of the night before flooded my mind.

Shaw had given me one hell of an orgasm. The best orgasm I'd ever had in my entire life. Feeling something hard under my hand, I looked down at the cover to see Shaw had also given me a mess to clean up. Maybe I should've been grossed out by it, after all, Shaw's little swimmers had found their final resting place on my duvet, but my bigger concern was finding a way to get it down to the laundry before Abby could see it.

And I should probably get a shower.

Minutes later, Abby popped her head into the laundry room just as I'd started the washer.

"There you are. Come on, we have to get breakfast going. What are you washing?" she asked, going over to look for herself.

They say the truth shall set you free, so I went with it. "It's just my duvet. It smelled a little musty, so I guess it hasn't been washed in a while." Half-truths were still better than outright lies.

"Oh," she said and then looked me over, shaking her head. "Good Lord, child. You're still not dressed?"

I looked down at myself to confirm what I already knew to be true. I was dressed, having found a pair of sleep shorts I'd worn during my high school years still tucked into one of my drawers, just not for the day.

"You've been away from Stonington too long. Keeping those movie star hours, I see." She laughed and then turned to walk out, waving her hands at me. "Go on. I'll get breakfast going, Hollywood."

I loved Abby. Everyone loved Abby.

My shower and dress routine didn't take long. Stonington women kept their appearances simple, and fuss-free. Though most of them didn't wear any makeup at all—and that was how their men preferred it—I wasn't one of them. Still, I decided on only a little eyeliner and mascara. I left my hair down and threw on a cami and one of my old flannel shirts with a pair of jeans and a pair of boots I hadn't seen since my last trip home, and then I made my way down to breakfast. Last thing I needed was for Abby to come up and drag me down by my ear.

I didn't need to worry about Abby, though. She was preoccupied with Shaw, serving him up a lumberjack portion of hotcakes and sausage links while he scarfed them down and leaned into the pat on his head. I'd never seen Shaw so . . . boyish. It was sort of cute in a very disturbing way.

"What's got you in a such a good mood?" Abby asked when she saw me in the doorway.

I felt my cheeks fall. Apparently, I'd been smiling. And why not? It was a gorgeous day and I felt good.

"Yes, please tell us what's got you glowing this morning," Shaw said, his voice a dare.

I shrugged on my way over to the coffeemaker. "You know,

I have no idea. I think I just got something I really needed last night." I paused, glancing over at Shaw with a grin as I poured my coffee.

He winked at me, chewing his food with a little too much sexy. It was the first time I'd ever seen someone make chewing a slightly pornographic event. I even shot a look at Abby to be sure she hadn't noticed.

"Well, a good night's sleep is always nice," Abby said, oblivious.

There was a ruckus at the front door then and we all turned in that direction. As I walked over and leaned into the doorway, I felt my smile broaden even more.

"Ma! You're home!" I said, setting my cup down and going to help Da.

Ma was in a wheelchair, bless her, with her cast leg elevated, and the two of them had been fighting the door to keep it off her while he got her inside.

"Why didn't you come in through the mudroom?" I asked.

Da grumbled. "I thought the gravel would make it harder to push her in this damn thing. Besides, we had that ramp out front put in for a reason. Might as well get some use out of it."

"He's an old, stubborn mule," Ma said, stretching her arms out for me to give her a hug.

"Here, let me help with that," Shaw said, stepping around Abby and taking the bag from Da.

"And who are you?" my father asked.

"He's a guest, so be nice," I told my father.

"Guest or not, I think I'm capable of carrying my wife's unmentionables," he said, nodding toward the bag.

Shaw held it out, surprised. "Oh, sorry. I was only trying to be helpful, sir. Shaw Matthews," he said, handing the bag back to Da and offering his handshake as well. "It's nice to meet you."

Da took his hand. "Duff Whalen," he said. "And this lovely daredevil is my wife, Anna. We own this place."

"I hope you've had a lovely stay so far." Ma smiled up at him. "Abby's so attentive to guests."

"She absolutely has been," Shaw agreed.

"Well, Ma," I said with a sigh. "It's a good thing your room is down here. Otherwise, I don't know how we'd get you into bed."

My da puffed out his chest and sucked in his gut. "I'd carry her," he said, not about to let anyone think he was incapable of it.

"Lucky for your back, you won't have to," I said, giving him a quick hug for still wanting to be Ma's hero.

"Come on, Ma, let's head that way," I told her, unlocking the brake on the wheelchair and aiming her in the direction of the back of the house.

Ma grabbed the wheel, stopping me. "I've been doing nothing but lying around in a bed for days now. If you think you're going to get me into another anytime soon, you better think again. Besides, there's no time for rest. We have to get ready for tomorrow."

Oh, dear God, what had this woman done now? "What's tomorrow?" I asked, even though a part of me already knew the answer.

"The whole town is throwing you a welcome-home party with a potluck picnic in your honor."

My shoulders sagged. *I knew it!* "Ma, come on. Seriously? You just got home from the hospital."

"And I'm just fine."

"You know you're fighting a losing battle, right?" Da asked.

"Oh, don't worry, Cassidy," Abby interjected. "My Anna's going to be the one giving out the orders while I do her heavy lifting." She winked as if that would somehow make me feel better. Maybe it did, but only a little.

Though I was concerned about Ma, I knew she was okay and Abby and my da would never let her overdo it. I think maybe I was more concerned with the big deal that was being made over my short return home. Because it *was* just a short trip. But like I'd said before, Stonington hated to lose one of its own. So this town get-together was nothing more than an attempt to convince me to stay with all of its residents pitching in. The women, anyway. As for the men, this was simply an excuse to eat, drink, and probably show off their boats.

"She's a tough cookie," Da said.

"And speaking of cookies," Abby turned to Shaw. "There's a fresh batch in the kitchen. Go put yourself a few in a baggie to take with you."

Shaw gave her a spoiled grin. "Aw, bless you, Abby," he said before giving her a kiss on the cheek and bounding off in that direction.

I was astonished. Shaw had been here, like, two days and already those two had a thing. Not a *thing* thing, but certainly something that surpassed guest and hostess territory and teetered over into "Is that your mom?" land. If Casey had seen that exchange and knew Abby was giving away his cookies . . . I shuddered to think of his reaction.

Abby turned to me then. "I'll take care of things around here while the two of you are out. Make sure you take him by the quarry. He seemed to really be interested in that when I told him about it."

She took Ma's wheelchair and headed to the back. No doubt the family room would become ground zero for Operation Make Cassidy Stay.

"And then there were two," I said with a chuckle to my father.

Da just studied me, something stirring up behind those X-ray eyes of his.

"Out with it, Da."

He shook his head. "Nothing. You go have your fun, but we're going to talk about this later."

"Talk about what?"

Da nodded toward the kitchen. "You and your new boyfriend under the same roof. *My* roof. You best be sleeping in separate bedrooms."

I rolled my eyes. "He's not my boyfriend, Da."

"When you were younger and got into trouble, you always thought someone in town was telling on you."

That's because they were, I thought.

"They weren't," he continued, and then he stopped, turning to point a finger at me. "You were telling on yourself. I always knew when you'd done wrong because the corner of your mouth twitches when you lie." He tapped the place to prove a point. "It just did it a little bit when you said that fellow isn't your boyfriend."

I didn't know how to respond to that. First, I apparently had a tic I wasn't aware of. And secondly, Shaw as my boyfriend? My inner teenage girl gave a mental *pfft* and an *as if.*

"The question is who are you lying to? Me or yourself?"

Da walked away then, leaving me to ponder the question. I didn't get to do so for long though because Shaw came strutting out of the kitchen with a cookie sticking out of his mouth and a baggie full of them in his hand.

"All set," he said with a spoiled grin.

I shook my head and laughed at how adorkable he looked. Abby's cookies had claimed yet another victim.

CHAPTER 8

Shaw

The tour around town was . . . short. Deer Isle was nothing more than a speck on the map, and Stonington occupied only about forty square miles at the tip, only ten of which was actual land, the rest, water. I got a lot of attention from the locals, especially the fishermen as they came in from their day out on the water to stock up on pizza—made fresh by the deli at the only convenience store—and booze.

Though most of the men were as young as me, if not younger, they looked at least a decade older, with their scruffy facial hair and sun-weathered skin. Each and every single one of them was so fit that I felt the need to suck in my gut and puff out my chest a little bit, and none of them missed the opportunity to look me up and down. I guessed my well-pressed attire sort of stood out in a sea of flannel shirts and jeans riddled with holes. At least my hair seemed to be in line with the local trend, though I'd say their messy dos were a result of rolling out of bed like that rather than product and sculpting time in front of a mirror.

They all knew Cassidy. Most everyone we encountered stopped to ask if she was back, though, duh, she was standing right in front of him or her, so of course she was. For the most part, Cassidy smiled and assured everyone she'd catch up with them at the picnic the next day, though she grumbled about it when we walked away. I couldn't understand it. The woman's freaking hometown was throwing her a welcome-home party and everyone seemed genuinely happy to see her, and she was grumpy about it. God, what I'd give if she and I could trade lives for just one day so she could see how lucky she was.

Walking down Main Street back toward the Whalen House, at least a dozen trucks sped by, honking their greeting to Cassidy. I started to pay attention then, looking around at all the vehicles parked on the side of the street, but particularly down at the dock. With the exception of maybe a handful, they all had one thing in common.

"Does everyone around here drive a truck?" I asked.

A breeze came in from the bay, blowing Cassidy's long, ginger hair across her face. She brushed the locks away, a playful sarcasm in her voice when she said, "Nah. Just the real men."

Hardy, har, har, I thought, seeing my tiny rental car parked in front of the Whalen House.

"I've heard men who drive big trucks are overcompensating," I countered.

"Well, we can flag one of the guys down and find out."

"Yeah, right. That wouldn't be awkward at all. *'Excuse me,'*" I said, switching gears and doing a very poor impersonation of a mousy scientist, " *'but we're conducting a survey to find out if men who drive big trucks have tiny penises. Can we see yours?'*"

Cassidy shrugged. "You don't know the men around here. They'll whip it out and not even have to be asked." She laughed. "Trust me, there is *no* shame in their game."

"You say that like it's a normal occurrence."

"You have to understand where you are. We don't have shopping malls or nightclubs. There's nothing to do around here but hang out at the convenience store or ride around drinking beer. Boredom equals shenanigans." Cassidy took my hand and started across the street. With an impish smile, she peered back over her shoulder at me. "Of course there is one other thing that can pass the time and ease the destructive behavior of a bored man."

I yanked on her hand, forcing a full stop. When she boomeranged back to me, I arched a brow. "If you tell me you played the part of Stonington's activities director, I'm going to need bail money. Lots of bail money."

The thought of Cassidy keeping men entertained made me want to decapitate every man within a thousand-mile radius and tear him limb from limb.

Cassidy's head fell back with laughter, her neck so long and graceful that it soothed the green-eyed monster inside me. "First, we don't have a jail. Our police force equals a whole whopping one, and he's more of a rent-a-cop. We just keep him around to badger middle-aged women over expired tags on their vehicles. We police our own. It's more effective that way. And second . . ."

Cassidy's attention was suddenly stolen and redirected to a girlish squeal down by the pier. It seemed Lobster Casey and Mia had returned from their fishing trip and Mia was having a hard time finding her balance while stepping from a rocking boat to the pier. As luck would have it, Casey had caught her, though so clumsily, she'd fallen back into his arms. Cassidy couldn't take her eyes away, and I . . . couldn't stop looking at her.

"And second," she continued without averting her attention. "Before you, I'd only ever been with one other man. But that was a very long time ago." She turned toward me then, an uncomfortable smile making her no less beautiful. "We'd better get inside so I can help with dinner before Ma hobbles out on that cast leg to round me up. And don't think for a second she wouldn't."

Cassidy headed up the drive, turning one more time to steal another glance toward the pier. Damn, it wasn't until then that I realized how very much we had in common. Maybe neither of us would ever be able to get over our past, no matter how far away we tried to run from it.

Blueberry bread pudding was the dessert at dinner. I'd given Abby high praise for it, only for her to tell me she couldn't take the credit this time because she hadn't been the one to make it. Right on, Mrs. Whalen could also throw down in the kitchen, but she, too, said it wasn't her. Imagine my surprise when I turned toward the only other possibility in the room to find Cassidy positively beaming with pride while studying the food on her plate.

Fuck, I wanted her. A fact I didn't think Papa Duff missed. In fact, I didn't think her father missed much of anything. He was a quiet man, but I could feel the weight of his stare on me as he studied every move I made and dissected every word I said. The same way Cassidy had always done, in fact. I supposed that was where she'd gotten it. I had to wonder how much Cassidy had told him about me because it sure as hell felt like she'd told him I'd been boning his daughter on the regular and he was planning to murder me in my sleep. No doubt a man like Duff Whalen knew how to hide a body. And if he didn't, I was positive the whole town would conspire for the cover-up. With Cock-block Casey taking the lead.

A little afraid for my life, I decided against sneaking into Stonington's favorite daughter's bedroom for a second night in a row. Instead, I thought maybe a little brisk sea air would put my food-induced hard-on at ease, and I went out on the porch to relax in the swing. Stonington was fast asleep again, quiet and dark. It dawned on me that it was probably the same old routine around here, day after day: wake before dawn, eat, fish, eat, sleep. Rinse and repeat. How boring. No wonder Cassidy ran away from home.

Speaking of, Cassidy came out to join me with a blanket wrapped around her shoulders. "Aren't you cold?" she asked.

Although it was springtime, there was still a chill in the air when night fell. Having been born and raised in Detroit, I was used to it, but that didn't mean I'd miss the opportunity before me.

"A little. Why don't you come share some of that with me like a good little hostess?"

Though she gave me a look, she still came over and sat beside me on the porch swing. I wasn't satisfied with just sharing the blanket, so I put my arm around her shoulders and pulled her into my side.

"There, that's better," I told her. I had no clue why she was looking at me like I'd grown two heads. It was cold. Body heat was a logical solution. So was taking my ass inside the house where the heat was on, but that wasn't the point. I really wasn't sure what the point was. I just knew that I wanted her closer and I was glad she didn't make me look stupid for it.

"So," I said, sighing. "Big picnic tomorrow, huh?"

I could sense the roll of her eyes even as her head dropped back onto my shoulder with a groan. "Don't remind me."

"Man, you're like a local celebrity around here," I told her, tightening my arm around her shoulders. "You should feel good about that. A picnic in your honor?"

"It's not as grand as it might sound. It's just their way of making me feel bad."

"No one's ever thrown a picnic for me. And if they ever did, I can't imagine it would make me feel bad."

"You have to understand this is nothing more than a trap. They lure you in with the promise of food and a good time, and then blammo! Everyone who has ever known you shows up to welcome you back home, *where you belong*," she added with air quotes, "and make you feel guilty about ever having left in the first place by telling you how they've suffered because of your absence. You're lucky you haven't had to endure the torture."

"Lucky? Cassidy, my parents don't even know where I am right now. Nor do they care. You think I abandoned them. I didn't. They abandoned me."

"Jesus, I'm so sorry, Shaw."

"Don't be. It made me stronger. But being here has really made me see what I've been missing all my life."

"Like what?"

"Like I haven't had a single meal by myself." When her brows furrowed, I explained, "I can't remember ever sitting down to the dinner table with my parents. In fact, they never even made me a warm meal. I practically lived off cereal, and most of the time, I had to keep my fingers crossed that the milk wasn't spoiled."

I had no idea why I was suddenly telling her all these things. I'd never told a single soul anything about my personal life. Cassidy knew more than anyone only because she'd kept digging until she found shit out. But not this time. This time I wanted her to know I wasn't a selfish bastard. This time I wanted her to know how lucky she was to have people care about her. Even if it was the entire population of her hometown. At least she had a home. At least she had a mother.

"Abby has been more of a mother to me in the couple of days I've been here than the woman who gave birth to me has over my entire lifetime," I admitted.

Cassidy turned her head toward me, that familiar pitying look in her eyes. And though I expected it to grate like a son of a bitch, it didn't.

"I'm sorry," she said.

Shit. Maybe it grated just a little bit. "Don't be. It's not your fault."

"No, I'm sorry for the assumptions I made about you," she confessed. "Back in Detroit. And in San Diego, for that matter. God, I was a total bitch."

She had been. She'd read me the riot act because she'd thought I was living in the lap of luxury while my parents lived in a shitty apartment smack-dab in the heart of a city well known for its crime and ruin. The assumptions she'd made had been my own fault, really, but I wasn't about to tell her.

"It's all good," I said, nudging her until she settled her head back onto my shoulder. I was surprised I'd taken that look for as long as I had. There was no sense in pushing it. "However annoying it might be, just please don't ever complain about someone caring too much about you. Because I promise, it could be a whole hell of a lot worse."

There was a stretch of silence then. Something had changed, and I wasn't really sure what that something was. When the fuck had I become that guy who talked about feelings?

Cassidy must have been thinking the same thing because she gave a soft laugh and said, "You're going soft, Matthews. You're supposed to hate me, remember?"

And I knew exactly how to respond. "I don't have to hate you anymore. I'm your boss now, remember?"

A jolt of pain shot through my ribs, courtesy of the quick jab from Cassidy's elbow. All in jest, of course, so I laughed because yeah, I'd probably earned it. And it was well worth the bruise that would likely be there by morning.

Every citizen of Stonington, young and old, turned out for the picnic the next day. It was amazing to me how this community came together all in the name of showing their support for one of their own. Maybe "community" wasn't the right word for it. Even someone like me who'd never known what it was like to be part of a family knew that that was exactly what this was.

Duff was tending to the fish fry and grill with Thomas and a couple of other burly men standing by to offer their support. Abby was running around like a chicken with her head cut off, bless her, but she still managed to find the time to come over and ruffle my hair and give me a quick peck on the cheek. I could've sworn I heard Casey growl a warning, which might have humored me. It had to suck for him to know I'd taken his girl and was on the verge of becoming his mother's favorite son.

But Anna? Anna was in beast mode. Despite her temporary handicap, she was all over the place, issuing orders, greeting guests, and generally being the ultimate social butterfly. With the exception of her ginger hair, Cassidy was a mirror image of her mother, which she should have been ecstatic about since Anna made for a decent MILF. But she definitely hadn't inherited the social gene. Though Cassidy seemed friendly with everyone who approached her—and believe me, there were a lot of people—I saw it for what it really was. She didn't like all the attention.

Seeing her unease, I couldn't help but remember the countless times I'd seen her in action during a board meeting or while romancing a client. In those situations, she was every bit as fierce as her mother was here. Then, it seemed like no big deal for the spotlight to be on Cassidy, it seemed natural even. Maybe that was because the light didn't feel as harsh when it was cast in a superstar athlete's shadow. If she treated this situation the same way, maybe it wouldn't feel so awkward.

I was just about to cross the yard to tell her that when a raven-headed beauty stepped directly into my path. She was petite, but curvy as hell. A fact that was obvious without the need to be dressed as provocatively as she was in short shorts. It wasn't even warm enough for shorts in the first place. That was one thing, but what really stuck out was her chest. Literally. She'd put an overly pronounced arch in her back to put her rack on display, which wasn't really necessary with the blouse that she was wearing. One wrong move and her tits were going to pop out all over the place. Though I doubted she'd be embarrassed by the wardrobe malfunction.

"Well, well, well . . . What do we have here?" she asked as her eyes made an intrusive sweep up and down my body. She cocked her head to the side and smiled at me. "I'm Brittnie, and this is Whittney," she said, pointing a thumb toward her sidekick. Said sidekick had opted to use her back arch to showcase her ass instead of her chest. It was a nice ass, I'd give her that much. Just not as nice as a certain redhead's I knew.

Giving them a polite nod, I responded in kind. "I'm Shaw. Nice to meet you."

Before I knew it, I was flanked by Brittnie and Whittney, each of them linking an arm through mine. Then they whisked me away toward an empty picnic table. There was a flurry of conversation between the two of them. A conversation I thought they were having with me, but since I didn't have to say a word, maybe not.

"Oooh, you're so strong," Whittney said, molesting my bicep.

"Someone should get you some food so we can keep you that way," Brittnie agreed. "Whitt, go get him a plate."

"You go get him a plate," she countered.

"And leave you all alone with him? I don't think so."

I let them have it out, not really wanting either of them to get me a plate, to be honest. I just didn't want to be rude. Though I felt a little smothered, they didn't particularly bother me. Both women were very pretty in a natural sort of way. Much like Cassidy. Maybe that was the sort of women Stonington bred. But unlike Cassidy, their behavior was a little too desperate for my taste.

Just then, a plate filled with a mountain of food slid before me. I looked up to see my Abby smiling down at me. "There you go, darlin'. Eat up." The smile dropped when she turned to regard my company with a warning glare. "Don't even think about it, you two. He's Cassidy's guest."

Whittney wore a mask of false confusion, her tone completely innocent as she said, "What are you talking about? He was standing all alone, so we just thought we'd be friendly and make him feel welcomed."

"Mmhm. I'm aware of your definition of 'friendly,'" Abby said. "And I know where your welcome mat is. You heard me. And if I have to say it again, I'm going to tell your fathers what that definition is, too. And then I'm going to tell them just how friendly the two of you have been all over town. I'm sure that'll make them proud."

I loved Abby in mama bear mode. Swear to God, I was going to put her in my pocket and take her back home with me.

Abby returned to her duties, but not before giving me a conspiratorial wink. As soon as she was out of earshot, Brittnie and Whittney straddled the picnic bench, waiting for me to take the seat between them. Instead, I picked up the plate Abby had brought me and dug in right where I stood, which didn't seem to deter the ladies at all. I could've walked away, but then that would be rude. Besides, if the way they were looking over the crowd of people was any indication, they were about to get their gossip on. And maybe, just maybe, some of that gossip would be beneficial to me.

I was not disappointed.

Whittney crossed her legs, shaking one so vigorously that her whole body moved in time. "So you're Cassidy's guest, huh?"

I nodded even though, technically, I wasn't. Guests were normally invited. I hadn't been, and certainly not by Cassidy. Maybe

Abby should've said I was Cassidy's creepy stalker. Something told me not even that disturbing title would've deterred these two.

"From California?" Brittnie asked, hopeful.

Again I nodded.

Brittnie adjusted her top. To show more cleavage, not less. "Oh, I'd love to go to California. I'd love to go anywhere that isn't Stonington."

Whittney rolled her eyes. "Why? You'd just come right back. Everyone comes right back."

Once I'd swallowed the creamy bit of potato salad I'd been eating, I finally spoke. "Really? What's that mean?"

"You're not from here, so you wouldn't understand," a gruff voice answered from behind me. I turned to see Duff Whalen standing there. "Run along, girls. I need a word."

Though they obviously weren't happy about it, Brittnie and Whittney did as they were told. For a second, I contemplated begging them not to leave me alone with Duff. Truthfully, he sort of scared me. Again, I wasn't really sure what Cassidy had told him about me, but the vibes I'd been getting off him hadn't been anything nice. I didn't know why I was so nervous; I knew how to handle men like Duff. I'd wooed my fair share of clients' mothers and fathers. This shouldn't be any different. But it was. This was Cassidy's father.

That's right. This was Cassidy's father. And I knew how much it irked her when she thought someone was placating her or wasn't being respectful of the things she felt were important. Clearly, this small fishing village was important to the man who'd made his life here.

I set my plate down and looked him in the eye. "Help me understand."

He just looked at me for a moment and then finally nodded.

"Look around you," he said, pointing toward the crowd. "You

probably wouldn't know it by looking at them, but a lot of these young men and women are well educated. That one over there," he said, pointing to a sandy blond guy standing with a couple of his buddies, "went away to college and got a degree in engineering. Know what he's doing now?" He didn't wait for my answer. "He's back here, lobstering right along with the rest of us."

"Why?" I asked, shocked. "An engineering degree pays very well."

"Lobstering pays better."

"Really? Wow."

"Most of these boys start going out with their pops the summer of their fourteenth year and start sterning, making their own money. Do you know what it's like to walk around with that amount of cash in your pocket at fourteen?"

I didn't. When I was fourteen, I was hanging out at stadiums, eavesdropping on conversations between athletes, coaches, and agents to learn the ropes. I didn't have any money, went hungry most of the time, and wore clothes I'd picked out of the lost-and-found bins.

"Some of them blow it, of course, on stupid stuff that don't add up to much. But if they're smart, they save up to get their own boat and gear. The ones that do that will probably drop out of high school before they graduate, and that's just fine because they'll be making plenty of money on their own." He sighed. "And some of them might use that money to go to college, but like I said . . ."

"They end up back here," I finished for him.

"That's right. Lobstering is what they know. It's good, honest money. But that's not the only reason they come back," he continued. "See, Stonington is its own way of life. The rules are different in the outside world, so most of them can't hack it out there. They might leave with big hopes of going away and staying away, but after about a year, two at the most, they find themselves right back where they belong."

He put his big paw on my shoulder, leveling a meaningful stare. "My little girl is one of the very few exceptions to that. She's the most stubborn and determined woman I know, and when she's faced with a challenge, she rises above it.

"All of this," he said, gesturing toward the picnic, "is for my wife, not Cassidy. And though I'd never tell the missus this, I don't want my little girl back here. Truthfully, I don't think someone who's been away from Stonington for as long as she has can ever really come back again. Not permanently, that is. She's changed. And there ain't a damn thing wrong with that. I'm proud of who she's become."

"Why are you telling me all of this, sir?"

He grinned. And for the first time since I'd met him, I felt like we had something in common that wasn't quite evident to me yet.

"You'll figure that out once she figures it out. And when you do, just remember: it's a mighty big ocean out there. An ocean filled with cage after cage of meaty bait." His laugh was as robust as his barrel chest and slightly serial killer-ish when he clapped me hard on the arm.

"And watch out for Whitt and Britt," he said, turning to stand beside me and giving a backward nod toward them. How he'd known where they were with his back to them, I'd never know. "They've been circling like a couple of vultures since I shooed them away."

Leaning in, he lowered his voice. "They're the number two and three. Cassidy's the number one, and they've been trying to take her spot."

Huh? I was definitely missing a key piece of information. "I'm sure you're trying to tell me something really important, but I have no clue what you just said, sir."

"I told you it's a different world here. There's a ranking order among the single boys and girls. The boys are ranked according to their earning potential, who's the best lobsterman. And the girls are ranked on beauty. Cassidy's the number one girl, and since Casey is a legacy, he's the number one guy.

"It was a given that those two would end up together, but when Cassidy left, it was free game. Now that she's paying attention to you, the other girls will try to lure you away." He shook his head incredulously. "These kids will step all over each other to land someone as high up on the ranking order as possible. Your best friend will steal your girl right out from under your nose, if you're not paying attention. Of course I never had to worry about that with Thomas. He's always been true blue."

"Sir, Cassidy and I aren't . . ." I didn't know how to finish that statement, but I didn't need to. Duff got it.

"Yeah, well, just remember what I said and you won't end up as lobster bait." With one more clap to my shoulder, he headed back to man his station.

On cue, Brittnie and Whittney reappeared.

"We're baaaack," Brittnie sang.

"I see that," I said, grinning and bearing it.

Brittnie linked her arm through mine again, pressing her tits against me. "How about if we get you out of here? Maybe show you some secret hiding places where *all three of us* could get to know each other better?" The suggestive tone to her voice couldn't be missed.

I chuckled, thinking how cute it was that these two thought they might be offering me something I'd never had. They weren't. Threesomes were okay, but really, they just made for more work on the man because he had two women to tend to while they shared the responsibility of taking care of one man. Doing the math, that didn't seem fair.

But I wasn't a lazy lover. And there was only one woman in the vicinity who could attest to that. Only one woman who I had an interest in putting that much work into. And she was standing across the lawn, staring down another couple that was engaged in what looked to be an entertaining conversation.

Casey and Mia. For Cassidy, this was becoming a pattern. Maybe even an obsession. One that I didn't much care for.

The set of Cassidy's body was all too familiar for me. She was pissed and having a damn hard time containing all that explosive energy running through her. Finally, her attention broke from Casey and Mia, but she was obviously determined to fixate on something else. Tossing her head back and forth, looking for that something else—maybe some*one* else—she stopped when our eyes met, and I knew she'd found it. Target located, Cassidy turned and headed in my direction, stomping across the yard, each step only fueled by her determination.

Her eyes flashed to Brittnie and Whittney, who'd become even more friendly while I'd been distracted. The sort of friendly that was just short of molestation. And then it occurred to me . . .

Holy shit. She was going to kill Brittnie and Whittney. Or maybe I was her intended victim. Either way, a murder was about to be committed. If I'd been a pussy, I would've grabbed one of the girls and used her as a shield, but that would've been wrong.

When she reached us, she set her shoulders and stepped past Whittney and into Brittnie's space.

"Excuse me, Mount Inappropriate," Cassidy said, waving a hand over Brittnie's exposed cleavage, "but I need to borrow him for a bit. Go find another bone to bury."

Ouch!

Grabbing my hand, she dragged me along behind her as she made her way toward . . .

"Where are you taking me?" Asking questions was a risk I had to take.

"Away from here."

Great, they'll never find my body. I started mentally ticking off the names of people who knew where I was. Demi, Sasha, Quinn? Nope, they'd probably help her with the cover-up. Ben? No, he'd keep his mouth shut so he could take my position. Chaz? Demi would threaten to cut off his balls and follow through on it. Landon? Yes! Landon was a soldier; surely he'd feel it was his duty to expose the crime.

But maybe there was a logical explanation and I just needed to keep my cool and ask her. So I did. With my fingers crossed. "Why?"

"Because I need to be away from here."

"Why do I have to go?" It was a fair question. One that I'd feel more comfortable knowing the answer to.

"Because I need to be with *you* away from here."

At least she'd said she needed to *be* with me and not that she needed to *kill* me. Still, I felt it necessary to point out that someone would notice her absence.

"You're the guest of honor. Don't you think people will start looking for you?"

"Probably, but they won't find me. Or you."

"That's what I'm afraid of," I mumbled.

CHAPTER 9

Cassidy

I was not Dorothy. I didn't own a pair of ruby slippers or a little dog named Toto, and I didn't have an Auntie Em. But Stonington was starting to feel an awful lot like Oz. All the people I knew were there, familiar yet different somehow. The same names, faces, and places surrounded me, but all I wanted to do was rip my skin off like it didn't belong to me. Like I didn't belong there among them.

Droves upon droves of people kept coming up to me, welcoming me back home and telling me I'd been gone for far too long. Each of them felt the need to fill me in on everything that had happened in their life while I'd been away, as if my leaving had caused their hardships in the first place and my return was suddenly going to make everything better. It didn't and it wouldn't. And I wasn't home for good, dammit.

That old smothering feeling I'd thought I'd left behind was back in full force, so naturally I searched out the one person who'd always whisked me away from it before.

Casey.

Popping up on my tiptoes and bobbing and weaving to see around the crowd, I finally found him. He was standing under the giant maple tree, one booted foot propped up on a picnic bench as he leaned over with his arm resting on his knee in that easygoing way of his. No doubt he was talking about boats and lobsters with one of his buddies because his hands were animated as he spoke, and a breathtaking smile was on his lips that magically swept me away from the conversation before me. And then the crowd parted and I saw that the company he kept was not one of the boys. It was Mia.

I made a mental note to check the reservation book to see how long this Mia would be staying with us because she was taking up a little too much of my Casey's time. Honestly, how much information could she possibly need to write her stupid book? And something about her must have been blocking Casey's Spidey senses, that knack he'd always had for knowing when I needed him the most, because as hard as I was willing him to turn and look at me, he wasn't. I needed him. He was my Tin Man, my Scarecrow, my Lion, my Toto, and my ruby slippers all rolled into one. But right now it felt as if I was looking at him through a crystal ball and he couldn't hear a word that my head and my heart were screaming.

I was mad and frustrated and jealous and my stupid feelings were hurt, and all I wanted to do was go home. Only I didn't know where home was anymore. But I knew who could help me find it. The wizard, of course.

Another search of the crowd and I'd found him. Unlike Casey, Shaw's attention had already been locked on me. Maybe I'd messed up and sent my damsel-in-distress vibes out to the wrong person. Then again, seeing the flying monkeys, Brittnie and Whittney, surrounding him, maybe he'd been the one to send out the SOS.

Excusing myself from the conversation Mrs. Paddock had all but been having with herself, I made my way across the yard. Shaw didn't break eye contact with me as I approached, though I thought I sensed a spark of fear. That was probably my fault. My lip may have pulled back to bare my canines when I saw Brittnie rub her tits all over his arm. He was mine, the only thing in this town that still was, and no one was going to stop me from staking my claim.

Grabbing Shaw, I pulled him along behind me, wanting nothing more than to get him alone somewhere. He'd been asking questions, which I'd answered, but I wasn't in the mood for talking. What I wanted was something exciting. Something that would remind me that Stonington's dull and boring existence was not my own.

So we set out on the yellow-brick road to hike the short distance to the park, not stopping until we reached the Emerald City, Stonington's only playground. The wooden jungle gym I'd played on as a child had been replaced with a bigger, fancier one with suspended bridges, nettings, swings, and slides. There was also a play tower that was covered by a green roof, though it still felt open and roomy. That was our destination.

"Come on," I told Shaw. Walking over to the ladder, I started my climb.

"Are you trying to relive your childhood?" he asked with a chuckle.

"Quite the opposite, actually." With quick footing, I crossed the suspended bridge, balancing out the tilts with my body weight until I'd reached the tower.

When I turned, I almost expected to see Shaw still standing on the ground, but he wasn't. He'd followed me, not really knowing what I wanted with him there. That was Shaw. He took risks, did things on a dare, leaped with blind faith. He was white-knuckled excitement. I wanted to be that. But more than anything else at the moment, I wanted to feel the adrenaline rush of having him inside me.

"Now what?" he asked once he reached me.

I fisted the front of his shirt and yanked him toward me, rising up on my toes to answer him with a kiss that should've told him anything he wanted to know about the purpose of our quest. Shaw kissed me back, his expert lips and tongue doing that thing that made me seriously wonder whether they, alone, could impregnate me. Jesus, the man could kiss.

I had no intention of wasting any time, so I got on with it, turning and walking him backward even as I worked his belt loose. Once I had satisfactory room, I slipped my hand down his pants to grip his long, thick cock firmly.

Shaw grabbed my arm and suddenly broke the kiss, but he didn't pull away. "Whoa, whoa, whoa, whoa! Here? Out in the open?"

Ignoring the brakes he'd put on, I revved the engine, my fingers continuing to stroke the soft skin of his hard length. "Yes. Right here. Right now. Because I want you."

"But what if someone sees us?" Though he was questioning whether or not we should be doing what we were about to do, he was moving against my hand. Yeah, he wanted me, too.

Leaning in again, I kissed his neck. "Don't be scared, Shaw. Everyone is at the picnic."

He chuckled. " 'Don't be scared,' she says. I'm a stranger in the middle of a town that doesn't even have a police station, and the town's most favorite daughter wants me to defile her on a jungle gym while its very scary residents could leave a picnic they threw *in her honor* and catch us." His words were a protest, but the tilt of his head to give me better access to his neck was an invitation to keep going.

"They won't," I whispered into his ear before taking his lobe between my teeth. All the while, I undid the button on his pants and lowered the zipper.

Shaw groaned, his large hands kneading my ass. "They might."

Pushing his jeans over his hips to set him free, I stepped back to ogle my prize. Shaw's cock was quite the sight to behold. I sighed, knowing I was about to have him inside me.

"I really don't care," I told him. Because I didn't.

I pulled my shirt over my head, leaving my cami in place, and then I spread the shirt over the wooden bench in the corner before giving Shaw's shoulder a push so he'd sit on it.

"I'm pretty sure your dad threatened to make me lobster bait," he said as I stepped out of my pants. He finally shut up when I straddled his lap and rubbed my bare pussy on his exposed cock.

"Please?" Rocking back and forth to let my wetness coat his cock, I took his bottom lip between mine for a soft suckle. Good God, but the man felt so good between my legs. And his lips tasted so sweet.

Shaw's hands gripped my thighs and then cupped my ass. His voice was raspy, quiet but sure when he said, "There's no need to beg. You can have whatever you want. All you need to do is take it."

There was a dare in his eyes, a challenge on the lip he bit into as he encouraged my movement. "What do you want, Cassidy?"

I lifted my hips, angling my body so that his cock was at my entrance. "You," I whispered, and then I sank down onto him.

I groaned at the sensation of the stretch and fill. Shaw did as well, the sound only doubling my pleasure. Holding on to his shoulders, I undulated over him, working his cock deeper and deeper until I'd acclimated to his size.

Shaw wrapped his arms around my back and pulled me closer as he nuzzled the cleavage of my still-covered breasts. "You don't want me. You want my cock," he corrected.

Whether it was true or not, it didn't matter. Being back in Stonington after having been gone for so long was like doing a zombie's frolic through a field of poppies, and it was time for me to wake up. Maybe Shaw had been onto something when he'd ignored the truth about his life for all those years and made people see what he wanted them to believe. The smoke and mirrors, the grand illusions . . . they were magical and awesome, and no one could say Shaw Matthews was a dull person. He was the wizard, and I wanted to live in his world.

Take me away from here, were the words I thought, though I wouldn't dare say them out loud for fear he'd get the wrong impression. But Shaw had suddenly developed a knack for reading my mind, something I'd have to evaluate further when I wasn't straddling the lap of an egomaniac with a massive cock. Taking my hips in his hands, he assumed control, moving me back and forth so that my clit was gifted that delicious bit of friction I loved so much.

"Jesus, woman. Why can't I ever get enough of you?"

The feeling was mutual. Even in this place where every nook and cranny held a memory of someone else, I still couldn't get enough of Shaw. I should've felt guilty, but I didn't. Why should I? Casey sure as hell didn't seem to feel guilty about spending all his time with someone else.

Shaw lifted me up and slammed me back down on his cock, like shocking my thoughts back to him . . . back to now. It worked. I opened my eyes and saw him there, his lips parted and pupils dilated, his brow peppered with beads of sweat even in the crisp air of Maine's spring. I fisted his hair and yanked his head back to crane his neck. And yes, I even relished the resulting warning growl and rough handling of my hips. He'd leave bruises and he wouldn't regret doing so because I'd earned them.

Yes, take me away from here. . . .

Casey would've never agreed to this. He would've insisted on something more romantic and respectable. He would've made love to me, tenderly stroking my face and hair while whispering sweet things that would make me feel all girly inside. He would've looked into my eyes in search of a deeper meaning . . . much like Shaw was doing now, I suddenly realized.

My head was a jumbled up mess then, a tornado of thoughts spiraling out of control. The faces of the two most prominent men in my life meshed like two worlds colliding. Where did one end and the other begin? My hero had become the person I needed rescuing from, and my enemy had become my savior. That wasn't what I wanted. And it definitely wasn't what I needed.

"Don't," I told him, and then I closed my eyes and buried my face in the crook of his neck.

"Don't what?" Shaw nudged me back, but I clung to his shoulders, refusing to sit up. "You just asked me to take you away from here. What does that mean?"

Crap. I hadn't realized I'd said the words out loud. God, what he must think.

"You're going to ruin it," I mumbled against his skin. "Please don't ruin it."

I was desperate then. Desperate for that dose of oxytocin, the connectivity that would undoubtedly make me feel whole again. My movements were hurried and awkward, selfish in my quest. Not Shaw, though. He was silent as I rode him, but it was too late. Try as I might, I couldn't erase from my mind the way he'd just looked at me. He'd seen something different in me. Or maybe I was see-ing something different in him now. Gone was his arrogance, his selfishness, the asshole I'd come to hate. When had the great and powerful wizard become just a man hiding behind a curtain?

"Hey?" Again he nudged me, his voice too kind, too soft to be ignored. I gave in, lifting my head and letting him see me. Shaw cupped my face, scanning it for the answer to an unspoken ques-tion. I supposed he found it when his expression changed to one of understanding.

"I'm not going to ruin anything," he said. His thumb brushed my bottom lip. "Use me."

And that was the tether I'd needed. With renewed fervor, I rocked back and forth, moving along his still-hard cock like my life depended on it, because dammit, it did.

Shaw kissed me deeply, his tongue stroking mine in time with the roll of my hips. And then he let go, gave up the control, sat back, and let me take the lead.

It was *exactly* what I needed.

I rode him. Hard. My knees burning from the scrape of the wood through the thin material of my shirt beneath. But I watched him. I maintained eye contact with Shaw even though I knew I'd regret it later. He was my anchor, my escape from a world that no longer made sense. Maybe he wasn't the wizard after all. Maybe he was Kansas.

Shaw

It was damn near nightfall by the time Cassidy and I made it back to the Whalen House. After she'd worn herself out on my cock, I'd gathered her in my arms and just let her be. I don't know why. I guess it felt like the right thing to do. I didn't even get off, and this time I didn't give a shit about it. For one, we didn't have any napkins or anything, and I wasn't about to come all over a bunch of kids' jungle gym—that'd be disgusting and just plain rude—and I *never* came inside a woman since baby-daddy material I was not. For two—probably the more important reason—none of what had gone down between us had been about me. It had been about Cassidy and what she'd needed. I knew it the second I saw that desperate look in her eyes when she asked me to take her away. Still didn't know what the hell she'd meant by that, but it didn't matter.

Cassidy Whalen was the most together person I'd ever known, all logical and business-minded, no girlie shit like being run by emotions. If that was ever the case, she'd done a damn good job of hiding it. Not today. Today, whatever fucked-up confusion she was feeling—and, believe me, she was definitely having a moment with some what the fuckery—it was spilling out of her eyeballs. Guess that was why they called them the gateways to the soul, or some philosophical whatevers. She wasn't together. She was all bedlam and disorder on the inside, and I'd been more than glad to let her use me to gain whatever perspective she'd needed.

Damned if Shaw Matthews wasn't "growing" as a human being. My mother would be so proud . . . if she'd actually given a shit about me. Cassidy's mother did give a shit about her, though. Which was exactly the reason she was all over her the second we walked through the door.

"Cassidy, my God, where did you run off to?" Two days in and Anna Whalen was driving that wheelchair around like a Nascar pro. Hmm, maybe I'd sign her if I ever decided to venture into the sport.

Cassidy huffed like a petulant child. "Don't be on my case, Ma. Shaw and I were feeling a little crowded, so we went for a walk."

Crowded? Her disappearance today had nothing to do with feeling crowded. Smothered, maybe. Discombobulated, definitely. Having an out-of-body experience . . . well, she was definitely in her body while it was riding mine, though I was confident her orgasm had felt out of this world. Just as mine had, all the other times.

We always had phenomenal sex.

Cassidy started toward the back of the house, but Anna refused to let her daughter make another escape, so she followed. "Oh, you did, did you? Well, thank you for leaving me there to make excuses for you. Everyone wanted to see the guest of honor, but the guest of honor was nowhere to be found. And then there's all the work around here that had to be done, but luckily, Casey and Mia pitched in. Honestly, Cass, I don't know where your head is. It's just not like you to . . ."

Her voice faded off as mother and daughter got farther and farther away. I sort of felt sorry for Cassidy, but in a way I was also jealous. My mother had never given a shit about where I'd been for whole days at a time.

On a different note, I finally understood where Cassidy got her argumentative powers.

"You made the right decision."

I turned to see Duff leaning against the doorframe to the kitchen with a pocketknife in one hand and an apple in the other.

"Excuse me?" I said, because what else do you say to a man holding a knife when you'd just let his daughter fuck you in a very public place and you weren't sure if he knew about it?

He sliced off a piece of apple and popped it into his mouth while nodding down the hallway. "Not putting your two cents in the pot with all that," he clarified.

I fought the urge to wipe the sweat from my brow. "Yeah, it seemed pretty intense."

"The wife will say her piece, Cass will apologize, and then all will be right as rain again." The knife carved out another chunk that he offered to me. When I politely declined with a shake of my head, he continued, "You made another good decision today as well."

"What's that?" I doubted he meant my sticking my thingy into his daughter's thingy, so I thought it best not to say it out loud.

"Getting her out of there this afternoon."

Oh, that.

"I didn't really have much choice in the matter. She sort of made me," I confessed. She made me do other things, too, but again, I didn't think it would be wise to kiss and tell.

Duff laughed. "That's my little girl," he said. "She's more like her ma than she'd care to admit. Whenever she and Casey would get into trouble, he'd always take the blame. But I knew better. Cassidy was the one wearing the pants in that relationship."

She might have worn the pants with Casey, but she'd taken them off for me. Again, wasn't going to verbalize that.

"Maybe he just didn't like to argue," I offered.

"And you do?"

"Yeah. I guess I do," I admitted, and then I leaned in, lowering my voice. "Don't tell her, but she's the only one who can give me a run for my money." It was the truth. In more ways than one.

Feeling the exhaustion from the day and knowing I still needed to check in with Denver before I called it a night, I stretched out a yawn. "Well, I think I'm going to head on up to bed."

"What do you have planned for tomorrow?" Duff asked, stopping me before I hit the first step.

Shaking my head, I answered with a shrug. "I'm really not sure yet, sir. Why?"

Duff stood erect and walked over to clap me on the back. "Get some sleep tonight. I'm taking you out with me in the morning, son. It's all hands on deck."

Dammit! Someone *had* seen Cassidy and me and I was going to be sleeping with the fishes by this time tomorrow. Though, wait . . . he called me "son." Did murderers call their victims "son"? I supposed they might if they were psychopathic killers.

Before I could err on the side of caution and bow out gracefully, Duff was nearly halfway down the hall. Clearly, I had no say in the matter. And clearly, Cassidy had gotten the whole "wearing the pants" thing from her father, not her mother.

CHAPTER 10

Cassidy

I couldn't be sure what had woken me so early in the morning, but I was bright-eyed and bushy-tailed before anyone else in the house. Try as I did to get back to sleep, it wasn't going to happen. So rather than continue to toss and turn in frustration, I dragged myself out of bed, though I wasn't entirely sure what I was going to do. The thought crossed my mind to pay Shaw a visit in his room, but after Ma's rant the night before, I'd found out Da had planned to take him out on the boat and I didn't want to risk getting caught.

Maybe I should've ridden to Shaw's rescue and kept him from being tortured by my father, but the truth was that I had a lot on my mind and could use the alone time to sort things out. So I headed for the one place that had always aided me in the past in my quest.

The polished wood floors were cold under my bare feet as I softly walked the hall to the end, opening the door that could've been the entrance to any room. It wasn't. On the other side there stood a winding staircase that led to the crow's nest at the top of the Whalen House. It was just a small room with a glassed panoramic view of Stonington, including the harbor. This place had been my sanctuary, the place where Casey and I would go to be alone when either of us had needed the escape or simply a really cool make-out spot.

I wondered how many times he'd been there without me while I'd been gone. How many times must he have been here thinking about me, missing me, wishing I'd been there with him instead of a million miles away? Maybe he hadn't at all.

Taking a seat on the red-cushioned bench that Da had built into the wall, I propped my elbow on the windowsill and rested my chin while looking out toward the harbor. Dawn was just coloring the horizon past Isle au Haut with its dusky pinks and oranges, surrounded by the still star-filled sky above that faded into blues and purples at the edges. Red and green starboard and port lights dotted the dark waters of the harbor, as gulls trailed behind in the wakes of boats silently easing through the peaceful tranquillity of a new day just at its beginning.

Stonington really was beautiful. To the people outside our little world, it was a thing of fantasy, something Photoshopped onto postcards, an illusion painted by movie creators in films. But this place truly existed. Maybe I had to leave in order to appreciate its beauty.

The pier below was already bustling with activity, dockhands moving equipment around in preparation for the fishermen who had just started to arrive in pickup truck after pickup truck. Casey would be among them. But then so would my da and, today, Shaw as well.

Jesus, the look on Shaw's face the day before, the intensity behind those baby blues . . . I'd used him as an anchor after seeing Casey with another woman. And he'd let me. Somehow I think he'd known it, and he'd let me anyway. My view of Shaw Matthews was slowly changing. Maybe he wasn't the selfish asshole I'd always thought him to be. Maybe I was the selfish one. The way he looked at me was a dead giveaway to the fact that he would've given me anything I'd asked of him in that moment. He'd looked at me like that a lot lately.

I had to close my eyes to push back the image before it over-whelmed me again. "Confused" wasn't even the word for how I felt about that situation now. I couldn't go there. I couldn't take it anywhere but where it was supposed to be. And that was just sex. Nothing more. If I allowed myself to have feelings for him, I'd be taking a huge risk with my heart.

Casey, on the other hand, was a different matter. He was the one constant I could always count on. The one person I knew would be in my corner, come what may. Maybe I'd taken it for granted that he forever would be, that things would never change, that no matter where I went in my life, he'd be there waiting for me.

"Wow. You are so selfish, Cassidy Rose. Selfish and egotisti-cal," I said aloud, needing to hear the bite of the words.

Maybe Shaw and I had more in common than I'd care to admit.

Because things between Casey and me had definitely changed. *We* had changed.

Even though we'd technically broken up a long time ago when I'd left town, I don't think I ever really felt, in my head and most definitely in my heart, that we were no longer together. Seeing him treat someone else the same way he'd always treated me, even making me an afterthought, hurt more than I'd ever imagined it could. And I knew that look. The way he looked at Mia was the same way he'd looked at me. The way he smiled at her with a bit of a twinkle in his eyes like he was looking at the brightest star in the sky . . . that was the smile that had been reserved for only me.

I'd been replaced. But then so had he. After all, it was Shaw whom I'd turned to when I'd gotten all up in my feelings about being ignored by Casey in the first place. Though that was a purely physical thing, right? Jesus, I didn't even know anymore.

It wasn't like I had any plans whatsoever of coming back to Stonington on a permanent basis. I had no desire to be with Casey; physical or otherwise. I knew it didn't make any sense for me to feel the way I was feeling, but I just didn't want to lose him. And I was losing him, my safe place. I could feel it. All the crazy that had accompanied this whole cat-and-mouse thing between Shaw and me, my inability to now separate the physical from the emotional, had made me want to desperately cling to something familiar. Casey was safe. But Casey was no longer mine.

Was he Mia's? And if he was, did that mean I'd lost Casey completely?

And the confusion just went up a notch or two on the WTF scale.

I was probably jumping to conclusions about Casey and Mia. Casey was always a nice guy. Yeah, that was it. He was just being nice to the outsider. Right? It didn't mean anything at all. Mia was a romance novelist writing about a lobster fisherman, and what better way to get that information than straight from the lobster fisherman's mouth? And Casey was probably playing up the part for her benefit: the strapping young hero, a little rough around the edges, with broad shoulders, a gorgeous smile, perfect body, deep voice, and eyes so beautiful and sincere that they made women want to drop their panties on the spot.

No doubt, Mia had been caught under his spell. It was just the effect he had on females. I almost felt sorry for the heartbreak she would inevitably endure if she'd allowed herself to believe he'd ever be hers. Many had tried and failed. I was the only exception. For Mia's sake, I hoped she'd get her information and then get the hell out of Stonington. Because unless you were from here, you didn't stay here.

Then again, I was the one feeling like an outsider lately. The familiar had a foreign air about it, and it didn't seem to fit anymore. *I* didn't seem to fit anymore. Which begged the question: once you left home, could you ever really go back?

It didn't matter. I wasn't planning on coming back. At least not for any reason other than the occasional visit. So I had to wonder why I was jealous of Mia in the first place. Casey deserved to be happy. I wanted that for him. Maybe I'd just never considered he'd be happy without me. And I was fucking another man, for Christ's sake! With some very mixed-up emotions about said man. What right did I have to be jealous?

"Jeez, Cassidy." I ran my hands over my face, frustrated and annoyed at no one but myself. I'd just done a complete three-sixty in my thoughts, bringing myself back around full circle with no progress toward a solution.

God, I couldn't wait to get back to San Diego, my friends, and my job. That was my life now. At least there I was too busy to get all caught up in my thoughts. A moment to contemplate wasn't always a good thing. There was such a thing as overthinking. Especially when it was to the point of driving yourself and those around you crazy. Screw it. Ma always said idle hands were the Devil's playground, so I decided to head downstairs to get breakfast under way for our lone guest.

And maybe . . . just maybe, I'd do a little recon to see what was up between her and my boyfriend. Er, ex-boyfriend. Whatever.

Hauling myself up, I stopped and did a double take when I spotted my father's boat getting under way with one other body on board that I hadn't expected. A lantern and the binoculars Casey and I had used to spy on people as teenagers were still sitting there on the sill, so I grabbed the binoculars to get a closer look.

Casey Michaels *was* the other body. Not that I couldn't have guessed it by his stance. A stance that was very much towering over Shaw in that "I am Poseidon, god of the sea" sort of way.

"Oh, this is so not going to end well," I mumbled to myself.

But there was nothing I could do about it from here other than to send up a silent prayer that Shaw's body would return instead of becoming shark chum. Served him right for being a stalker and following me cross-country in the first place. His one saving grace would be if he managed to keep that sarcastic mouth shut, which I knew wasn't likely to happen.

Oh, well. I'd deal with the aftermath of the testosterone-filled lobstering excursion later. For now, I had a little fishing of my own to do. After all, the intense research of a subject of interest was what I did best.

Just as I'd stood to get on with my investigation into Mia's story, I noticed something odd down at the pier. The dockhands weren't moving equipment and preparing to bring in the day's haul when the boats returned. Rather, they were removing equipment and securing the cranes. Something they did only when a wicked storm was approaching. I looked out toward the water to see the puddle pirates preparing their boats to ride out the weather as well, and not getting under way to check their traps.

Turning to scan the view to the right, I noticed for the first time the blackened clouds coming in from the southeast. All that peaceful tranquillity I'd just noted had been nothing more than the calm before the storm. Crap. Though I hadn't been paying attention at the time, my very organized brain had recorded and stored the discussion Mrs. Paddock had been having with an otherwise distracted me at the picnic, and said brain was now playing back the details. She'd been talking about the hurricane moving in.

We're not ready, was the thought that screamed through my mind. How much time did we have? There was so much that needed to be done, and the Whalen House had not yet been secured. Or had it? Was that the thing Ma had been going on about last night? Damn. Now I knew why I'd waken so early. Once again, my brain had been keeping tabs on things while my emotions had whisked me off to some nonsensical place where I'd been exploring my feelings and becoming increasingly oblivious to the real world around me.

That was going to end right here. It was time to kick it into gear and do something productive, something that made sense.

I made a quick stop off in my bathroom to wash my face, brush my teeth, and change out of my nightclothes, and then hurried down the stairs to check on Ma. Ma, of course, was already up and about and watching the news in our private den.

"Morning, Cass," she said with a worried smile and then patted the arm of the couch next to where she'd settled in her wheelchair.

"What are they saying?" I asked, folding my legs under me as I sat.

Ma shushed me just as the broadcast got under way.

Harmony Hale was poised behind her news desk with a bright smile on her face as if Mother Nature hadn't gotten her panties in a wad and decided to take it out on Stonington. "Batten down the hatches, Maine . . . Tropical Storm Ayla has been upgraded to a Category 1 hurricane and is making her way closer to shore. For more about that, let's turn it over to our weather anchor, Kipp Edgington. Kipp?"

The camera angle changed to a tall, lean man with perfect posture, bleached teeth, and a spray tan. Kipp was so obviously not from Maine. "That's right, Harmony. Everyone has an eye on the sky, and for good reason." He moved around the screen behind him, pointing out this and that as he continued, "The current trajectory of Ayla's path is centered on the island coasts of Maine, but it is uncertain if she will actually make landfall. Though it's unheard of to have a threat of this magnitude this early in the year, the unseasonably warm temperatures of the Atlantic Ocean have pushed up along the southern and eastern coastline to create the perfect recipe. And make no mistake about it, folks, this one has the potential of turning into a demon. She'll likely be upgraded to a Category 2 or 3 by the time all is said and done.

"That's the bad news," he said. "The good news is that a warm front coming in from way down here in the Gulf of Mexico is going to keep us from getting feet upon feet of snow. Flooding will, of course, still be an issue, as will the wind damage, but at least when it's over, there won't be mounting snowbanks to contend with."

He went on and on about meteorological stuff that I was sure he explained in layman's terms for the viewing audience, but I was already in damage-control mode.

"What still needs to be done?" I asked Ma.

Ma looked at me, a worry-free and determined expression on her face as she set her shoulders in confidence. "Breakfast," was her response. And then she unlocked the break on her wheelchair and began to maneuver herself to head toward the kitchen.

"Ma . . . the storm?"

"Doesn't keep our guests from getting hungry," she said. "Besides, we don't know how much time we have before we lose power, so we need to get in there and see what we can whip up now that will hold over for as long as we might need it."

Food? Food was her concern? "What about the house?"

Ma stopped and pivoted the chair around to face me. Impressive move. "Did you not hear anything I told you last night? While you were out gallivanting around, everyone else pitched in to help get the house ready. Including our guest."

Confused, I looked toward the windows in the front sitting area. The storm shutters had not been pulled closed yet, but they'd certainly been hung. How had I missed that when Shaw and I had returned last night? Jesus, maybe all the sex I'd been having with Shaw lately had jarred something loose in my head.

Shaw!

"Da took Shaw out to pull in the traps, didn't he?"

Ma was already turned again and nearly at the kitchen, so I quick-stepped to catch up.

"He needed the help, Cass."

Panic set in. I knew how choppy the waters got when a system was moving in, and they were even worse as far out to sea as legacies fish. "But Casey can help!"

"Casey *is* helping." She didn't even glance back at me when she said her next words. "Are you as worried about him?"

"What? I don't need to worry about Casey, Ma. He's used to this. Shaw isn't. I don't know if he's even ever been out on a boat, let alone in storm waters. He could get killed!"

Ma waved me off. "Stop worrying. You know your father and Casey will take care of him."

My father? Yes. Casey? Well, I couldn't be so sure of that. He was as protective as they came, and with all the bad things I'd told him about Shaw and our standoffs back in San Diego . . .

Shaw may never be heard of or seen again.

"Good morning!" came the too cheerful voice of the Whalen House's other guest as we came into the kitchen.

Mia Morgan was sitting at the island in the middle of the room with her tiny fingers wrapped around a piping-hot cup of coffee like she was about to get cozy in front of a fire. Her dark hair spilled over her shoulders as she adjusted the crocheted blanket she wore like a shawl.

There was a dreamy look in her eyes as she said, "So our men are out braving the elements to get everything prepared for the long night ahead, leaving the three of us at home to wait for them and do what we can here. Where should we start?"

I cocked a brow. "'*Our* men'?"

That disillusioned smile dropped from her girl-next-door face as her cheeks flamed pink from embarrassment. "Oh, I'm sorry. I just meant that . . ."

She didn't finish, though she didn't have to. I knew what she meant. She was trying to be cute, which might work on everyone else, but she didn't know me like that yet. What I did know was that "our" men were not ours. They were *my* father, *my* best friend, and *my* . . . Well, whatever Shaw was, he was mine. So sayeth my vagina. And each one of them was a part of my story. A story that was getting rough, both figuratively and literally. *My* men were out there on a very fickle ocean in dangerous conditions, and I just wanted them all to get back home safe before all hell broke loose.

Miss Mia Morgan needed a reality check. This was no romance novel. The Whalen House was not a cabin in Vermont. There was no fire to cozy up to, we were not settling in for a romantic snowstorm, and she would not be snuggling naked with Casey under a blanket for body warmth.

It wasn't until Ma stabbed a boney finger into my ribs that I realized I'd been staring Mia down like I was daring her to utter another word. Not that Mia was even making eye contact at that point. Her head was bowed in submission and she was studying that cup of coffee like there were sea monkeys putting on a water ballet show inside of it.

I cleared my throat and relaxed the muscles that had coiled tight in preparation for a pounce. What had gotten into me? "No, I'm sorry. I didn't mean that the way it sounded," I lied, like a seasoned pro, I might add. Guess Shaw had been rubbing off on me. "I'm just worried about them."

Ma gave my hand a reassuring squeeze. "They'll be fine, Cass. We, on the other hand, need to get to work."

Shaw

In Detroit, the only people awake at four o'clock in the morning were thieves, murderers, rapists, prostitutes, crack heads, and the boys in blue tasked with the responsibility of keeping them all in check. Scary-ass creeps that thrived during the hours of darkness right before the dawn. In Stonington, only the fishermen and dockworkers were out. And they were no less scary.

Casey was waiting on the pier when Duff and I had arrived. The prick made it a point to tell us he'd been waiting for a while before Duff explained the clothing faux pas we'd had that morning, what with the two of us having to work together to make his oversized rubber pants and beat-up jeans and shirt fit my much smaller frame. It wasn't like I'd packed for the occasion. Not that it was any of Casey's business, but apparently he'd already gotten his own boat secured for the storm and had volunteered to tag along on team Duff to help him do the same. It might have been nice to know that tidbit of information beforehand, though I didn't suppose it would have changed Duff's mind about dragging me along. I was doing it for Cassidy, and because there was a real sense of urgency about it all. I'd never been anywhere near a tropical storm. I didn't even know the damn things came this far up north. But I was willing to help in any way I could. If nothing else, it would certainly be one adventure I wouldn't soon forget.

It was dark, cold, wet, the water was getting choppier by the second, and I almost slipped about half a dozen times while trying to get down the ladder and onto the boat from the pier. The last thing I needed was to fall and bust my head open, but to do so in front of Cassidy's father and ex-boyfriend would have been more insulting than the injury itself.

Don't get me wrong; I was tough, but I was street tough, whereas these two were rugged-seamen tough. I'd fought thugs. They'd fought Mother Nature. So technically, they were the bitches, because who fights a chick?

Once we'd loaded all of our gear—and I couldn't tell you what any of it was—Duff manned the helm and the engine roared to life. Despite the deep rumble, the buzz of smaller engines whipping past us was the thing that most caught my attention.

"Why are the other fishermen in smaller boats?" I instantly regretted asking the question when Casey looked at me like I was stupid. My jaw ticked a little bit because I absolutely detested people thinking I was ignorant.

"You mean the skiffs?"

Whatever. How was I supposed to know the technical word?

"Their boats are the ones you see anchored out in the bay. They ride skiffs back and forth because they can't tie off to the pier."

"Why not?"

Again with the look. "Because that privilege is reserved for legacies."

"And legacies are what?" At some point, my questions stopped being less about curiosity and more about wanting to annoy Lobster Casey.

It worked.

Lobster boy huffed. "Legacies are the families that have been fishing the longest. The slip where they dock is reserved for only them. Duff is a legacy. My father is a legacy. And when he retires, I'll be a legacy."

"So your boat is anchored in the bay, too?" This was a question I'd wish I hadn't asked.

He pointed across the way to a shiny white boat with blue accents. "Yep. She's right there." The name *Shooting Star* was scrawled in elegant script across the aft end. My jaw ticked a little more when I recalled an identical shooting star etched onto Cassidy's hip with this numbnuts's name beneath it. I guess this was their version of matching tattoos.

"Beautiful, isn't she?" Casey asked, and all I could do was nod because yeah, Cassidy was very beautiful, indeed.

Duff yelled down from the helm, "Time to get under way, boys. The weather's moving in faster than I thought. Let's not get caught in it."

Casey hopped down from his perch and pulled in the mooring at the bow. "You ready for this?" He pointed toward the stern, and I went over to pull in that line as well.

No. Not really. But I wasn't going to tell him that. So with a shrug I simply replied, "Sure. How bad can it be?" The line was simple enough, anyway.

I took no comfort in the foretelling chuckle he and Duff shared at my expense.

"I guess you're about to find out." The boat took off with a jerk and I nearly lost my balance again while Casey's Captain Morgan stance on the bow hadn't been displaced in the least.

What had I gotten myself into?

CHAPTER 11

Shaw

What was once a blue ocean had turned black as night with wave caps of white that dotted the expanse without any rhyme or reason. Buoys tossed back and forth, bending so far over onto their sides at times that I didn't think they'd come back up. The clouds that had been slowly creeping in were now upon us, blocking out the sun and throwing us into darkness. I had to admit, I was intimidated by the sheer, raw power of Mother Nature.

Five miles or so off the tip of Isle au Haut, Duff was fighting against the force of an unreasonable current. Even I could see the skill it took to maneuver that boat, and he had it in spades. He would forever have my respect.

Casey had said I'd find out how bad it could be, and man, did I ever.

I'd worked hard for all my life, struggled every single minute of every single day for my job, but all of that had been a mental struggle. This? This was pure physical labor. Seven hundred steel traps had to be hauled on board Duff's vessel. Seven hundred waterlogged, weighted traps that required a great deal of arm strength and the shoulder and back muscles of an Olympic weight-lifting champion. No amount of topical pain relief was going to cure the ache screaming through said muscles, but I did a damn good job of hiding it. I think.

We were being pummeled by heavy winds and rain. Cold rain that stung like a son of a bitch and was likely leaving welts on my skin. Plus the boat was getting tossed around like a rubber ducky in a rambunctious toddler's bath, so I could add a churning stomach on top of it. Damn if Casey didn't notice it.

"Looking a little green around the gills there, city boy. Maybe you should sit the next one out," he said as Duff used those mad skills to move us to the next spot. The last spot, thank God.

I straightened my shoulders and plastered on a mask. I'd been used to donning it in every other situation. I just had to reach deep into my bag of tricks for this particular one. As afraid for my life as I was, no way was I going to let Lobster Casey think I couldn't handle anything he could. He'd yet to break a sweat, hadn't shown the slightest hint of strain, and rode the rocking boat like a seasoned cowboy on a bucking bronco. The only victory I could take away was that at least he was drenched also. He wore it better, though.

I hated him.

Swallowing down the urge to upchuck all over the place, I gave him the same smile I gave to every prospective client. The one that assured him of my confidence and tendency to win. He would not beat me. No one would ever beat me. Except for the fact that Cassidy already had, technically, but I'd come out the victor in the end of that situation as well.

"Shaw Matthews does not sit one out," I said, quoting him.

He grinned at me and then shook his head. "Cassidy was right about you. You *are* an egomaniac."

"She told you that?"

"She tells me everything." The expression on his face begged me to read between the lines, but I doubted she'd told him I'd had my cock inside her on multiple occasions. I wondered if he'd be so smug if he'd known that.

"Though even if she hadn't, I'd have figured it out the second you referred to yourself in the third person anyway."

The boat pulled alongside the next trawl, so Casey and I went over to start the haul. The sooner we got the traps in, the sooner we could make it back to land, and I was very partial to that idea.

I likely looked like a drunk crossing the street as I made my way across the deck, but I'd given up on trying to walk a straight line and considered it a personal accomplishment if I got to the other side without falling on my ass. "I see nothing wrong with having a high opinion of myself. I happen to think I'm a pretty great guy."

"You're the only one." He hooked the line and brought it closer, grabbing and hooking it onto the wench once it was within reach.

"What's that supposed to mean?"

Casey grabbed the first cage and then stopped to look at me. "Why are you even here?"

I shrugged. "Same reason you are. I'm helping Duff."

"No, not here, here," he said, referencing the boat. "Here in Stonington. And you haven't earned the right to call that man by his first name, so don't. Show some respect."

Wow, that one kind of threw me for a loop. I looked toward *Mr. Whalen* to see his reaction and apologize, only to find him in his own world with captaining the boat. But there was something else Casey had asked me, a question that I realized the answer to only at that moment.

"I'm here because I couldn't let her run away." The words shocked me just as much as they'd apparently shocked Casey.

"If Cass was running away from anything, it was you. But

don't give yourself that much credit. Truth is, she was running to something."

"You think you know her that well, huh?"

He arched a brow. "You think you know her at all? Cass and I are childhood sweethearts, best friends. I know her better than anyone ever has or ever will."

"Is that right? Well did you happen to notice how it's affecting her that you're spending so much time with Mia? Because I did."

Casey yanked the next trap on board and straightened, his face hard and the muscles in his body even harder. Classic defensive mode. "Who the hell do you think you are?"

"I'm the man paying attention. You should try it sometime. It comes with its own rewards." Maybe I'd said too much, but I didn't care. I just kept seeing the desperation in Cassidy's eyes the evening before, feeling the way she'd clung to me. And all of that was after I'd watched her heart break from across the yard as she watched this man with another woman; this man that she'd trusted so much.

"Cassidy hates you, and I'm done talking to you about her. Get back to work."

Casey grabbed the next cage and slid it toward me. Ignoring the searing pain in my muscles, I snatched it up like it was nothing and turned to stack it with the others.

"Maybe you're right. Maybe she does hate me. But you know what they say . . . There's a fine line between hate and love. Only in this case, I suppose we'd have to trade out love for lust."

I turned back around to give him my famous smug grin, only I was met with a sucker punch to the face. There was no way to prepare for a blow I never saw coming, but should've expected. It had all the impact of a wrecking ball to a brick building, only much faster. An instant throb pulsed through my jaw that I wasn't entirely sure hadn't been dislocated. What was with these people and their violent tendencies? In Detroit, I expected that sort of thing. But in a quiet little fishing community, not so much.

Duff yelled something from the helm that I couldn't quite make out for the ringing in my ear, but whatever it was it didn't matter. I saw red then, anger gushing through my veins, which probably didn't help the throbbing in my jaw. Finding my balance, I swung at Casey. He ducked, but I followed through with an uppercut to his chin that knocked him backward.

The boat tossed to the side, making me have to think quick to stay on my feet. If there had been anything I'd learned on the streets of Detroit, it was to never let your opponent get you on your back. But everything was working against me: the weather, the ocean, the wet deck, and Casey's agenda. He charged forward and tackled me, sending the both of us crashing against the lobster traps that had once been stacked neatly. The unforgiving corners of the steel cages dug into my back, adding insult to injury.

Having had enough of that bullshit, I fisted Casey by his stupid rubber jacket and used all my strength to toss him off me. It bought me enough time to get to my feet, but in my effort to do so, one of the cages got me good on the head. Not to mention that all that time had also given Casey the chance to regroup and set up for another charge. I braced for the impact, knowing that this one would knock the breath from my lungs, but I couldn't predict what happened next.

One second I was planting my feet, and the next I was swallowing seawater. I'd been knocked overboard and the ocean was claiming me for herself. Instinct got my legs and arms into gear and I propelled myself upward, gasping for a breath of air the second I broke the surface. I'd only barely gotten it when I saw a wall of water barreling down on me. It crashed with a force that felt like someone had grabbed my head and held me underwater. Again I fought, not really sure which direction was up by this time, but determined to find it. I kicked and clawed until finally I burst out of the water with another sharp inhale.

I shouldn't have bothered. It was a cruel tease. Having a moment to tread water, I twisted and turned myself around, searching for Duff's boat. It was still there, but I'd somehow been pulled very far away.

"Over here!" I yelled. At least I thought I'd yelled. Thanks to the gallons of salt water I'd swallowed, my voice was croaky and my throat raw.

And then another wave took me under. This one was bigger than the last, stronger and more determined in its quest to send me to the bottom of the ocean. Pulling and pushing, kicking and twisting, I tried so hard to find my next breath again. Everything was dark. I couldn't find the light of the surface, and I wanted nothing more than to take a breath. But I couldn't. Because if I did, it would be over. Of one thing I was sure: Mother Nature was not going to let me go.

At some point, I just became too tired to move my arms anymore. I wasn't even sure if they'd been working for or against me in the first place. My legs were the next to go. Everything was fading in and out and I was struck with the realization that this was the way Shaw Matthews was going to die. I'd survived Seven Mile and a life in which the odds had been stacked against me only to succumb to a force that could not be stopped.

I *could* be beaten. And I was.

Releasing the breath I'd been holding, I gave up and just let go. It was odd how peaceful the ocean felt beneath the tumultuous surface. It would be a fine resting place for my remains. And I could've sworn it cradled me as my body sank.

Casey

I should have let him drown. I really should have. I thought about it, even thought about the explanation I'd give Cassidy and the authorities.

"Oopsie! He fell overboard and there was simply no way to get to him. Tragic loss," I would've said, while hanging my head and pretending to feel bad about my inability to rescue him.

But I was the hero, dammit. Always had been. At least that was the way Cassidy had seen me. And the one thing I never had been and never would be able to stand was knowing I'd disappointed her.

Sometimes it really sucked to have to be the bigger man.

Putting my own life at risk, I jumped into the frigid abyss and swam to the last spot where I'd seen Shaw. It wasn't easy either. The elements worked against me, but I was a seasoned sailor and, therefore, one hell of a swimmer. Not to mention strong. Diving deep, I caught a glimpse of the bright yellow raincoat that had been way too big for him in the first place. With any luck, it would still be on his body because no, I couldn't see shit else.

By the time I got to him, he wasn't moving. Pale skin and blue lips, he looked for all the world like a lifeless corpse floating in a laboratory tank. I really didn't know if there would be any bringing him back, but if nothing else, I could at least make sure he wasn't lost at sea.

Grabbing his outstretched hand, I made my way toward the surface with his body in tow. Jesus, my lungs burned with the need to take a breath. The light from Duff's boat penetrated the darkness like the light at the end of the tunnel. Fat lot of good it would do for us both to die here. And damn, all I could think about was how devastated Cassidy would be to lose us both at the same time.

Summoning all my strength, and it took a lot with Shaw's deadweight, I made like a porpoise and jumped out of the water with a huge gasp for air. The waves had gotten even bigger, something I had to be wary of while hooking an arm under Shaw's chin to keep his head out of the water. Not that it mattered by then. As far as I could tell, the guy wasn't breathing.

Duff was already hanging half off the side, prepared to lift him on board, and that sucked like a motherfucker because what if he got tossed into a watery grave like Shaw and I had? The old man was a sea dog, though, so he was good to go.

"Is he alive?" Duff called over the howling wind and rain.

"I don't think so," I told him.

Once I reached the boat, I grabbed the rope ladder Duff had thrown over and yanked Shaw within his reach. I helped as much as I could, but that wasn't saying a lot considering all the energy I'd expelled just getting him to that point. When Duff nearly took a tumble, I got a sudden jolt of adrenaline and lifted Shaw up, shoving him over the port side.

By the time I got myself out of the water, Duff was already getting down with the resuscitation. "Goddammit! He doesn't have a pulse!" he yelled.

I let him have his way with the mouth-to-mouth because no way was I kissing the asshole, but I did rip open that jacket to take over the chest compressions. Thirty quick pumps later and Duff checked for a pulse again. Nothing.

"Keep going!" he said, abandoning his post and heading toward the helm.

Shit. I kept working on the compressions. "What are you doing? He's still not breathing," I said.

"I'm getting us the hell out of here and back home. Now save his goddamn life!"

The motor kicked into high gear, feeling more like a surfboard riding a wave as Duff got us under way. I did my best to keep Shaw in place while still trying to bring the son of a bitch back around. Swallowing down my pride, I pinched his nose shut and put my mouth over his, pushing air into his stubborn lungs. Fuck it. Only the two of us would ever know my lips had touched his. Even if Shaw pulled through, he'd not remember it, and I'd take it to my grave.

Leaning down, I put my ear to his mouth to listen for a breath, but I couldn't hear jack shit over the wind, the sloshing waves, and the engine. I searched for a pulse, but my fucking hands were frozen, my whole body was frozen and probably on the verge of hypothermia, so I couldn't feel a thing.

I went for thirty more chest compressions and then finally, Shaw went into a coughing seizure, expelling seawater from his lungs. The poor bastard's throat was going to hurt like hell for a few days after that. His eyes popped open in a panic, and for a second I saw his fear. Not wanting to have gone through all of that just to watch him choke to death, I rolled the guy onto his side and let him get it all out. Within a few minutes, he was holding himself up with a palm to the deck, still coughing, but very much alive. I clapped him real good between the shoulder blades, only to help him out—kind of, sort of—and then backed up to give him some room.

Shaw tilted his head and gave me an evil glare.

"What? No thanks for saving your life?"

"My . . . mistake," he said, trying to catch his breath. "Thanks for the sucker punch and knocking me overboard to begin with, asshole."

I simply grinned. "You're welcome."

I should've let him drown.

The engine began to back down and I got to my feet, seeing the pier coming closer and closer. Also coming closer were my mother, Mia, and Cassidy. Of course. They were sprinting toward us with panicked and worried faces. I'd never seen my mother run so fast. I'd never seen her run at all, in fact. But I had seen that fear in Cassidy's eyes before.

It was a really long time ago. She and I had just stepped out into the parking lot of a store when those thug wannabes, Jeremy and Kennedy—what kind of thug name was Kennedy, anyway— had pulled a gun on me because of some beef they'd had over fishing territory. They'd ventured too far into my family's, so I'd cut their lines. Fuck 'em. And fuck their pussy-ass gun. Said pussy-ass gun had gone off during the scuffle that had followed, and the bullet found a temporary home in my shoulder. Even wounded, I'd taught those boys a lesson they'd never forget. You didn't mess with legacies. Legacies were some crazy bastards.

But what had once been a look of fear at the thought of losing me was now directed elsewhere. Cassidy was damn near in tears, hyperventilating when she saw Shaw.

"Oh, my God! Move out of my way!" she shouted to the dockworkers scrambling to get our mooring in place.

When Cassidy got into position to climb onto the boat, Duff put a stop to it. "We don't need to be dragging your butt out of the water, too. You just stay right where you are."

"What? Who fell overboard? Shaw! Are you okay? Somebody call nine-one-one!"

Yeah, thanks for your concern, Cass. I'm fine, too.

"No! Do not call nine-one-one!" Shaw shouted back. "I'm all right."

"You do not look all right. Da, we need to—"

Duff cut her and the engine off. "No, he's right. Doesn't

make any sense to anyway. It would take them too long to get here, especially with the hurricane barreling down on us like she is. We need to get to the house. Now."

Duff and I waited until Shaw was off the boat, Cassidy and my own mother lending a hand, before we followed. The dock-hands took orders from Duff to secure his vessel to safely ride out the storm, while I watched the mother and girlfriend thief being escorted back to the Whalen House for, I assume, some much-needed TLC.

Mia remained behind with me, trying to appear calm, cool, and collected even though her eyes told a different story. That was what I liked so much about Mia. Her eyes were stunning on their own, but add to that the truth they spoke, and I never had to wonder what was on her mind.

Mia was shivering, her arms crossed over her chest for what little warmth she could get from them. Standing there, drenched by the pouring rain, her beautiful hair dripping wet and clinging to her face, and her voice so meek when she said, "Casey? Are *you* okay?"

Finally, someone showed a little bit of compassion and concern for the unsung hero.

I did something then that I hadn't planned. Ever the protector, this time for a different woman, I put my arm around Mia and pulled her into my side. I didn't have much warmth to offer either, but she could have it all. "I'm good. Let's get you somewhere safe."

CHAPTER 12

Cassidy

I'd been pacing the house, going from one window to the next, waiting and watching for any sign of Da's boat. Hurricane Ayla had really gotten her bitch on, upgrading to Category 2 in record time. Abby and Thomas had come over to ride out the storm with us because our families always did everything together, and if we were all going to die, we were going to do that together as well.

I wanted to yell at Thomas for not being the one to go help my father and his son, but I got it. He'd been securing their home before they left it and couldn't have helped them even if he'd wanted to. Which I was sure he probably did.

Ma and Abby had done most of the work in the kitchen, shooing me away because I was apparently making them nervous wrecks with all my worrying. Mia got to stay, though, because she was "so eager to learn" and "such a joy to have around." I might have given her a dirty look or two on my way out. I didn't need to learn how to cook. I might have spent a lot of time in my early years down by the dock, but when I wasn't there, you'd better believe I was in the kitchen with Ma. She'd insisted.

Whatever. I was glad to have the time to stalk the harbor, even if only from the living room window.

The sky was dark and getting darker with each passing second, and the first of the rain bands had already come to shore. But the worst of the worst was the wind. My imagination had gotten well away with me as I kept picturing all these scenarios where the boat had capsized or had been broken in half and was bobbing around in the ocean like the *Titanic* before it sank. And the water . . . The Gulf of Maine was absolutely frigid in the spring. I didn't care how unseasonably warm the weatherman said it was, it wouldn't have had that much effect on the water.

Relief flooded me, much like the streets of West Main Street, when I finally caught a glimpse of Da's boat. The closer it got, the more convinced I was that something was wrong. I ran up to the crow's nest, ignoring Ma when she yelled after me to slow down before I fell down the steps, just like she always had when I was a child. Once I got to the top, I went for the binoculars and saw for myself that I was right. Shaw was down on the deck with Casey hovering over him. Without a second thought, I dropped the binoculars and ran back down the stairs.

But Abby was blocking the way once I got to the ground floor. "Where do you think you're going? There's a hurricane out there, or have you forgotten?"

"Sorry, Abbs." I moved past her and wrenched open the door. "You can yell at me later, but they're out there, and something is wrong."

"Something's wrong?" I hadn't meant to panic her, but I didn't exactly have time to offer her reassurances that I didn't have, either. "I'm going with you."

"Me, too," Mia said, popping out of the kitchen where she'd obviously been eavesdropping.

I paid no more attention to it. I didn't give a crap about her at the moment. And I knew I should've stopped to convince Abby to stay inside, but all I could think about was getting to Shaw. So I ran. As fast as my legs could carry me, jumping puddles and juking obstacles along the way like a wide receiver gone pro. I paid no attention to the rain, didn't give the wind a second thought. My focus was trained on the end zone, which just happened to be Da's boat and the men inside. One man in particular.

My heart fell into my stomach once I reached the boat and saw how pale Shaw was. The color of his lips didn't look normal, he was shivering, there was a gash on his forehead, and his jaw looked slightly swollen.

I tried to get to him, but Da wasn't having it. And there was also no convincing any of them to call an ambulance, though my father did have a point about that. I was just grateful that everyone was alive and breathing and back home where they belonged. And all I wanted to do was get Shaw back to the house so I could see for myself that he really was okay.

Mama bear, Abby, was all over that, though. She helped me get Shaw back up to the house, while along the way, Shaw ignored questioning by both Abby and me about what had happened out there.

"Nothing. I'll explain it later," he said as if it was no big deal. It was a very big deal. "I'm freezing and I just want to get inside."

Da had managed to catch up, most likely due to the slower pace we had to keep for Shaw's sake. He climbed the ramp to the porch where Thomas was already busy closing up the Whalen House. I went ahead to hold the door open for Abby and Shaw, but before I could follow them inside, my father stopped me.

"Cass, start securing those windows," he said, nodding toward the other end of the house.

"But Da, Shaw—" I began, though I should've known he'd cut me off.

"Will be just fine. Abby's got him. We're running out of time. Go on now, do as I said." He used the tone that indicated he meant business.

"Wait, where's Ma?" I asked Thomas.

Thomas snapped a shutter closed and punched the sliding bolt in place with the palm of his hand. "She's doing what she does best, wringing her hands and worrying herself to death while staying plastered to the news and giving a minute-by-minute update on the weather as if we don't already know it's a shit storm."

And there was just one more person unaccounted for that I had to worry about. Though by the look of things, maybe I didn't need to worry about him at all. Casey and Mia came up the ramp, Mia snuggled in close to Casey's side. It sure as hell didn't look like she was trying to hold him up, either. That was definitely a snuggle. Maybe I'd been wrong. Maybe romance novelist Mia Morgan was going to get her cuddle under a blanket in front of a fireplace with my Casey, after all.

I slammed a shutter closed as well, giving the two of them the evil eye as they stepped onto the porch. Casey noticed and suddenly pulled away from Mia, the look on his face apologetic. He should be sorry. Not for Mia, but for Shaw. Because I'd bet my bottom dollar that he'd somehow been responsible for all his injuries. So when he rushed over to help me with the shutter, I stiff-armed him.

"I've got it."

Casey pulled up short, no doubt shocked that I wouldn't let him play my hero this time. "Let me help you, Cass."

"I said I've got it. Just take your little friend inside." That one looked like it hit home. For both Casey and Mia. I wasn't sorry. "I'll deal with you in a bit."

He put his hands up in surrender and slowly backed away. "Fine. Have it your way."

"I always do," I mumbled, getting back to work.

I'd forgotten how many windows were on our house. Though I don't know how I could've possibly forgotten since cleaning them had always been one of my monthly chores while growing up. It was fine. I needed the time to calm down, but I wasn't going to get that time because Da couldn't stand to see his little girl out in all the weather and had sent me inside. I bolted at the chance, anxious to see how Shaw was doing and find out what in the world had happened in the first place.

He was in mid-conversation with Abby when I walked in, already stripped of his wet clothes and wrapped like a burrito in a heavy-duty thermal blanket. I didn't want to interrupt, so I was careful to hover just outside the doorway to do a little eavesdropping of my own.

"I know it wasn't any of my business, but that look Cassidy had on her face while she was watching him with another woman at the picnic . . . He really hurt her. Whether she'd admit it or not."

"And she probably wouldn't," Abby agreed.

"I don't know why it bothered me so much. It just did."

"Well, maybe you like our Cassidy a little more than you thought." Abby soaked a cotton ball in alcohol.

"Honestly, I've always liked her. Admired her even. She's smart, funny, and beautiful." He suddenly went quiet as if he'd just realized he'd said too much. "If she knew I said that, she'd find some way to use it against me."

Abby smiled down at him. "Your secret's safe with me. Now, hold still. This is going to sting a little."

Shaw winced with a hiss when she dabbed at the cut. The big baby.

"Sorry, sweetie. Probably takes you back to a time when your mother used to clean your boo-boos, huh? You'd think as you get older it wouldn't sting so much, but it does."

"Actually, no. The lady who gave birth to me wasn't really a mother, you know? If we'd had a first aid kit in the first place, she just would've told me to do it myself." Shaw's uncomfortable chuckle was a failed attempt to make light of a very sad situation.

I wanted to hug him. I also wanted to add his piece-of-crap mother to the list of people I wanted to punch in the throat.

Abby put the cotton ball down and sat on the stool facing him. "A boy needs a mother, darlin'. I can't imagine why any woman wouldn't want to be yours, but some simply aren't equipped to do the job in the first place. Lucky for you, I've got plenty of love and attention to go around. So how about if I unofficially adopt you?"

Shaw looked stunned, his expression morphing into childlike wonderment. "I think I'd like that very much," he said. For the first time ever, I heard some genuine warmth in his voice.

Abby took the hug I'd wanted to give him, and I wasn't even jealous about it. I was glad she was there for him. Though I wasn't sure how Casey would feel about it once he found out.

"Wow," Shaw said when she pulled away. "That almost made the sucker punch from your other son worth it."

"He sucker punched you?!" Abby and I said at the same time.

Shaw and Abby turned to see me there. I probably looked like Carrie at the prom, my Irish skin flaming as red as pig's blood with my anger. A sucker punch? That wasn't how we did things around here. We faced our opponents and let them know what was coming because that was the only fair, non-pussy way to do it. I was outraged that Casey, of all people, would pull a stunt like that. And he was going to face my ire.

"Cassidy, calm down," Abby said, knowing full well what was about to go down.

"Abbs, don't even try to defend him," I warned.

"I'm not," she assured me. "I just want you to calm down. Everyone is okay, and that's what's important."

"Really? Everyone's okay? Shaw fell overboard!"

"That wasn't from the sucker punch, though," he said, actually defending Casey.

My hand went to my hip. "No? Well then how about you tell me how that part happened?"

Shaw started to say something but then stopped. "It doesn't matter. The point is, I can take care of myself, Cassidy. I don't need you to fight my battles."

"It does matter. And if you won't tell me, I'll just ask Casey," I said and then turned on my heel to go find the big jerk for myself.

"Cassidy!" he called after me, no doubt jumping off his stool to give chase.

"Let her go," I heard Abby tell Shaw as I climbed the stairs. "Listen to your mother on this one, sweetie."

Yes, Shaw. Listen to your mother. Despite my anger at Casey, my heart warmed for Shaw.

I knew exactly where Casey would be, and I was right. But I was surprised to find he wasn't alone in our crow's nest. I guessed I'd found the answer to my earlier wonderings; Casey had indeed had other women there. It pissed me off even more that he would violate our sacred place. *Our* place. Not his and Mia's. Yet when I opened the door to the staircase that ended in our place, I distinctly heard her voice.

Casey had some nerve. We'd see if he still had it by the time I was through with him. But first, a little more eavesdropping. Hey, Mia had done it earlier. Why couldn't I?

"You're still in love with her," Mia was saying. "It's perfectly normal for you to be upset about the situation."

"I lost my temper. I shouldn't have. I swear I didn't mean to knock him overboard."

"But you're the one who rescued him, Casey. You put your own life at risk to save his. That makes you the hero, not the bad guy."

I could just imagine her batting those long, fake lashes at him. Okay, so I couldn't prove they were fake. But come on, they had to be. Either way, the vision nauseated me. She probably thought she was going to play Lois Lane to Casey's Superman.

"She won't see it that way, though. It's probably only a matter of seconds before she comes up here to rip me a new one."

"I think maybe you're making more of it than what it really is."

No, Miss Morgan, he isn't. And you should probably mind your own business before I make you victim number two.

Casey's guffaw was low. "You don't know Cassidy like I do. When that woman gets mad, whew!"

"So she'll yell at you. Big deal."

"No, she won't yell. I wish she'd yell. She'll hold a grudge."

I grinned a little to myself, remembering some of the spats we'd had as teenagers. This one time I'd gone a whole month of giving him only one-word responses and never even looking him in the eye when I did that much. All because he'd avoided my phone calls for an entire day, and I'd found out that it was because he'd gotten a call from Brittnie, who'd told him her car had broken down and her father was out fishing, and she didn't know who else to call. Well, she could've called anyone except my boyfriend. But the point I was mad about was that he could take her phone call but he couldn't take mine, nor could he pick up the stupid phone before he left the house to let me know what was going on. It looked shady as all get out, and I figured if he couldn't talk to me, I wouldn't talk to him. Yes, I'd taken it a little too far, but again, we were teenagers. And Casey had never let something like that happen again, so I'd say it was a lesson well taught.

"Oh. The silence routine again?" Mia asked.

What? She knew about that? Good God! Did he give her every single detail of our life together?

"You got it," Casey answered, and I was pretty sure it was the correct answer not only to her question, but to mine also.

"Well, if I were her . . ." Mia began.

Ha! You wish.

"I'd want you to tell me the truth about what really happened, what really set you off. She needs to know how you feel. And if she doesn't feel the same way, at least you'll know and you can finally move on."

Apparently, being a romance novelist qualified her as a couples therapist. Not.

That seemed like just about as perfect a time as any to interrupt. I made my presence known by the sound of my footsteps on the stairs. Casey and Mia got quiet, and when I reached the top, they were both staring right at me.

Well, didn't they look cozy in their mirrored positions, sitting knee-to-knee with one leg crossed under the other? At least they weren't naked, though I couldn't help but wonder if they'd changed out of their wet clothes together.

The lantern was on, casting a romantic glow around the room that was amplified by its reflection on the glass behind the two lovebirds. It would've been the perfect setting for one of Mia Morgan's sappy love scenes had it not been for the rain pelting the windows—which sounded more like someone throwing handfuls of pebbles at them—and the ferocious wind that was shaking them in their frames. Hurricane Ayla was barreling into town, and she was on her period.

But I was more concerned about the storm inside than outside. Inside my head, inside my heart, and inside this room.

"I'd like a word with you," I told Casey, crossing my arms over my chest. "In private, if you don't mind. And even if you do, I don't care."

Mia put her hand on Casey's knee like it was the most natural thing in the world. I wanted to smack it off, but I pushed back the urge. "I'll see you later?" she asked him.

He nodded, the corners of his eyes crinkling with the reassuring smile he gave her. It wasn't my smile, but it was unlike any smile I'd ever seen him give to anyone before. And then she took her cue and stood to leave, smart despite all her whimsy.

I didn't budge as she maneuvered her way past me, which was rude, but I didn't feel like being polite at the moment. She'd obviously done enough research to write a book about me, so she should've understood my mood and not taken it personally. Fine, I'd apologize later. I honestly had no reason to be mad at her. I was just jealous, unreasonably so. It was the age-old "I don't want you, but I don't want you to want anyone else" thing. Maybe men were right. Maybe women really were crazy. I knew I was certainly borderline at the moment.

Casey was on his feet, his hands tucked into his pockets and his shoulders sagging as he cautiously came toward me. He had the same look in his eyes that he'd had the last time we'd said goodbye. The same look he'd had every time we'd said goodbye. It was always as if he'd thought that *this* time might be our last. And though I wanted to rage at him for what he'd done to Shaw, my instinct was to make sure he was okay.

There were no lumps or bruises, no cuts or scrapes to his face or anywhere else that I could see. He didn't walk with a limp, and he didn't grimace in his movements. He looked perfectly fine. If I hadn't known better, I'd say the fight had all been nothing more than a nasty rumor. It was nasty, all right, but not a rumor.

Meeting him in the center of the room, I took Casey's chin between my fingers and turned it from side to side to be sure the shadows hadn't been hiding any marks. "Did he even get a punch in?"

He pulled back, finally showing a modicum of discomfort. "Yeah. One hell of an uppercut to my chin that jarred my teeth. I think I might have chipped a molar."

"Oh. Sorry," I said, not entirely meaning it. "Do you want me to take a look, or did your little girlfriend already do that?"

Casey rolled his eyes and turned his back on me. "Cass . . ."

"What?"

When he faced me again, he hung his head and shook it. "She's not my girlfriend."

"No? Because the two of you sure seem pretty inseparable to me. Since I've been here you've spent all your time with her, time you'd normally spend with me. Jeez, you were practically finishing each other's sentences at dinner, Casey. And then she ran down to the pier tonight, so worried about her big, strapping lobsterman, that she felt the need to give you a personal escort back . . . snuggled into your side like she's your girl."

He finally looked up at me. "Yeah? What do you care? You were more concerned about that asshole than me!"

I don't know what it was about what he said, but it really set me off. "Because you sucker punched him in the face, Casey! Really? Why? Why would you do something like that?"

Casey tried to answer, but I was so pissed, I wouldn't let him get a word in over my rant.

"It wasn't bad enough that you and Da had him out there in the middle of hell's soup, you had to go and start a brawl with him on top of that! You didn't even fight fair!"

Again, he tried to defend himself, "I didn't mean to—"

"And then you both ended up overboard! You could've died, Casey! Shaw could've died! It was so *stupid*! And for what? I know Shaw has a mouth on him, and believe you me, there have been a lot of times that I've wanted to punch him in the face—and well, I did once, but he'd earned that one—but you? You're better than that. You're better than a *fucking* sucker punch, Casey Michaels. So you tell me . . . what could've possibly made you stoop so low?"

Casey didn't say anything. He just stood there, grinding his teeth with his jaw ticking and head shaking, not even looking me in the eye. I could tell there was something on the tip of his tongue, but he was fighting hard not to say it. And the more he hemmed and hawed over it, the madder I got.

"Spit it out!"

Jesus, he pinned me with a wild glare then. "Fine! I saw you, Cassidy! I saw you with him on the playground. *Fucking*."

I was stunned, shocked into silence. Casey's face was twisted up in pain, the hurt in his eyes like a cannon that shot through my chest and into my heart. I felt it break for him then. No, not break. Shatter.

"Oh, my God, Casey. I'm so sorry." I tried to go to him, but stopped short when he backed away.

"Don't."

What had I done? "I never meant to—" This time, I was the one unable to finish.

"Do you have any idea how goddamned much it killed me to know I've been waiting for you all this time only to see you with another man? I'm right fucking here!" Casey pounded on his chest with each word, the ferocity like the rumbling of an earthquake that made me flinch in tandem, but it was the aftershock that shook me to the core. "I've always been right fucking here. Waiting. Like the biggest dumbass in the world."

I didn't know what to say. I don't think I ever thought Casey had been waiting for me. Though really, how could I not have seen that? He'd always been available to me when I'd called, had always been available when I'd come into town. There was never another woman around, he'd never talked about any relationships, and we'd had sex during each visit. I knew Casey well enough to know that he wouldn't have done that if someone else had been in the picture.

"I thought you hated him. So I'm confused. How do you go from hating the guy to fucking him on a playground?" They were valid questions. His words held venom, but I knew he was just hurt.

"I don't know," I said with a shake of my head. "But I don't hate him anymore."

"Well, that's great," he said, throwing his hands up. "Glad the two of you could work it out. Hope you didn't get any splinters during the mediation."

That was unnecessary. "Casey, don't be a jerk."

"Don't be a jerk? Did you not hear me? I've been waiting on you, Cassidy. Wasting all these years on something that was nothing."

Waiting for me? Well, I was sure that was a romantic gesture his new friend could appreciate and maybe even swoon over. But me? I was a mover and a shaker. I didn't wait on anything. If there was something I wanted, really wanted, I did something about it. So it was hard for me to make sense of his words when his actions spoke something different.

"That was a choice you made, Casey," I reminded him. "You stayed here in Stonington and you let me go across the country to live another life. A life separate from yours."

"I gave you what you wanted, Cassidy. Like I always did. Like I continue to do even to this day. What was I supposed to do? Move to San Diego and be a good little wifey waiting for you at home?"

"No. You were supposed to love me enough to ask me to stay." The words just fell out of my mouth. I didn't even know I'd felt that way. Maybe in all my effort to be independent and in control, I'd convinced myself I'd been fine with his decision all along.

"Oh, Cass . . ." He sighed. "Don't you get it? I loved you enough to let you go."

"That's right. You did. You let me go, Casey, and you waited." I paused. "But Shaw came after me."

That last part looked like it stung. I hated hurting him, but it was the truth.

Though his voice was low, I still heard every syllable of every word he said next. "He doesn't love you. I love you."

"I know you do."

"So what do you want now? *Who* do you want?"

I ran my hands over my face, frustrated with myself, frustrated by the situation, frustrated by the question. "I don't know. I'm really confused right now."

Shaw could be a real egotistical ass most of the time, but he'd shown me something different the last few days. Casey had consistently been that man that other men aspire to be, good to the core, and that wasn't likely to ever change. Choosing Casey was exactly what every other woman in my position would do, but I wasn't like every other woman.

I needed a man who would let me stand on my own two feet, make my own decisions, and clean up my own messes. And at the same time, someone who instinctively knew when to rescue me from myself, when to step in and say, "Enough. I've got you." I needed to be in control of my own life . . . outside the bedroom.

But inside, I wanted to be dominated, devoured, and devastated. But would the walls of that bedroom adequately confine the devastation to my sexual needs and not infiltrate my emotional sense?

Casey was the safe choice. But he wasn't Shaw.

"Well, I'm not confused. I want the same thing, the same person I've always wanted. You." He moved closer, encircling me in his arms and pulling me against his chest as he dipped at the knee so he could look me in the eyes. "I've missed you, darlin'. The way you smell, the way you feel . . . the way you taste." Casey's breath was warm and sweet, like Abby's fresh baked cookies being pulled from the oven, the enticing aroma teasing my senses and confusing me even more.

I closed my eyes, falling prey to the familiarity of it all. And then I felt his lips on mine, soft and supple, tender in his silent plea for me to kiss him back. I'd missed his kiss. I'd missed Casey. And although my mind told me it wasn't right to do so, that I'd regret it later, I gave in and kissed him back.

The moment I parted my lips, Casey's passion took over. He cupped my face and held me there as if he was afraid that if he let me go, I'd pull away. Covering his hands with mine, I removed them with every intention of doing just that, but instead I guided them to encircle my waist again. And then I wrapped my arms around his neck, cradling his head and holding him to me. Tilting my head, I gave him better access to my mouth, inviting his tongue inside to sample the taste he'd said he'd been missing. And taste me he did. Our tongues met and I melted into him. Casey's kisses had always been fueled by his emotions for me, and I felt it all then. Mia was right. He was still in love with me. And judging by the hardness growing and pressing against my belly, he still wanted me, too.

Casey's hands moved to my ass and he lifted me up so I could wrap my legs around his hips. I was lost to him, to his kiss, to a world I'd once known long ago. My back met the cushioned bench and Casey was on top of me. His lips left my mouth and started a hot trail down my neck even as his hardened cock rubbed against my center with slow but deliberate strokes.

"That's my good girl," he said against my neck.

And then I freaked. Those were Shaw's words, but that wasn't Shaw's voice.

"Stop . . . Casey, stop," I said, pushing him away and wiggling out from underneath him.

Casey sat up to give me room, but still hovered close. His breathing was heavy and he was obviously still aroused, which made me feel like the biggest tease in the world. But what I noted most was the pained expression etched into his ruggedly handsome face. He looked like I'd just slapped him. "Why? What's wrong?"

"I can't," I said, shaking my head. "I'm sorry, but I just can't."

"Because of him?"

"No. Yes. I mean, no." I jumped up and growled, frustrated and mad at myself. Taking a deep breath, I tried again. "I can't because it's not right, Casey. I love you. That's never going to change. But the way I love you has."

I remembered a time when I'd been with Shaw and felt like I was cheating on Casey. Now, the tables had turned. Whether Shaw felt the same way about me or not didn't matter. I did feel something for him. And although I had no clue what that something was, I knew I had to figure it out.

Meanwhile, it wasn't right to treat Casey like a safety net. He had been my constant; the one person I knew would always be there to catch me if I fell. Maybe some part of me had sent him mixed signals to keep him in that place, should everything in my life go to hell in a handbasket. It wasn't fair and it wasn't right. And I refused to do it to him again.

Casey sat back and his shoulders slumped. "So that's it, then? There's no more you and me?"

"No, that's not it, Casey. You're my best friend. You always will be. We're just not meant to be together in any other way." I paused, not to let the words sink in or because I was waiting for his reaction, but because there was something else I needed to say and I was having a hard time pushing the words out of my mouth.

He was no longer *my* Casey. I had to let him go.

"You're free, Casey. Really free. Be happy. That's all I've ever wanted for you."

"And you're going to be happy with Shaw?"

That wasn't a question I could answer. Not yet. I didn't know if Shaw wanted me. I didn't know if I wanted him. I just didn't know anything right then, but I definitely didn't want Casey to wait for me any longer. So I gave him a smile and leaned in to kiss my best friend on the cheek. I realized then that this was the only sort of kiss we would ever share again.

Rubbing my thumb over the spot when I pulled back, I told him, "I'm going to be happy knowing you're happy."

And I meant it.

CHAPTER 13

Cassidy

I was absolutely exhausted, having ridden some epically emotional highs and lows throughout the day, not to mention the mental strain of trying to figure out my life, and then the physical exhaustion of readying the Whalen House for Hurricane Ayla. Despite said hurricane making landfall and sounding like a train whistle doing the nasty with a banshee scream, all I wanted to do was crawl into my bed and hide under the covers until it and all the dramatic bullcrap had passed.

I'd just finished my shower, changed into my nightshirt and panties, and gotten comfortable in my bed of a million fluffy pillows when there was a knock at my door. With an aggravated huff, I threw back the down comforter, landed my feet hard on the floor, and stomped over to greet the intruder of my sanctuary.

Abby was standing on the other side. Not that I was surprised, really. There was a freakin' hurricane outside, so of course the parents would be worried.

"You're lucky it's me and not Anna," she said, registering my attitude. "If she could've gotten that wheelchair up here—and trust me, she tried—she'd have probably tied you off to the back and dragged you down the stairs."

It wasn't an exaggeration. Ma would've done it.

"Jeez . . . Abbs, will you please get her to chill out? I'm in the house, safe and sound. If the roof starts coming apart, I promise I'll be down there. But for now, I just want to be left alone."

"All right. I'll do my best," she said, that understanding ever present in the fine wrinkles of her face. "Where's my boy? Did you leave anything of him to bury?"

"I didn't lay a finger on him," I told her. Well, I had, just in a nonviolent sort of way. "Find Mia, and I'm sure you'll find him. What about Shaw? Is he okay?"

She shrugged. "Seemed to be when he went up to his room. A little shaken still, contemplating life maybe, but physically fine."

"Thanks for what you did for him, Abbs. I don't think you understand how much that means for him."

Abby patted my cheek. "I understand more than you think," she said with a wink. "Get some rest, sweet girl. I'll hold the fort down. And put some pants on in case you've got to scatter in a hurry."

She turned to leave and I closed the door behind her. Screw the pants. Shuffling back over to the bed beckoning me to get lost in its comforts, I snuggled in deep and tried to concentrate on nothingness, willing the sleep to come. But the more I tried to think about nothing, the more I thought about everything.

Had I made the right decision where Casey was concerned? Yes, definitely. Most women were never lucky enough to find one good man. I, as it turned out, had two. Choosing between them had not been easy, but when I put my analytical powers to work, I could see the differences between my best friend and the man who had become the long shot.

Where Casey always let me find my own way in my own time, Shaw pushed and shoved. Where Casey supported whatever decision I made without putting up much of a fuss, Shaw never let me become complacent and issued new challenges. Where Casey was my loudest cheerleader in the stands, Shaw ran alongside me as I raced to the finish line to meet those challenges. And where Casey helped mold me into the woman I had become, Shaw helped me realize the woman I wanted to be.

Yes, Shaw was a long shot, the last of the draft pick, but somehow he'd still managed to make the playoffs despite his less-than-impressive stats. With the big game at hand, I realized I was no longer playing referee, but rather I was the opposing team. Would he be the one spiking my heart in the end zone with the game-winning play?

There was another knock at my door, which irritated the living daylights out of me. Jesus, Ma had probably dumped herself from her chair and hobbled all the way up the stairs. Again, I stomped across the floor like a petulant child preparing to throw a tantrum. But when I opened the door, Ma wasn't standing there. Neither was Abby.

I nearly tripped over my own feet as I tried to move out of the way of a charging Shaw, as he blew past me and into my room. If our turbulent history had taught me anything, it was that when Shaw Matthews was in a tizzy, as he seemed to be now, a less-than-quiet confrontation was about to go down. So I closed us in together, hoping the fit that Hurricane Ayla was throwing would keep the parents and Casey from overhearing. Especially Casey. The last thing I needed was to give him a reason to bust down the door so he could finish the brawl he and Shaw had started earlier.

When I turned around, Shaw was so close that I nearly collided with his chest. But it didn't keep me from noticing the way those jeans sat sinfully perfect on his hips, or the way they hugged his thighs, or the way they accented the bulging package in the center. His white T-shirt was stretched too tight across his toned shoulders and chest, the collar snug around a perfectly sculpted neck. For the first time in my entire life, I wanted to mark a man. I wanted to mark *this* man.

It was yet another difference in the way I saw Shaw versus Casey. With Casey, I'd wanted to snuggle into the warm protection of his embrace. But Shaw? I wanted to climb him. Climb him and sink my teeth into him. And I wanted him to shove me away so that I'd have to work for it. There was something unhealthy about that, disturbing even. Then again, he was the one person who'd always managed to make me insane.

Judging by his expression, now was not the time to attack. There was no cocky smirk on his lips, no ticking of his scruffy jaw, and no high-and-mighty set to his chin. His eyes were electric, swarming with white lightning. Yet there was a gentleness about them. He hadn't come here to argue. So what had he come here for?

"I almost died today, and it made me realize something."

My heart plummeted, and the thought of Shaw dying made me sick to my stomach. I don't think I'd thought about how much his near-death experience had affected him, which was so incredibly stupid of me. None of this was about me. It was about him. I had to find a way to fix this.

"Shaw," I started, but he cut me off.

He grabbed my shoulders, holding me in place, and though it was firm, it wasn't meant to be forceful. "No, let me finish. If you don't, I'll never get it out."

"Okay." I looked down at my shoulder and he eased his hold as if he'd just realized what he'd done.

"I almost died today and I was alone. Just like I have been for my entire life. And I always thought I was okay with that, but I'm not." He stopped, cupping my face in his hands. "Cassidy, I don't want to be alone anymore. Not tonight. Not any other night."

Before I could even process what he'd said, Shaw was kissing me. And though his body was taut with restraint, his lips were tender. I couldn't put my finger on what was different, but something had definitely changed. Maybe it was his near-death experience. Maybe it was the hurricane beating down with all its fury outside. Or maybe it was Shaw's internal fury, rising to the surface to finally surrender.

A contradiction to his kiss, Shaw's hands were at my hips, his fingertips pressed into my skin with a firm grip. And then he fisted my shirt and broke the kiss to pull it over my head before fusing his lips back to mine once more. He was still dressed, and even though I wanted nothing more than to rectify that situation, Shaw was running the show.

He walked me backward, his mouth moving to my neck, my shoulders, and the valley between my breasts until he pushed them together to devour first one and then the other nipple. When the back of my knees hit the bed, his hands abandoned my breasts to cup my ass and lift me up to sit on top of the mattress. The crown of Shaw's disheveled pecan brown hair was all that I saw and felt against my lower belly as he went even farther and . . .

I gasped. "Oh, my God," I groaned when I felt the warmth of his mouth soaking me through my panties.

Well, maybe his mouth hadn't been fully responsible for the soaking. My wanton vagina probably had a thing or two to do with it as well. But Christ, the man knew how to awaken the woman in me. I'd have to remember to check this pair of panties to see if I'd purchased them with a bull's-eye over my clit because Shaw had managed to find it with absolutely no problem. Even hidden as it was.

Gripping his hair in both hands, I held on for dear—"Sweet baby Jesus"—life. The interruption to my thought was a very welcome one, indeed. Though I wasn't sure how I'd been able to think of anything when Shaw was doing that thing he was doing . . . through my freakin' panties.

I tried to lie back in order to enjoy the gift being bestowed upon me, but Shaw's muffled "Mm-mm" and tight hold on my sides kept me from going anywhere. So I did what any other woman in my position would do. I watched him, and I was ever so glad I did. Slow and steady was his pace as his head moved back and forth while his tongue made love to me. And then finally, the panties were breached when he pulled them to the side and plunged two fingers deep inside.

My back arched, and this time I was permitted to recline back onto the mattress. Shaw's tongue, lips, and teeth aided him in his quest to drive me insane. Back and forth he moved his fingers, alternating with knuckle-deep thrusts meant to keep it unpredictable. I couldn't stand it anymore. I couldn't stand that he was so far away, and I couldn't stand the damn panties that were keeping him from doing anything more than teasing me into oblivion.

I could've come. And I was sure that was Shaw's intent, but I didn't want to. I wanted my first orgasm with him tonight to be on his cock.

"Shaw, I need you."

He stopped what he was doing, and for a moment I almost changed my mind about letting him continue. But when he looked up at me with that same sense of surrender coupled with a hungry need in his eyes, goosebumps broke out across my flesh.

"You have me," he said with a quiet conviction.

I don't know what it was about his choice of words, but I sat up and took his face into my hands to kiss him, to taste myself on his lips. He needed to know he had me, too, and I tried to convey as much with that one simple, yet passionate action. Because words were meaningless without the physical proof.

Shaw gripped my thighs and pulled me closer, and I felt the warmth of his chest through a shirt that was every bit as annoying as my stupid panties. It had to go, so I gave it a tug and pulled it over his head. When he sat back and looked at me as if to say, "What now?" I put the words to good use.

"I meant I need you inside me."

My onetime adversary, now turned lover, got to his bare feet. Remaining focused on me, he undid the button and zipper of his jeans. My attention shifted to the toned planes of his chest, the ripples of his abdomen, and the sloping curves of the Adonis belt he wore so well. Chancing movement, I reached out and let the tips of my nails gently comb through the fuzzy trail of hair that started at his navel and ended at his groin. Shaw took a deep breath, the muscles there flexing involuntarily under my touch.

He was beautiful.

And impatient.

Shoving his jeans over the narrow hips that paired well with his muscle definition, Shaw kicked them free of his feet and then stood erect once more. And speaking of erect . . . His cock was already hard for me, almost begging me to have a taste in the way it jutted out from his body toward me. But there was no time for that before Shaw leaned in, forcing me to recline back once more. It was a good thing, because when he hooked his fingers under the waistband of my panties and gave them a yank, I didn't even have the chance to lift my ass to aid him. He didn't need a lovely assistant; he just needed me naked and bare for him.

As Shaw followed onto the bed, he scooted me up to lay on the pillows, the palm of one of his capable hands planted next to me to hold his weight. And then he did something too sweet for the Shaw Matthews I knew. With a tender touch, he raked his fingers through my hair, being sure to brush it away from my face, almost methodical in the way he arranged it like a crimson halo about my head.

The veins in his forearm were so mesmerizing, I couldn't turn away and I couldn't squelch the savage craving for a taste. So I selfishly took what I wanted, my tongue following a vessel ripe with pulsing blood beneath his skin. The sound Shaw made was half protest, half approval—as if he didn't know whether to stop me in favor of his own control, or to encourage me so he could lose it.

My mouth closed over his skin to give him a suckle, and that was when he made his decision. With the dominating insistence of a lion, he leaned forward and nudged my mouth away from his arm so he could capture my bottom lip between his teeth. He could have his way. I loved him like this.

Except I didn't love him, did I? Confusing love with lust was one sinkhole I wouldn't fall into. Not with a man who had the power to devastate me. Not with a man like Shaw.

My lion's thick mane of hair was soft between the fingers of my clenched fist. I tugged, attempting to force him to release the hold on my lip before he broke the skin, but there was no victory to be had. Mercifully, Shaw's appetite for flesh subsided in exchange for that same tender, yet fiery passion he'd shown when he'd first entered my room.

Wedging first one knee and then the other between my own, he forced my legs to part so he could occupy the space. And Jesus, his cock lay heavy and thick in the crook of my thigh. His kiss intensified, becoming almost impossible to match until, without warning, he abandoned it altogether to look down at me. I was sure I must have looked confused, dazed, and breathless at the sudden charge in the air crackling with anticipation.

And then he entered me. The broad head of his cock penetrated my tight opening, the defined ridge leading the way through the narrow channel to prepare me for his girth. My breath hitched at the slow intrusion, the stretch on the cusp of painful thanks to his large size. But the pain would subside and he would give me nothing but pleasure. I'd come to expect nothing less, and Shaw had never disappointed.

Once he'd pushed all the way inside, he began a slow pace, filling me completely before retreating again. The next push forward was accompanied by the reward of a purposeful grind to stimulate my clit. Oh, and how very delicious it was.

I closed my eyes, absorbing Shaw's presence on my skin, in my mind, inside my body, letting him burrow deeper into a space I'd never imagined he would ever occupy. My heart.

"No, Cassidy. I told you I don't want to be alone. I need you to be here with me in this moment. Not just physically, but in every way imaginable. See *me*."

I really didn't know how to process those words, but I knew that no matter how much it would likely destroy me in the end, I wanted to give him anything he asked for.

With a barely perceptible nod, I whispered, "Okay."

I wasn't even sure he'd heard it over the sound of the shutters straining at the hinges and the debris hitting the roof overhead, but something must have convinced him that all systems were Go because the way he moved inside me, the way he kissed me . . . may the powers that be have mercy on my soul as it crossed over into the afterlife. Because this new Shaw was going to be the death of me.

Though we'd just begun, we had to stop to catch our breaths, and not even that kept us from wanting more. He kissed me again and again, resting his forehead against mine in between and staring down at my lips. This was the sort of kiss that went straight to your head and made you forget about everything else, including how to breathe. No oxygen to the brain tended to make one dizzy, so I had to hold on to keep from falling. But Jesus, I was too late. I'd already fallen, and fallen hard. There was no safety net, no bottom in sight. All I could hope was that Shaw would be there to catch me.

Clutching him to me, my thighs squeezed his hips even as I tried desperately to bring him closer. His hands cradled my face while my fingers sought to find purchase in his hair. It wasn't enough, so I dropped my arms and wrapped them under and over his shoulders instead. Finally, safety. Something to hold on to. Something to give me balance.

I wanted even more control, but Shaw wasn't giving it. For each time I tried to take the lead, he showed his dominance, countering every move with a redirect or a nip to my lip. No. God. I couldn't let him. I couldn't let him have that much control and I couldn't let him know it was his to give. If he knew how I felt, if he knew I was in love with him . . .

My breath hitched. I was in love with him. Crap.

Everything went still under the weight of my realization as if some higher being had hit the pause button on the world. It was quiet. Too quiet. Even the howling winds and pounding rain had come to an end.

Shaw slowed his movements, his hips abandoning the thrust to focus on the grind instead. He was so deep. So very, very deep inside me. Closer than he'd ever been before.

"It's the eye of the storm," he whispered. "But it isn't over yet. In fact, things are about to get rough again. Are you ready?"

I knew he was talking about the back end of Ayla, but I couldn't help but think how well his statement fit everything that was going on between us now.

"No. I really don't think I am. But I've never backed down from a challenge," I told him. And I meant it.

"That's my girl," he said with a slow and steady grind that nearly made me orgasm on the spot. "My girl."

And then he nuzzled my neck, sucking and nipping . . . marking me. His girl. God help me, but it was true.

Running my hands along his back, I reveled in the flexing muscles there until I reached his ass. Closing my eyes, I stepped through the looking glass of my mind and recounted the memory of the way his back looked in the mirror while he'd fucked me in the bathroom of that private jet. Only, he wasn't fucking me now. He was making love to me. Maybe it was wishful thinking from a mind that was still freaking out about my most recent revelation, but even if that were the case, I didn't care. I'd let myself believe he loved me, too. If only for this one moment.

I sank my nails into the cheeks of that divine ass, feeling the flexing of muscles underneath my fingertips as he ground against me. Closer. I wanted him closer. So I lifted my legs until my knees were at his ribs and then wrapped them around him, cupping his ass and drawing him deeper inside me.

Shaw moaned at my ear, whispering, "Fuck, sweetness, you feel so good. I never want to not be inside you. Not ever again."

God, I didn't want him never to be there either. But I couldn't tell him that. It would give him way too much power over me. Though, truthfully, the power was already his.

I loved him. And for the first time, I felt like we were truly connected. Not just physically, but on some other level. A level that penetrated the core of me that was almost as deep as what his cock was penetrating now.

His groin massaged my clit with a delicious pressure that beckoned my climax forward. I couldn't have called it back, even if I'd wanted to try. And I didn't. I wanted to come on his cock, wanted him to feel the pulsing pull of my orgasm, and I wanted to milk him of his own.

His skin was hot against mine, fevered more by his passion than the blood running through his veins. Each grunting thrust forward propelled me further, his thick cock moving so purposefully inside me and the broad head doing something very wicked to that gland of pleasure. It had to be swollen from the stimulation. Swollen and ready to burst. Oh, but I was ripe and on the verge of a dual orgasm; one from my G-spot and the other from the pressure on my clit.

"Shaw, I'm almost . . ." I moaned out, unable to finish the sentence.

"I know, sweetness. Me too. I'm trying to wait for you, but you're so goddamn tight—" He paused, grunting through another deep grind.

I bit into his shoulder and he bucked forward.

"Fuck, you can't do that. You're going to make me come."

I didn't care. I was almost there myself and it set off a sort of feeding frenzy inside me. I wanted to taste him, to feel his flesh between my teeth and savor the salty flavor of his skin. So I went for his neck, sucking with the groaning pleasure of the orgasm at its cusp. And then Shaw really got busy, the thrusting grind jarring my body with its force. My hypersensitive nipples ached in a wonderful sort of way under the compression of his chest, and the raging beat of my heart became heavy and dense.

I moaned, the sound no doubt vibrating against his skin. Every muscle in Shaw's body went even more taut, his ass still flexing beneath my hands. He needed more control, more room to move.

I started to release the lock I had around him with my legs, but Shaw stopped me with a shake of his head and a raspy "No. Hold on to me, Cassidy. Don't let go."

So I tightened the embrace, undulating beneath him and meeting the rolling grind of his hips. Oh, my God . . . the slippery stroking of his groin against my clit, the engorged cock moving inside me, the feel of his skin on mine, and the sound of his grunted pleasure at my ear . . . I had no choice but to succumb to it all.

My moan started low, building and building in tandem with the mounting orgasm. With a one-two punch, the clitoral release hit first and the G-spot followed hot on its trail. Shaw pulled back to watch my face.

"Oh, fuck," he mumbled, and then his lips covered mine as he moaned into my mouth.

I felt it. The pulsing heat of his semen as he came. Not on my belly. Not on my thigh. No, his orgasm mingled with mine deep within the protection of my pussy. I could feel my walls contracting around his cock, milking him while still indulging in the pleasure he gave as his movements slowed to a stuttered pace.

And then finally, Shaw's kiss became less carnal, tender in the way his mouth softened and his tongue retreated. With one last suckle to my bottom lip, he pulled back to catch his breath and allowed me to catch mine.

Shaw wasn't moving, but I could still feel his cock throbbing inside me, and it was the most intense thing I'd ever felt before. Almost as intense as the way he was looking down at me. His lips were parted to ease his breathing, and a light sheen of sweat kissed his skin. But the thing I noticed most was the way his brow furrowed with a mix of contemplation and confusion. He wasn't the only one confused.

I felt his absence before he'd even completely withdrawn his cock, but somehow I still felt fulfilled. Lowering my legs, I gave him room to roll off me, but he stayed right where he was.

What was it about the way he was looking at me that made the butterflies in my belly go berserk?

"Do you want me to leave?" he asked.

I didn't even need to think about it. I'd done enough thinking tonight to last a whole lifetime. And if this one night was all I'd have with Shaw in this way, I'd take it. Without regret.

So with a shake of my head, I answered truthfully, "I don't want to be alone anymore, either."

The smile that spread across his face nearly took my breath away. And then he flopped onto his back, slipping his arm under my shoulders to gather me to him so that I was forced to lay my head on his chest.

"Good," he said, and I could still hear that smile in his voice.

Yeah, it was very good.

CHAPTER 14

Mia

I was fast at work back in my room, cataloguing every detail of the storm raging outside, making notes of everything I saw and heard because if ever I found myself in a position to write a hurricane in the future, I knew that retelling the experience from my own point of view would make it as real as possible for my reader.

But the hurricane wasn't the only thing I was making note of.

Casey had had some extreme emotional reactions that had led to a fistfight, a man overboard, a near-death experience, and the heartache of losing the one woman on the face of the planet that he'd ever cared anything for. Well, at least I assumed he'd lost her. He'd seen her screwing another man with his own eyes, for goodness' sake. And if I'd learned anything about Casey while I'd been studying him, it was that he was as loyal as they came and expected the same in return.

I was as shocked as he was by the interesting twist of Cassidy hooking up with a man she'd supposedly despised. We'd talked so much about her and their life together that I felt like I knew her personally. Though truthfully, she intimidated the hell out of me. She had it all: a loving and supportive family, a superstar career, local fame, and a boyfriend (excuse me, ex-boyfriend) who was a one-in-a-million rare find. How could she have left it all behind?

People fascinated me. I was completely obsessed with figuring out what made them tick. I studied the way a subject walked, talked, dressed, gestured, their facial expressions, words they chose and the inflection upon them, the choices they made . . . everything. All those things that made each of us an individual. Not only did I study all the things of the present, but also of the past. We were a product of our surroundings. The way we reacted to situations was part genetic makeup, part the surroundings in which we grew, and part the lessons we learned on our own. Everything we did was preprogrammed at some point along our journey, and I wanted to reason it all out. It was a game, a riddle to be solved.

But getting to know these people—getting to know Casey—had put an end to the game for me. It was real. His emotions were real. And I just wanted to live in his world. So I did it the best way I knew how. I wrote about it. Within the pages of my own musings, I was in control. I could feel his touch, taste his kiss, and calm his hidden fears . . . I could give him his happily ever after. And I could imagine it was with me. Though the line between what was a matter of my imagination and what was real had become blurred.

Casey and Cassidy were the fictional characters within a made-up world inside an overactive romantic mind. It was every author's dream to be able to reach out and touch them, to interact in a way that was tangible, real. My Jayson Bass and Janell Kain had come to life right before my very eyes, and I couldn't help the overwhelming excitement it had given me. Of course that might have also meant that I'd become too familiar with their real-life counterparts in my own world, a familiarity Casey and Cassidy couldn't understand and certainly didn't feel. But in them, I saw my characters. They likely saw a crazy lady who they'd probably thought was being way too intrusive. Hopefully, they'd indulge my fantasy for just a little while longer so I could get my manuscript completed.

I should've already been gone, but then Anna had hurt herself and Casey had told me Cassidy was on her way back home. I just couldn't leave without meeting this infamous woman and seeing if she was anything at all like my Janell. Admittedly, after all the discussions about her—all the *ooh*ing and *ahh*ing over how smart she was, how beautiful, how successful, how loved, and how absolutely perfect—I'd developed a girl crush. But she didn't like me much.

Cassidy was less than receptive toward me, but I tried not to take it personally. After all, I was a stranger and I'd been spending an awful lot of time with her ex-boyfriend, who didn't quite get that he was an ex per all of our conversations. It was so obvious to see. Casey was still over the moon for her. In fact, he'd sworn the moon *was* her. Apparently, that had been their thing.

I wished I'd had a thing with someone.

A knock sounded at my door, giving me a start so that I nearly fell off my bed. Then I literally did fall off when I tried to get out of it and got tangled up in the sheets. Again with the knock, more insistent this time, urgent. Jeez, with the hurricane raging as it was outside the Whalen House, I hoped it wasn't some sort of emergency.

Finally gathering myself off the floor and finding my clumsy feet, I went over, willing myself to stop overthinking things. I had a really bad habit of doing that. But my instinct to do so kicked into overdrive when I pulled back the door and saw what was waiting on the other side.

Casey was standing there, his chest rising and falling in that "quiet just before the storm" sort of way. Which was poetic because the actual storm outside was deafening. Soft baby blues that once promised comfort and security now matched the lonely, tumultuous dark waters of the bay and gave thought to a sailor lost at sea, looking to use every tool at his disposal to find his way back to the shore. Ooh, that was good. Where was my notebook?

Swallowing the clichéd lump in my throat, I decided to say something rather than continue to stand there looking like an idiot. "Is something wrong?"

"Yeah. Something is very wrong." Casey's voice sounded even more gravelly than normal in a very sexy, though dangerous sort of way.

I was forced to back up as he walked inside and closed the door behind him like he owned the place. There was something in his eyes, something that changed everything and excited me while also putting the fear of God into my soul.

"You said you could tell a lot about a person by the way they kiss."

I nodded.

Getting right to the point, he grabbed the back of my head, holding me in place as his mouth came down hard on mine and his tongue pushed inside. There was nothing sweet about his kiss. No light nips of my lip, no precursory suckles at the corner of my mouth, no sweeping tease of the tongue begging for entrance like you read about in all the cookie-cutter romance novels. It wasn't slow, nor was it gentle. It was desperate and rough and looking to prove a point. So unlike the man I'd thought I'd come to know, but still exactly what I'd expected.

The intensity of his gaze when he pulled back was no different from the kiss. "And what did that tell you?"

Again I swallowed, and then I said the first thing that came to mind: "You need to be fucked." I couldn't believe I'd been so bold.

"Wrong. I need to be the one doing the fucking. If you don't want to be on the receiving end of that, you better say so now."

I didn't say a word. Even if I'd wanted to, my lips would've denied my brain's request. But he must have seen my acceptance of the offer in my expression because the already supercharged atmosphere ignited into something I wasn't entirely sure I'd been prepared for.

"Get undressed."

I followed the order, not because I was terrified of him, but because I was terrified he'd change his mind if I didn't. I wanted to be his outlet. I needed to be his outlet. So I made fast work of shedding my yoga pants and oversized T-shirt, and thanked the powers that be I'd just had a shower and hadn't bothered with the panties or bra. Once I was done, I stood there, awkward and very naked, waiting for Casey to finish undressing himself. I wanted to help, would've helped, but something told me my assistance would be unwelcome.

Casey stood when he'd finished and I gawked. And probably drooled. Holy fucking shit, but the man was even more glorious naked than I'd imagined my Jayson to be in my wildest fantasies. And yeah, there'd been a few of those during my special alone time since I'd come to the island. Casey's chest was thick and firm with a small patch of hair between the pecs, his gorgeous arms were veiny and bulging, and that trail down his abdomen was worthy of a paragraphed description. But there was no time to write now because even farther below, there was a granite trophy in need of attention. Casey's erection hung long and thick from his body, and I was feeling mighty attentive.

He didn't take the time to check me out as thoroughly as I

had him. I was almost grateful he hadn't. I wasn't built like the women I wrote about. My breasts were only about a B-cup, and my figure didn't look anything like an hourglass. I was average— not skinny, not fat—with the sort of thickness that came along from sitting behind my laptop day in and day out while snacking on junk food.

Taking me by the arm, Casey walked me over to the bed and turned my shoulders so that I faced it. All business in order to get down to the business. I liked it. And then he nudged me forward until I was bent over the mattress. I liked that, too.

"Are you ready?"

More than. "Yes."

Without any preparation—though, truthfully, I was already more than wet for him—Casey pushed inside me, burying his cock balls deep. My back arched as I whispered, "Oh, my God. Yes . . ."

"No talking," he said as he leaned forward, the heat of his body nearly scorching the exposed skin of my back. "And you might want to hold on to something."

I felt the swift retreat of his cock, which nearly made me shout a protest despite his order of silence, but then I was again gifted with every agonizing inch of the next drive forward. His pace quickened and the power of his thrusts became more demanding. He was right; I needed to hold on to something, so I found purchase on the sheets right next to his hands. The way he covered me with his body, those perfect teeth buried in the skin of my shoulder . . . it was carnal, intense. Perfect.

Pinning me down by the neck, I was trapped and unable to move. I couldn't see Casey's ruggedly handsome face, which meant he also couldn't see mine. And that was just as he needed it to be. However, I could definitely hear the grunting at my ear. Closing my eyes, I let the sound of him, the feel of him, the smell of him whisk me away to that place inside my mind where I'd recorded every nuance of my Jayson, and the two became one.

Much like the kiss, there was a purpose to his fast and steady strokes. No deviation from the angle from which he worked, no slow and steady grind. He wasn't working to bring me pleasure. He was seeking his own, though I couldn't help but wonder if his release would bring him anything other than pain.

I had no grand delusions about what all this meant. His cock wasn't inside me because he'd fallen madly in love with the woman who'd come from out of nowhere when he was at the most desperate point of his life. It wasn't even there because I was voluptuous and seductive and he simply couldn't resist me. And none of this was about my sassy mouth turning him on and making him want to fuck some manners into me.

Casey was not Jayson Bass, and I was not Janell Kain. But I wanted him all the same.

Yanked from my imaginary world and thrust back into reality, I was confused when the glorious cock that had been occupying my very needy vagina suddenly disappeared. And even more so when Casey snatched me up like I didn't weigh a thing, only to find myself in a straddled position with that beast of a man between my thighs.

Apparently needing no help from me, Casey guided my hips until he was completely sheathed again. I groaned, relishing the stretch and feel once more. But this wasn't about me, a fact proven when he began to move me up and down on his cock, fast and hard. So I did the only thing I could do; I held on to his shoulders and let him have his way, regardless of how contradictory the position may have been.

As a woman and a romance author, I'd always considered cowgirl style to be a position of dominance over a man, my chance to be in control. That simply was not true with Casey. Like a horse without reins, he controlled the ride. He was wild and free, the lean muscles of his body flexing with each movement, the huff of his labored breaths every bit as powerful as the momentum behind them. Casey was a thoroughbred free of fences, free of restraint. Finally.

I was going to write about this. I was going to immortalize him and this moment in the pages of one of my books. Because it was worthy of immortalization. Inside my writer's brain, I memorized every minute detail—the flex of his strong shoulders, the grip of his capable hands, the feel of the rough calluses from his palms against my cheeks, the exquisite pull of my anus with each lift up, and the sound of skin meeting skin with each push down. But most of all, I'd remember and hope to capture every shade of the raw emotion behind eyes as blue as a marlin on a hook making its last-ditch attempt to free itself from its captor's line. Because no matter how free his movements seemed to be, those eyes told a different story.

I was locked on his gaze, unable to turn away for fear I'd miss something intrinsically important. What Casey saw as he looked back at me wasn't me at all. In the place of dull brown hair, he saw robust locks of shimmering auburn. In the place of amber skin, he saw flawless ivory. And in the place of boring brown eyes, he saw orbs the color of springtime leaves. What he saw, *who* he saw, was Cassidy.

The grip on my ass softened, but the cock inside me was still very rigid. When Casey also stopped moving me up and down, I wondered if he'd changed his mind and no longer wanted to follow through on the task he'd started. So I stopped moving as well, waiting for him to tell me to get off him. He didn't.

Instead, he pulled my hips forward, encouraging me to take over, to move as I wanted . . . to ride him. My heart raced in my chest, thrilled by the opportunity to have this man the way I'd wanted him from the moment of our very first greeting. Casey was tall with broad shoulders, sturdy and strong, a mountain of a man that made we want to get out my climbing gear and go for his summit. But I'd somehow managed to control my impulses, intimidated by his mere presence as he towered over me. Now he was between my thighs, all that raw power mine for the taking. So I seized the once-in-a-lifetime opportunity and accepted his offering.

Leaning into him, I positioned my hips for an easier glide, rolling forward and back with a pace that was much more sensual than the pounding he'd been serving up. I didn't want him to feel angry. I wanted him to feel needed, desired, worshipped. Holding him close, I nuzzled his neck. When I heard his slow exhale as he craned his head to the side to give me better access, I took full advantage. But I knew I needed to be careful not to spook him. So I took my time, gently sucking at his skin and taking nips, though I was sure not to mark him. He was not mine. I was only borrowing him.

When my lips captured his earlobe and my teeth scraped it, his breath stuttered. I took great power from being able to affect this man in such a way. I'd found his button and my research was complete. But I wasn't quite done with him. There had been one other thing I'd wanted that I hadn't yet had the opportunity to do. It was a risk, but one well worth taking. So I suckled his earlobe one more time to hopefully guide him to a more receptive state, and then I kissed along his chiseled jawline to his mouth.

Casey hadn't kissed me since the one and only kiss we'd shared before all of this began. I wasn't even sure if it would be okay to go there again, if it was too intimate for him to handle. But kissing Casey wasn't the plan. I simply wanted to sink my teeth into the meaty flesh of that damn bottom lip of his. So with the forward roll of my hips, I took his cock deep inside me, inhaling sharply and throwing caution to the wind as I covered his mouth with mine.

And oh, God, yes! Casey's large hands splayed across my back and he held me to him, his mouth receptive and his tongue seeking the comfort of my own. His taste was sweet and I grew lightheaded from the sugar rush. He was so hard inside me, so warm and naked against my skin, so fucking manly in every way. For one brave moment, I pretended I could have my way with him. My arms wrapped around his neck and I fisted his hair, pulling back ever so slightly and forcing him to release my mouth. And then I did it. I took that sin-worthy lip between my teeth and scraped the tender flesh with my bite.

Casey growled. Not in warning but in approval. I gave him my best seductive smile, the kind all the sassy heroines in my books gave their male leads to drive them bat-shit crazy with lust, and then I bit him again. This time I didn't pull away. I deepened the kiss, taking control of it and giving him a taste of his own medicine. Maybe I was sweet, but innocent I was not. If this was the only time I'd ever have him in this way, I was going to make damn sure it was as memorable for him as it would be for me.

Holding on to his shoulders, I used my body the way a woman's body was meant to be used in order to please a man. The arch of my back put me in the perfect position to ride his thick length while still teasing his lips with the brush of my nipple. I wanted him to take it, and he did.

Casey captured the pert bud between his teeth, gently scraping it with a delicious sort of pain. Though I was careful not to say a word—he still hadn't given me permission to—I whimpered at the sensational tease. More. I wanted more. Reading my cue, he took the wanton peak fully into his mouth, suckling and licking, while looking up at me. There was a shift behind those eyes, and I got a glimpse of the man who lived to please his woman.

I watched as he moved from one breast to the other, kneading them both with his strong and roughened hands. Each draw backward and push forward of my undulation teased my G-spot and sent me higher and higher, like an elevator climbing to the top floor of a tall building. Anticipation to reach the final destination dueled with the impatience of the long ride up, but I knew once those doors opened, my orgasm would come flooding in.

Second floor . . . third floor . . . fourth floor . . .

Quickening my grind, my focus shifted to the sensation of my swollen clit against that sinful patch of hair on Casey's groin. It tickled yet stimulated the highly sensitive button to my pleasure, so I bore down, pressing closer and closer. So enraptured was I—by the expression in Casey's eyes, his mouth on my breasts, every minute detail of his engorged cock deep inside me—that I hadn't even noticed I'd been biting down on my lip until it started to throb in warning that I was about to break the skin.

Fifth floor . . . sixth floor . . . seventh heaven.

Destination reached. No sooner had the doors opened than the elevator went crashing down, the sudden shift sending wave after wave of euphoria through every nerve ending in my body. My chest felt light and airy, almost cold in the absence of the blood that had vacated it to converge upon my center only to explode and then spread through my veins like a wildfire demanding the scorch and burn. I swooned and swayed, basking in the aftermath of a rush that left my head dizzy with bliss.

I'd only barely registered the stillness of my movements when Casey took over, pushing and pulling at my hips to prolong the event. The walls of my pussy gripped his impossibly harder erection, squeezing and tugging, begging him to join me in a place that should be shared by lovers.

And I almost believed we were exactly that. Until I opened my eyes and came face-to-face with reality once more.

The shift I'd seen only moments before had suddenly changed, like he'd snapped back to some reality I couldn't fathom. Gone was gentle Casey, desperate Casey having resumed his place, and I found our positions changed yet again.

Lying flat on my back with my arms pinned to the bed above my head, I felt exhilarated. Yes, I wanted this.

"Wider," was his order, and I was his to command, though he didn't give me the chance to comply. Instead, he hooked an arm under one knee and spread me to his liking. Angling his hips, that very thick cock entered me again with a delicious stretch and fill. Sweet Jesus, but I wished I had the power to rewind time so I could feel it again.

Holy shit, but his glorious cock was abundant and . . . and glorious. It was also unyielding in its selfish endeavor. Casey pounded into me hard, each punishing thrust shoving my body forward on the mattress with only a quick reprieve before being jostled again.

Although he was rough, I craved the next retreat and advancing drive. But as they had been at the start, these thrusts were not for my benefit. They were for his. I was merely a willing participant. He could use me for his purpose. I didn't care. I just wanted to feel him, just wanted to keep him inside me, just wanted to have that one fleeting connection with him. His pleasure was my own.

Casey's grunts became more anxious, his hips more insistent, his rhythm direct and hurried. And then finally, his cock was free of my pussy and lying thick in the crook of my thigh and pelvis. I felt it throb with each stuttered release of his erupting orgasm and relished the carnal sensation of his teeth at my neck while hot semen coated my skin.

Closing my eyes, I held him to me because I knew I'd never feel him like this again. I wished I could say that for that one moment in time he was mine. But he wasn't. He would never be mine because he would forever be hers. What a stupid, stupid girl Cassidy Whalen was.

Breaking free of my hold, Casey rolled off me to rest at my side. The chill of the room was unwelcomed against my flushed skin and I was aware of my nakedness for the first time. Chancing a glance at Casey, I found him with an arm arched over his head, his eyes shut, and his chest heaving with breaths he was trying to get under control. I wanted to lay my head over his heart to hear its loud pounding. I wanted to snuggle into the crook of his arm and throw my leg over his, peppering his sweaty skin in thanks. But I wouldn't because I couldn't. He was not my boyfriend and we were not lovers. We just were.

Casey's eyes popped open and he turned to look at me. No doubt he'd felt my stare. I turned away, not quite sure what to say in the awkward silence that followed or if I should say anything at all. I had my answer when he jumped up and grabbed his pants, pulling them up in a hurry and not even bothering with the button. His socks and boots were next as he sat on the edge of the bed. He didn't look at me as he went about his task, didn't utter a word. When he finished, he stood and grabbed his shirt, holding it in his hand with his back, toned and fanned like a cobra's hood, to me.

"Sorry," he said, and then he made for the exit like he couldn't get out of my room fast enough.

Once I heard the door click into place, I chanced my own words. "I'm not."

CHAPTER 15

Shaw

I'd barely slept a wink all night. Not because of the storm but because I'd been contemplating the meaning of life. Okay, so maybe that was a slight exaggeration, though not by much. I had nearly lost my life the day before, after all. Shit like that tended to make you take stock of the things you had and didn't have. Not the materialistic stuff I'd coveted for most of my life, but all the other more meaningful things those self-help gurus wrote about. Things like family, happiness, self-actualization, core values . . . and time—what I had left of it and how I was going to use it. I'd thought those things were absolute bullshit before. Not now. Now, instead of a warehouse full of shiny toys, all I saw was a prideful waste of space. Needless to say, I wasn't very proud of who I'd become.

Despite all my efforts to be nothing like my parents, my self-ishness had made me *exactly* like them. My father's greed and my mother's addictive personality were both nestled inside a bouncing baby boy who wasn't a bundle of joy, but rather a giant pile of regret fueled by a lifetime of self-indulgence. If I'd died in that ocean, there'd be no legacy, nothing of Shaw Matthews left behind.

I'd never wanted that before, wouldn't have given two shits about it. But now I was obsessing over it. What the hell had changed? Damned if everything in my noggin wasn't topsy-turvy and in complete disarray.

To add to the chaos, I'd come inside Cassidy. And that just wasn't the type of shit I did. So I'd been trying to figure out why I'd done it in the first place, and why Cassidy. That was enough to explain the restlessness on its own, but then there was also the matter of my not wanting to miss a second of that woman sleeping in my arms. The way she fit into my side perfectly, her quiet snore, and even the endearing way she drooled just a little bit made me one happy and content motherfucker. Happy, content, and befuddled.

Sleeping alone would just plain suck now.

Cassidy stirred in her sleep, snuggling closer though her head was already on my chest, her legs entwined with mine, her beautiful breasts pressed against my side, and her arm draped around my waist. Fuck, was I smiling? Yeah, I was.

Turning toward her, I pressed a kiss to her forehead while stroking her hair, loving the way she settled in with a sigh of contentment as if my attention had been what she'd been seeking. Whether it was or wasn't, it didn't matter. She had it. She had my full attention. And like the creep I apparently was, I sniffed her hair because her scent was simply amazing and did some shit to me that I couldn't explain.

I was going to make her mine. Though the fear that she'd reject me was scary as hell. If she'd have me, if she'd give me just one chance to prove myself to her, I'd make damn sure she'd never regret it. Christ, I was willing to relinquish the title of partner at Striker Sports Entertainment, the same title my little ice queen and I had gone toe-to-toe over, because I knew it was the only way we could be together openly. I didn't care. Cassidy Whalen was fucking worth it.

Yep, Shaw Matthews was on some new type of shit, all about becoming a better person, someone she might be proud to call hers. But the kicker was that I wasn't going to make changes to make only her happy; I was going to do it to make myself happy. And there wasn't a damn thing selfish about that.

First things first, I needed to check on Abby, who just happened to be the sweetest lady in the world and who was quickly changing my perspective on the whole parental thing. Jesus, this perma-grin thing was going to get painful after a while.

While I knew Abby had Thomas and Casey to look after her, I'd taken on that responsibility as well. It was a badge that a good son—adopted or not—wore with pride, after all. I was going to be that for her. I was going to make her proud, and I'd even try to get along with Casey because I knew it would make her happy. Not that I'd have to kiss his ass because, you know, sibling rivalry was a real thing and all, but still. We had something in common now. Something other than the fact that we'd had our cocks inside the same woman. Which made me growly to think about, so I smashed and banished the thought from my mind, never to be heard from again.

Cassidy was my girl, Abby was my mom, and nothing else fucking mattered. Period.

Except the fact that I was going to have to wake up Cassidy in order to get out from under her. Not that I wanted to—because, hell no, I didn't—but I knew we couldn't stay there like that forever and my help would be needed for whatever shit storm the hurricane had left behind, and I was all about pitching in. The problem was, I was suddenly a nervous wreck about waking her. What if she'd have the same reaction she had the morning after we'd spent the night together in Detroit? It had been fine then, but now I'd messed around and caught some feelings for her. Funny thing about feelings; they were some fragile motherfuckers, prone to hurt. Hence the reason I'd avoided them all my life.

Nah, I wasn't going to go back behind that brick wall. If she flipped out, she flipped out. I'd deal with it and find some way to move past it. But I'd damn well respect her wishes. Either way, I couldn't avoid the unavoidable.

Giving her a slight shake of my shoulder to nudge her awake, I kept my voice soft to avoid a total freak out. "Sweetness?"

Yeah, I called her "sweetness." So what?

She stirred with a "Hmm?" and her hair fell over her face.

I brushed it away with my fingertips and tried again. "Sweetness, we need to get up."

"No," she mumbled in this pouty sort of way that made me want to flip her onto her back and kiss her hard.

"Aww," I fucking aw'd like the girly man I'd apparently become. "Is someone still sleepy?"

Cassidy's eyes remained closed, but she answered nonetheless. While snuggling in even closer, I might add. "No. I'm just really comfortable and don't want to move."

Fuck it; I wasn't going to make her. Except damn it, I had to.

"I'd be perfectly content with letting you stay right here for the rest of forever, but the truth of the matter is that reality is right outside the door, and before long, your father will be as well." I leaned in and whispered conspiratorially, "Gotta tell ya, I do not want to be caught naked in bed with Duff Whalen's baby girl when he comes knocking."

Cassidy giggled. "He's not going to do anything because he likes you."

"Yeah? He likes me?" Admittedly, I found this new information a little hard to digest. I'd fallen overboard from the man's boat, while brawling with a guy he'd considered a part of his own family, for Christ's sake. Oh yeah, and I'd been screwing his daughter on the regular.

Cassidy nodded, her cheek doing this cute little smooshy thing against my chest. And she wasn't freaking out. Not in the least.

"What about you? Do you like me, too?"

"Maybe a li'l," she mumbled, and then this smile pushed at her cheeks that made the cute smooshy thing go away, but I couldn't be sad about it because, yeah, she fucking liked me.

"Oh, maybe a li'l, huh?" I mimicked her, which made her giggle again, so of course she had to be punished for laughing at my pain.

While the fingers of one hand found her ribs, the tips of the other slipped beneath her arm to give her dainty armpit a tickle. Cassidy startled and bucked, those gorgeous green eyes of hers popping open while her pearly whites stole center stage with a hearty laugh accompanied by a snort that wasn't anything near dainty.

Good God, but she was beautiful.

Seizing the opportunity, I rolled with her and assumed the dominating position overtop to continue my tickle siege. Cassidy laughed so hard, slapping at my shoulders and doing her best to push my hands away, to no avail. There was even a really close call between her knee and my boys, but I managed to dodge that unnatural disaster with a quick juke of my hips and some pretty fancy footwork that earned me the spot between her thighs. Eat your hearts out, every pro running back who ever existed.

My girl's head was thrown back, her hair a tangled mess on the pillows, and tears of delight glistening at the corners of her eyes, and all I could think about was how much I wanted her to always look like that. It wasn't until Cassidy began to show signs that she was having a hard time catching her breath that I eased up.

Before she had a chance to come down completely, I took advantage of our position and pushed inside her. Yeah, my cock was fucking hard as all get out and even if morning wood wasn't a thing, we were both still naked and rolling around together, and that tended to do shit to a man.

Cassidy gasped at the unexpected intrusion, but not in protest. All that *hee-hee–ha-ha*'ing was replaced by a moan that made me want to come on the spot. Holy fuck, but I loved this woman.

"What's wrong?" Cassidy asked.

It wasn't until then that I realized I'd stopped moving and was just staring at her. Raging hard-on inside a beautiful woman aside, my befuddlement suddenly made sense in a nonsensical way. I loved her?

"Baby? Are you okay?" Cassidy's brow was furrowed with concern while her nails brushed through the hair just behind my temple in an endearing sort of way.

She fucking called me "baby" . . . and I suddenly felt like the Grinch on Christmas morning, my heart swelling to three times its size.

"Yeah. Leg cramp," I lied. An absurd kind of lie, at that. But I didn't want to press my luck on the whole "Cassidy not freaking out" thing, and balls deep inside the woman of my dreams wasn't the proper time to blurt out something I needed to evaluate further. I'd never loved anyone other than myself. Did I even know what it meant?

Faking the shake off of the cramp, I found my stroke again and settled on the pace she seemed to favor from last night. Deep and purposeful with a grind that brought us as close as any two human beings could physically be without wearing each other's skin. But I'd flay myself alive, too, if she'd wanted that.

Christ, she felt so good around my cock—warm and tight yet soft at the same time. It was all too much and I was going to come way too early like this. Easily fixed, I flipped us over so that Cassidy was on top, a move she clearly hadn't been prepared for. Then again, I'd been throwing us both for a few loops this morning already, so what difference did another make?

Cassidy giggled at my abruptness, the walls of her pussy constricting my cock with each contraction of her abdomen. My brain started concocting all kinds of ways to make her do it over and over again, but it wasn't necessary because my girl was riding me, her fingernails were digging into my chest, the tips of her hair were tickling my face, and her fucking gorgeous breasts were full and round with hardened peaks that begged to be palmed and plucked. It occurred to me then that it didn't matter which position we were in, who was in control, or whether I was all up in my feelings or not. She just did things to me that no other woman before her had ever done. And I'd been with a lot of women.

Cassidy Whalen was special. Cassidy Whalen was . . . the one.

So I let her have her way with me because, truth be known, she always had. And though she was wrapped around my cock at the moment, I was wrapped around her little pinky. Yeah, I fucking loved her. Now if I could just figure out a way to tell her.

CHAPTER 16

Casey

I was an asshole.

As I stood there under the shower with the water beating down on top of my head, I realized it didn't matter how far I turned the knob to the left because I could Bugs Bunny it and bathe in a pot over a blaze and it still wouldn't be hot enough to wash my asshole-ishness away. Maybe I should just set myself on fire. Or better yet, tie myself to a stake at the heart of a pyre in the middle of town, with angry waving pitchforks all around me, and let the masses torch me to death while I am forced to look Mia in the eye.

I'd used her. Plain and simple. Mia. Sweet, innocent Mia.

She hadn't deserved the way I'd treated her last night. She'd simply been caught in the cross fire of the great Casey and Cassidy tragedy. Or maybe it was the cease-fire. Because things between Cassidy and me had definitely come to an abrupt halt. Though that had happened a really long time ago, so maybe it wasn't quite as abrupt as I'd liked to believe. I'd just been clinging to something that was no longer there.

I think maybe we both had. Me more than her.

I hadn't ever been with anyone other than Cassidy, hadn't

even considered it, really. But Mia? Mia had come into town with the wind change, and she'd been like a breath of fresh air despite the near-constant breeze from the sea. All that innocence about her in the midst of a seemingly untainted environment. Those doe eyes, a natural beauty that needed no makeup to cover up who she really was, hair that flowed about her face like the waves that danced on the ocean's top under calm weather, and the body of a mermaid. She was every seaman's dream come true. And I'd ruined her.

I'd be lying if I said I hadn't had an inkling about her attraction to me. I'd known it was there, had seen it in the subtle hints. The way she leaned in ever so slightly to be closer. The way she looked at me like I'd hung the moon. The things she'd said; her choice of words were so intimate, familiar yet not, at the same time. She'd been unbelievably cool to talk to, and for the time I'd held Mia's attention, I truthfully hadn't thought about Cassidy. And hadn't that been the nitty-gritty of why Cassidy had been upset with me?

Damn. Hadn't seen that one coming, though I didn't have to strain my brain trying to figure out why that was either.

So unlike any woman I'd ever known before, Mia had hung on my every word. I'd thought it was about nothing more than gathering the information she'd needed for her research, but more often than not, she'd put her pen and paper down, rested her chin in her hand, and just listened to me. She'd made me feel important, more than the other half of a whole. Not like I wasn't complete unless I had Cassidy Whalen on my arm, but like I was a man with his own story to tell. I think it had surprised even me. I think it had changed the way I started to see myself.

But that hadn't stopped me from trying to salvage what I could of my relationship with Cassidy. We'd been together our entire lives and I'd always believed we'd be together until our dying days. So when Cassidy had caught me with Mia in the crow's nest, a place that had been ours, I'd felt the sudden guilt of having another woman there. And I could see the disappointment written all over Cassidy's face. She was jealous. And that had confused me even more.

I'd seen her with that bastard on the playground, of all places. The playground we'd frequented as kids. My Cassidy was in the arms of another man. She was in the arms of a man she'd supposedly despised. Not only that, but she was riding him. Everything I'd thought I'd known had come crashing down around me in that moment.

It should have been me. Me, the man who'd been waiting for her to live her dreams and eventually come back into my arms, where she belonged. But it wasn't. And she'd left me in that crow's nest with a cock as hard as the devil's and a very wicked seed looking to make a break from the fiery pits of hell. You'd think Cassidy breaking my fucking heart would've made my erection deflate like an anvil popping a balloon, but it hadn't. And I'd needed to relieve the pressure.

Mia had been all too willing to play Cassidy's understudy. But somewhere in the middle of the phenomenal sex we'd had, something had changed. I saw Mia. I saw Mia seeing *me*. She'd wanted it, wanted me. And that had been more than I could handle with a wound as fresh as the one left behind in my heart from Cassidy. What made matters worse was that being with Mia had felt right. How could that have been?

Stepping out of my guest room at the Whalen House, I heard the voices of our parents down below. For whatever reason, I really didn't feel like facing them yet, so I went to the crow's nest to look out and survey the damage left in the wake of Hurricane Ayla. She'd finally blown past sometime in the middle of the night, and as far as I knew, everyone in the house was okay.

Though I'd really hated leaving Mia alone to ride it out, I knew I couldn't be with her after what I'd done.

The hallway was dark, but there was a faint light coming from under the door of one room. Mia's room. She was up. My conscience pushed and shoved at my morality, refusing to allow me to avoid the talk I needed to have with her. I owed her one hell of an apology, and though I knew I'd never be able to come up with the flowery words to give her the one she deserved, I supposed a half-assed one would be better than none at all. Stalling wouldn't be right, and the longer I waited, the worse I would feel. Manning up, I decided to get it over with.

The floor outside her room creaked under my weight as I stepped forward to meet whatever awaited me on the other side. She'd be completely within her right to refuse my apology, even justified if she decided to throw a lamp at my head. And I'd stand there and take it like a man because whatever it took to make her feel better, she'd have it.

Not wanting to clue in the rest of the house on the massacre that was about to go down, though I'd deserve their admonishment as well, I rapped lightly on the door with one knuckle.

"Come in!" I heard her call from inside. Selfishly, I was glad she was soft-spoken by nature.

My hand shook as I lifted it and gave the doorknob a turn. Damn. I was nervous. That was a first for me. Then again, I'd only ever had to beg for forgiveness from Cassidy, and I'd always known she'd eventually give it after some groveling. With Mia, I couldn't be so sure.

Other than the glow of the white light coming from the screen before Mia, the room was mostly dark when I went inside. Of course it would be when the electricity had been knocked out somewhere in the middle of Hurricane Ayla. There was just enough illumination to see that the sheets were still a crumpled mess on the bed, and I wondered if her tears had stained the pillows. Jesus, but that mental image was a punch to the chest. Yep, I was an asshole, all right.

But you couldn't tell it by looking at Mia.

She was sitting cross-legged in the chair before the desk, looking for the entire world like a coed student trying desperately to finish up a term paper right before class. The oversized T-shirt, yoga pants, and messy bun didn't do anything to distract from her beauty. That was Mia. She was fucking gorgeous without even having to try.

"Good morning." Mia didn't look at me, and I really couldn't blame her. She just kept hammering away at the keyboard of the laptop in front of her. It was her tool of the trade, which was probably the only reason she hadn't chucked it across the room at me.

"Mornin'. You're up early," I said. Because stating the obvious seemed like the best way to baby step it into the daunting conversation to come.

"You mean I'm up late," she countered, obviously having been awake all night.

"You haven't been to bed?" Fuck, that was because of me. I really was worse than an asshole. I was the whole ass.

"Well, when inspiration strikes, you have to go with it or risk losing it forever."

The glow from the laptop was harsh on her normally angelic face and I could see the dark rings under her eyes. "You look tired." Again, I was baby stepping it.

Her eyebrows lifted, but she still didn't turn away from the screen. "Do I? Because I don't feel tired." She gave a halfhearted laugh. "Besides, it's kind of hard to sleep with a hurricane in full force right outside the window."

Well, didn't that just make me feel like the biggest douchebag on the island? An ass and a douchebag, now that was one hell of a combination. "Shit. You were scared. I should've stayed here with you."

Mia finally sat back in her chair and turned away from the screen to give me her undivided attention. "Casey, honestly . . . you're just entirely too hard on yourself." When she smiled, I swear the whole damn room lit up despite the boarded-up windows and powerless lamps. "I wasn't scared. And before you go there, I wasn't upset about what happened between us last night, either. I couldn't sleep because Jayson was in the mood to talk, so I had to purge him from my mind."

"Jayson?" Was he her boyfriend from back home? The little green monster inside me stuck his head out of the cave where I'd banished him after I'd nearly let a man drown to death all over a woman.

"Oh, I never told you," Mia said, her eyes lighting up with excitement. Sitting forward, her whole body came to life as she explained further. "Jayson Bass is my protagonist's name. I swear I'm not crazy. The voices I hear in my head are completely normal for an author and not a Sybil complex or whatever. Says my therapist," she added with a wink. It was the cutest thing I'd ever seen.

Putting an index finger to the tiny dimple in her chin in thought, she continued, "Though we can't rule that out completely when there are so many personalities bouncing around in there. Hmm . . ." She cocked her head to the side. "Maybe writers cover up a multiple personality disorder under the guise of artistry, and we're just really good at fooling everyone else."

She laughed, the sound fluttering toward me like a thousand butterfly wings. My flesh pebbled all over from its delicacy, which was weird as fuck because laughter was not a tangible thing that could be physically felt.

"So you've been up all night writing?" I asked because, of

course, a douchebag of an ass would egotistically assume he had been the reason.

"Yep! That's my happy place." She put her hands on the desk and maneuvered herself back toward the laptop, getting busy with her fingers on the keyboard again. Man, but the woman typed at the speed of light.

"A happy place in the middle of a hurricane, huh?" Not just in the middle of a hurricane, but in the middle of my douchebaggery as well.

If Mia could only hear the assholes inside my head, she probably wouldn't be as calm as she was. "My happy place is always there. The weather has no bearing on it. Writing is a way for me to escape. Do you know what I mean? Sort of like how I imagine fishing is for you."

Well, damn. She'd pegged that one. But I was no doubt the reason she'd needed to escape in the first place. Though there was no way for me to take it all back, even the feel-good parts, I knew I had to find some way to fix the unfixable.

"I need to apologize for last night," I blurted out before I lost my nerve.

She remained facing forward, her expression unchanged. "Need to or want to?"

"Both."

Leaning in toward the screen to read over what she'd written, she still managed to answer me. "Don't. Really. It was great inspiration."

It was hard to tell by the inflection in her voice whether she'd meant that or not. "Can you look at me, please?"

"I *can* and I will," she said with a sassy grin.

Note to self: Remember to use proper grammar when speaking to an author.

"Just let me save this real quick," she said, moving the wireless mouse around. With a simple click, she closed the laptop and turned back toward me. "What's up?"

I looked her in the eyes, not only so I could tell how she really felt about what I was saying, but because that was what a man was supposed to do when owning up to his fuckups. "I don't want you to hate me."

She linked her fingers together in front of her and casually propped her elbows on the armrests of the chair. "Why on earth would I hate you? Didn't you hear me? It was great inspiration. I should be thanking you."

Nope, didn't see that one coming. "You were inspired?" Admittedly, I was confused. I hadn't even put forth my best effort. The sex we'd had was good, but it wasn't great. If given another chance, I was sure I could blow her mind. Because, yeah, I wanted to give it another go. Whether it ended up in her book or not.

"Oh, definitely." She cocked her head to the side and studied me for a moment before continuing. "You're obviously out of sorts about it, so I'll make a deal with you. I'm willing to tell you all about what I wrote, if you promise you won't get mad."

Not that I had any right to get mad, but like I said before, whatever it took to make her feel better, she'd have it. Plus, I had to admit I was a little curious. "Deal."

"No, you have to say you promise," she said, pointing a finger at me, which we all knew was the international sign for *I mean business.*

Again, author, so I was sure that meant I literally had to say those words to satisfy her. My lips parted to do just that, but she interrupted before my vocal cords formed the first syllable.

"Before you do, just know that I take promises very seriously. So if you say the words, you have to mean them."

I sighed, which made her brows lift in question.

"Okay," I said, finally. Taking a seat on the bed across from her, I leaned forward to put my elbows on my knees and spoke the words she wanted to hear. Not only because she wanted to hear them, but also because I meant them. "I promise I won't get mad."

That spoiled grin that made its way across her gorgeous face made me want to promise her anything she'd ever wanted. "So Jayson has just found out that the woman he loves, Janell Kain, no longer loves him back. And it's sort of a mess because Janell is in love with someone else."

Wow, she really was writing my life. I'd been expecting her to tell me about some mind-blowing sex or about how the dude made a giant ass out of himself. I wasn't sure how to feel about my broken heart serving as inspiration. Then again, Mia had always been pretty insightful where I was concerned, so I was curious as to how it had all played out in her "fictional" book. Because those sorts of stories always had a problem and a resolution, right?

"And what does Jayson do about it?" I asked, hoping she'd gotten that far.

Mia's teeth tugged at her bottom lip. "Um . . . Well, he um . . . He sleeps with another woman."

Her face drew up like she was waiting for me to blast her over it, which I had zero intention of doing. But damn. Talk about opening wounds. Mine weren't only open, they were oozing crimson gunk all over the place. I wasn't mad. I really wasn't. I'd earned all four knuckles of reality's punch to the teeth.

"Why would he do that?" This was where I got to see Mia's feelings about what I'd done to her. Hard as it was going to be to have to hear, I had to know.

Damn, but I wished she wouldn't look at me with so much pity.

"Because he's hurt and frustrated and he just needs to feel something other than the pain."

Hearing her say it out loud was like having salt poured into those wounds. It stung like a son of a bitch, only because that was some real shit. And through my own pain, I couldn't help but be in awe of Mia. Not only did the woman write books about people, she read people like they were books, as well.

But the truth was the truth was the truth, so I put it out there. Blunt as blunt could be. "So he uses one woman to get over another? What a dick."

"I don't see it that way, and neither does his concubine."

"Concubine" was an interesting word choice. I wondered if that was the way she saw herself when she looked into the mirror this morning. Because I really wasn't okay with that.

"Oh, really? And what's this concubine's name?"

She hedged, and then her voice was soft. "Maria."

Maria . . . Mia . . . Nope, not a coincidence.

"Maria knows she's being used and she's okay with that?"

Her eyes glassed over while the tip of her nose turned a shade of pink. Fuck me, she was trying so hard not to cry. Mia swallowed and forced a smile before saying, "Of course. *She* actually gives a shit about him. Besides"—she blinked away unshed tears and then shrugged—"what are friends for?"

Bullshit. I was going to kick my own ass. Any douchebag that could make someone as virtuous as Mia cry had it coming. The woman had a heart of pure gold, good to the core, and she didn't deserve to be made to cry. Not one day in her life. No one would ever convince me otherwise. Yet I'd done it. I'd fucked her with a total disregard for her feelings. What kind of friend does *that*? And the thing was, I'd never even seen Mia as just my friend. She was something I couldn't explain.

She was . . . a possibility.

I slid off the bed and onto my knees before her. "Mia, when you look at me, what do you see?"

It took a moment before she answered. A moment during which she seemed to study everything about me, leaving my eyes for last. And when she looked into them, it was as if she'd found her answer there. "I see Jayson . . . just a figment of my imagination."

For whatever reason, that wasn't okay with me.

"You know, when you came to town and said you wanted to interview me for the book you're writing, I figured you were trying to get some of the technical details about lobstering and a lobster fisherman's way of life. I didn't realize you were going to write my life."

"I honestly didn't intend to. But, Casey, you're the ultimate alpha hero: flawed yet perfect; confident, not cocky; passionate about everything you do; strong and strong willed; smart without being a smart-ass; you have the swagger of a bad boy with a boy-next-door's heart; you're dominant, yet not aggressive; and you are a *very* capable lover."

That last part made my cock flinch in my jeans. Huh. I didn't have the heart to tell her an alpha male would never use an innocent woman to get over another.

Mia must have taken my contemplative silence as a sign that I was insulted because she said, "I'll scrap the whole manuscript. I promise. Contracts be damned. I'd never want to offend you or make you feel like your whole life is on display."

That wasn't at all what I wanted. Truth be told, I was honored that she thought me worthy of being a topic in the first place. And to make me the hero? Well, I didn't feel very much like the hero at the moment. Be that as it was, she saw me that way. Maybe she was the only one. And I didn't want that to stop. Having had an insight into her beautifully creative mind, I wondered if the answers were hidden somewhere within all that brilliance.

"No, you don't have to scrap any of it. But maybe you can help me with one thing."

Her voice was soft again, a gentle swallow drawing my attention to a neck I suddenly wanted to mark. "Anything."

"Tell me what happens to Jayson."

"You know what happens, Casey. . . . You *are* Jayson."

"No, not that. I meant, what happens to him at the end of the book?"

"He sails off into the sunset and lives happily ever after, of course."

"With who?"

A meek smile tugged at her lips and a flourish of pink tinged her cheeks. "Guess."

"Maria?"

She nodded. "He's all she's ever wanted but never knew she'd been searching for."

"I don't see how that's possible after what he's done to her. Maybe you should just kill him off."

Mia laughed. "That's impossible."

"Why is that impossible?"

Her smile never fell, but those eyes? Those eyes did some wicked shit to the rhythm of my heart. "Because, silly . . . if a writer falls in love with you, you can never die."

My eyebrows reached for my hairline and damn near permanently relocated. "You're in love with me?" Shaking my head, I made a quick correction. "I mean, Jayson?"

"I'm in love with all of my characters."

"Mia—"

She cut me off before I could say another word. "Casey, please don't freak out on me, okay? I'm a romantic. It's not a big deal. Really. I do this all the time—with fictional characters, not actual men—and I eventually get over it. I promise. You don't have to worry that I've dreamed up some real-life scenario born of fantasy in my head. And while it's true there's a fine line between brilliance and insanity for artists, and we walk it every single day, I haven't yet crossed over to the delusional side. I know I'm not Maria, and I know exactly what last night was all about. You needed a concubine, and I was glad I could be there for you. And hey, I got a breakthrough in my plot and a couple of really awesome orgasms out of it. So it's cool. We're cool." She stopped and took a much-needed breath before her shoulders drooped with the exhale. "Right?"

Catching her completely off guard, I grabbed her around the waist and pulled her to me, forcing her legs to unfold and form a cage around my ribs. Just as I'd wanted. And then I kissed her. She'd told me she could tell how a person felt by the way they kissed, and that was something I'd used the night before to let her know I wanted to fuck. This time, I used it to show her something else.

Her lips were so sweet, so pliant beneath mine, and when I deepened the kiss, her mouth was receptive. Mia moaned, a sound that went straight to my cock, and then she wrapped her arms around my neck to push her fingers through my hair. With an arch to her back, she pressed her center to my chest, the warmth nearly scorching me through my shirt. Mia was no concubine. And she was more than a possibility. She was . . . everything.

I pulled back ever so slightly to allow her a moment to catch her breath. She kept her arms and fingers just as they were and pressed her forehead to mine, simply breathing.

"Wow," she whispered, and I had to smile because, yeah, my message was received.

"You don't get seasick, do you?" I asked, knowing damn well she didn't.

The shake of her head was almost imperceptible, but I caught it. I also caught the sexy little way her teeth pulled at her bottom lip.

"Casey, please be sure. If you're just looking for a rebound—"

"I'm sure," I said, not letting her go there. "What man wouldn't want to live forever? Make me immortal, Mia Morgan."

Leaning in for a soft, chaste kiss, she said, "You're already half-way there."

"Yeah? Does that mean I'm like bulletproof or something?" I asked, because I sure as shit felt like there was a giant *S* on my chest at the moment.

Mia laughed. She laughed and my heart soared like a bird, like a plane, like a speeding bullet, like it could leap tall buildings in a single bound. I'd be her hero in the flesh, despite the fact that she was the one who'd rescued me.

But I'd fight for her because I knew she'd fight for me. Fuck it; we could be some dynamic duo or whatever. I didn't care as long as we could take on the world together; her with a gold lasso on her hip, and me with a red cape blowing in the wind.

And no, I wasn't delusional either. She'd be leaving Stonington, just like Cassidy did. I knew that. Though this time, I wasn't going to leave fate to the wind. This time, I was going to get off my ass and make damn sure I convinced Mia to stay.

CHAPTER 17

Shaw

People always talked about the calm before the storm, but no one ever mentioned how deafening the silence afterward could be. Cassidy and I were fine within the four walls of her bedroom, but outside those walls lurked the reality I'd warned her about. The only way to identify that reality was to open the door and walk out to meet it. Together.

Right after we showered. Together. I'd had to sneak into my room to grab a change of clothes for that one, but we managed to pull it off without getting busted. I didn't want this thing between us to be a secret anymore, though I wasn't sure how she'd feel about it. Not that I was planning on hiring a blimp with a scrolling neon advertisement to proclaim my feelings. Especially when I hadn't even told Cassidy, but still, I was all about making damn sure that happened in the very near future. Telling Cassidy, not the blimp thing. That would be overkill.

Cassidy tightened the laces on her second gym shoe and looked up at me while tying the bow, a graceful smile lighting up her entire face. Jesus, the woman even made tying her shoes look sexy as hell.

When she was done, she slapped both knees and stood with

her hands on her hips. Hips that were covered by yoga pants that she'd pulled up to her knees to show off those toned calves, by the way. I thought about asking her if she'd brought any of those fuck-me heels with her, but the distraction wouldn't have been conducive to the work waiting to be done.

"Well, are you ready to see what the aftermath looks like?"

I was sure she meant from the hurricane, but really, the question could apply to not only that but whatever had taken place between the two of us last night. A near-death experience and an emotional awakening within a man who'd prided himself on not feeling anything at all was a recipe for a whole lot of what-the-fuckery. Things were going to get *very* messy. Especially if she was still in casual-fuck mode, the way we'd started. The only way any of this thing between us had ever been meant to be.

Taking a moment to appreciate her bare shoulder, courtesy of the oversized V-neck raglan she'd chosen to wear for the cleanup process, I gave her an answer that could also apply to both situations. "Is anyone ever really ready for something like that?" I for damn sure wasn't, but I'd never backed down from a challenge before, so I was full steam ahead. On both counts.

"Good point," she said, seeming to be in good spirits despite the inevitable work that lay ahead. "Time to face the music, then."

Reaching for the doorknob, I stepped back as I swung the door open to let her pass through, because that was what a gentleman was always supposed to do for his lady. Whether she knew she was his lady or not. But once we stepped out into the hallway, we stopped in our tracks. It wasn't the music we'd come face-to-face with. It was Casey and Mia, side by side in the exact same stance as Cassidy and me.

No good-mornings were uttered, not a sound was made, but I noticed the look Cassidy and Casey shared. Right before she reached out and took my hand, lacing her fingers through mine.

It surprised me, though, thankfully, not enough to make me do something stupid. I did, however, grin like a motherfucker because, yeah, I'd won the girl and my position as the alpha male was set in stone.

And then Casey reached out and took Mia's hand. Huh . . . two alpha males occupying the same space? Well, there was a new and interesting concept. Another interesting twist was the tender smile exchanged between Casey and Cassidy, followed by a quite intense stare-down from him to me that ended with a respectful nod. I heard him loud and clear: I'd better take damn good care of her. And I would.

It was funny how so much information could be exchanged without one word being said between four people. But it was quite clear that Casey was with Mia, Cassidy was with me, and Casey and Cassidy were genuinely happy and okay with that. All was where it was meant to be.

Casey and Mia were closest to the steps, so Mia was the first to head in that direction with Casey at her side. Cassidy and I followed, the four of us descending two-by-two, like animals off the ramp from Noah's ark after the flood. It was a fitting visual considering the bit of epic-ness that Mother Nature had thrown at us during the night.

Filing into the kitchen where the parents were already moving about, also quiet, four sets of eyes turned toward the two newly emerging couples. And still, no word was said. Abby, Thomas, Duff, and Anna all took in the sight before them, with a particular interest in the hand-holding. Hmm, I made a note to do a lot more of that everywhere Cassidy and I went after this so that everyone would know she was my girl.

Abby's face lit up with complete approval of the way things had worked out. For both Casey and me. I really didn't notice what the other parents thought because Abby's approval was all

I needed. Well, Abby's and Duff's, of course. He gave it in his own way.

With a loud clap of his hands, Duff finally broke the silence. "Well, all right, then. Let's go face the music," he said, and it made me smile because it was obviously a phrase he'd used often enough for his only daughter to have picked it up as well. I was so going to love this family shit.

We cleared the path as Duff escorted his wheelchair-bound wife toward the front door. When everyone else had gone ahead, Cassidy looked at me and sighed, not altogether prepared to see what ruin might have been left of her hometown. I gave her hand a squeeze, and with that, we brought up the rear.

The morning sun was bright, in contrast to a house darkened by shuttered windows and no electricity, and the seabirds were calling just like they would have on any normal day. But standing shoulder to shoulder with two families stretched eight wide across the porch, each person in absolute shock from the scene before them, it was clear to see that this was anything but a normal day in Stonington, Maine.

The Whalen House's position on the side of the hill, coupled with its very strong foundation, had been its saving grace. Others in town hadn't been so fortunate. Looking out over Main Street, it was hard to tell where some properties began and others ended. The streets were littered with the normal debris you might expect to see—gobs of seaweed, tree limbs, shingles off roofs and siding, and just plain garbage—but what you didn't expect to see were whole-ass trees that had been pulled up by their roots and smashed through houses, or homes crushed, their contents spilled out into the streets and bobbing around in the bay.

Mother Nature's power was something to be respected. The way she picked and chose which families lost everything, which suffered only minor damage, and which remained untouched was a puzzler indeed. We still didn't know how much actual destruction had been done to the Whalen House because we hadn't stepped out to really survey the property, but no way could it have been as bad as most of the other homes.

Quite a few of the townspeople were already out and about, some of the elderly shaking their heads in disbelief while mothers hugged their children close, helping them over piles of who the fuck knew what it had once been. Instinct kicked in and I released Cassidy's hand to go help, not shocked in the least that Casey was already on the move as well. But I pulled up short when I heard a sniffle to my right.

Looking over my shoulder, I was frozen in place when I watched a tear stream down Anna Whalen's face. That was my girl's mother and she was heartbroken for her town. I was heartbroken for her. This was real shit. Not a negotiation gone south, not a major deal missed, but a real-life catastrophe.

Duff put his hand on Anna's shoulder and gave it a loving pat. "It's okay, darlin'. Everthing's going to be okay. You'll see."

CHAPTER 18

Cassidy

Hurricane Ayla was a nasty bitch. She'd reached Category 4 before making landfall and had ripped through Stonington, shredding it to bits like confetti. So much destruction had been left in her wake; homes broken, lives turned upside down and inside out, and crippling financial ruin.

And she did it all without a care in the world for those who were left to pick up the pieces.

The townspeople of Stonington wouldn't wallow in self-pity, though. They were resilient, tough, determined to get on with their lives and salvage what was left. Stonington would come back from this. We would all come back from this.

In the hours following Ayla's departure, we'd gone through all five stages of grief: denial, anger, bargaining, depression, and acceptance. Acceptance was where we all shined and showed the stuff we were made of. The cleanup process had already begun, and by some miracle the power was back on. Hope and strength were the foundation upon which this island had been built, and no storm was going to change that.

Lives had been spared. I'd yet to hear of a single one lost, and most of the injuries were to the pride of hardworking lobstermen. As competitive as each one of them could be, they pulled together for the sake of their community. I was proud to be counted among its people.

Despite all my moaning and groaning about coming back to Stonington, I realized I'd never really left. A tether attached at birth had bound me to it, and even though I'd stretched that tether as far as it would go—to the extreme opposite end of the country—it was still tied to Stonington.

I looked up from a pile of debris I'd been sorting and wiped the sweat off my forehead. It was hot out here, with loads of moisture still in the air and the sun beating down so hard I turned to give it my WTF brow, as if it and I had a casual relationship like that. The sky was painted an azure blue, with wispy white clouds streaking through the color like the world was nestled inside a marble. I snorted thinking how very Dr. Seuss the idea was. Though Dr. Seuss's stories all had happy endings and a moral to be learned.

There was a grunting sort of growl behind me, one that a giant gym junkie might make when lifting a barbell loaded down with three times his own weight. Shaw had been in that direction, as had Casey, so I turned to be sure those two weren't back at each other's throats. Imagine my surprise when I saw they were working together to raise what appeared to have once been the roof of the Harbor Master's shed.

Shaw Matthews, a man who'd never cared about anyone other than himself, had pitched in to lend a helping hand. And my very dearest friend, the man who had sucker punched him the day before, was now watching his back. Yes, natural disasters were devastating, but they always seemed to bring people together in a way that might not have ever happened otherwise. I was proud of my boys.

To my right, Mia was struggling with dislodging a microwave

from the mountain of mud surrounding it. Throwing all of her weight behind it, I saw the end result before she eventually lost her footing and fell flat on her derriere with mud splashing up all around her. But I wouldn't delight in her predicament, nor would I sling even more mud in her face. If my boys could be big enough to bury the hatchet, so could I.

Propping my foot on the same microwave, I stretched out a hand in Mia's direction. She looked up at me, puzzled at first, and then she smiled. I totally got what Casey saw in her. She really was pretty in an unassuming way, sweet like the girl next door, and just Casey's type. Plus she was a romance author, so yeah, I was sure he could get down with that.

Mia took my offered hand, an unspoken truce passing between us as I hauled her to her feet.

"So . . . You and Casey, huh?" I asked.

The smile that radiated from her overshadowed the beams of sunlight streaking down from our marbled sky. Oh, yeah, she was smitten. She was also looking down at the ground as if she hadn't wanted me to see it. And that just wasn't right, so I lifted her chin to look her in the eyes.

"It's okay. Honestly," I assured her. "He really likes you."

Mia turned, her whole body gravitating in his direction. "You think so?"

I laughed. "Oh, yeah. Trust me, no one knows him better than I do. He's my best friend, and that's never going to change, but I'm really happy for you two."

That bright smile turned demure as she attempted to knock the mud from her pants. "Thanks. It means a lot coming from you."

I decided to help her with the mud situation by wiping what she couldn't see from her cheek. Her situation with Casey was still new, and I was sure she wouldn't want him to see her that way. Chicks had to band together on these sorts of things, after all. Unless you were being catty, in which case you "accidentally" smeared even more. I wasn't in a catty mood.

"A word of advice?" I offered.

"Oh, sure!" she said, eagerly.

"Don't lead him on. Casey is Stonington. This is his home, and it's all he knows," I told her while moving to clear the mud from her hair. "I'm not sure how a long-distance relationship between the two of you would work, but if you just visit often and stay true to him, I promise he'll remain loyal to you."

Mia nodded. "I promise to be good to him, Cassidy. For as long as he'll let me."

Pointing a finger, I gave her a playful smile. "You'd better. Oh, and if he messes up, just give him the silent treatment. He can't stand it. Works every time," I said with a conspiratorial wink.

Just then, Ma called down from the house, "Cass, go tell that husband of mine his dinner is ready. The rest of you come get your bellies full, too."

"Okay, Ma! Where is he, anyway?" I asked, looking around and not seeing him.

"Where he always goes when he's trying to get out of work," she said.

"I've got him!" I knew she was exaggerating because that was her way. Besides, my da never shirked on responsibility. He disappeared to get away from her nagging, and it was always to the same place: the beach.

Before I even had a chance to say anything, Mia was quick on the draw. "You go ahead. I'll get the guys together." She was a take-charge type of gal, too. I liked that. Casey was in very capable hands, indeed.

"Don't worry about the mud. Guys around here like a woman

who isn't afraid to get a little dirt on their hands," I told her, and then I set off to drag my father back to the homestead with the lure of Ma's cooking.

Shaw

A few weeks ago, no one would have ever believed their eyes if they'd seen me getting down in the dirt with a village full of fishermen. Hell, I wouldn't have believed it myself. Still didn't, but there I was . . . lending a helping hand to my fellow man. And better? I was doing it right next to the guy who'd been swinging at me just the day before. And I didn't even want to get square with him for the whole attempted involuntary-manslaughter thing.

What I did want, however, was an ice-cold glass of sweet tea and my girl.

"All together now, boys," Thomas barked his direction after I, along with four other young men, got into position to lift the roof of the Harbor Master's shed.

At the count of three, we put all we had behind it, managing to elevate it enough so that Casey could run steel cables underneath, which would then be attached to a crane that would do the really heavy lifting. Damn thing weighed a thousand tons, and every muscle in my body was putting in 110 percent to make sure Casey got to do his thing safely. Unfortunately, Billy Jo Bob on the other end had himself a case of the slip-'n'-falls and lost his footing.

"Whoa! Whoa! Whoa!" Thomas yelled, running in and trying to take the guy's place before the aftermath of Hurricane Ayla claimed her first victim, his son. "Get him out of there!"

Casey was right in front of me, the rooftop bearing down on

his legs and leaving him no room to move. Not an ounce of fear registered in his features, though I knew he had to have been saying his final prayers.

"Gimme a little more room!" I called back.

With another burst of energy, I shoved upward, using all my might to help as much as I could with my left arm while extending my right for Casey to grab hold of. His gloved palm clasped mine and he looked up at me, pupils dilated even as his brow furrowed in determination. A fierce sort of sound came out of me, somehow giving me strength I never knew I'd possessed, and I yanked the shit out of his arm.

The next thing I knew, a whole bunch of incidental shit was flying up around a rooftop that had come crashing back down to the ground. A swift glance to my right, and I found Casey lying safe and sound on the concrete next to me, those wild eyes turned toward the sky and his upper torso making with the breathe in, breathe out.

Thomas came around and gave his son a once-over. "You all right, son?" he asked. When Casey nodded, Thomas clapped me on the back with a "Good job" and granted us both permission to take a break before he stalked off and yelled at the boys to get back to work.

Casey and I looked at each other like the old man was off his rocker, and then we both started laughing. Once we'd gotten that out of our systems, I took a deep breath to get my heart rate back under control and then offered my palm to Casey yet again.

There was something in the way he looked up at me that made my chest swell with pride, an unspoken truce that accompanied a newfound trust. He took the damn thing, and I pulled him to his feet.

"Thanks, man," Casey said, dusting himself off, an act that was probably a force of habit since it really didn't make a difference.

"You did the same for me," I reminded him.

Casey chuckled. It was the kind of chuckle that was every bit an admission that he'd been the reason I'd almost met my maker, but we'd let that go. "Guess we're even now."

"Yeah, guess so," I said, fidgeting in the awkwardness between us, and knowing there was still a pink elephant doing the squeeze on us.

"Hey, about Cassidy," I started.

Before I could go any further, Casey looked me square in the eye and asked, "Do you love her?"

He was methodical with the way he tugged at each finger of a glove to remove it. Damn, maybe we were going to go for round two. Okay.

"I . . . um . . ." I hedged, not because I was afraid of him but because I wasn't entirely sure I wanted to exchange that bit of information with anyone when I hadn't even had the conversation with Cassidy about what was up with my feelings.

"Look, man, you don't want to tell me? I respect that," he said, tucking the first glove in his armpit and moving to the next. "But if you do, ya gotta fight for her. Don't be an idiot like I was and let her get away from you. Ya know?"

I nodded, knowing it had to take some mad nerve to admit his folly.

"As for Cassidy and me," he continued. "Don't sweat it. Had nothing at all to do with you. Truth of the matter is that Cassidy was just too much of a woman for me." He laughed in spite of himself, shaking his head. "Damn, she's headstrong. Loves to argue. She was definitely the one wearing the pants in our relationship. I need a woman who's a little more docile. One who's willing to be the little lady while I treat her like a princess. Ya feel me?"

I laughed along with him. "Mia that for you?"

Casey put both of his gloves in one hand then fisted it on his hip as he looked toward the house. I turned to see Mia walking in our direction with a definitive sway to her hips. Casey grinned like the cat that ate the canary. "Maybe . . ."

"Well, all right then," I said, finding I was sort of happy that he was okay, maybe even better off, with how things had turned out.

Cassidy

Stonington's beach wasn't anything like the beaches in San Diego. Firstly, because San Diego had too many to count, while Stonington had only the one. And whereas San Diego's beaches were usually smooth and flat, Stonington's was mostly giant boulders. The thing that made Stonington win out was the natural beauty, clean and without the thousands of visitors throughout the day, or their litter. Not today, though. Thanks to Ayla, there was debris everywhere. Still, sea moss and driftwood made for a much better view than just plain garbage.

I found Da perched atop his favorite boulder looking out over the cove with surprisingly small waves lapping at the stone. I knew before I reached him that he'd have a handful of pebbles, their smooth edges a weird sort of contrast to his calluses. My father had been a hardworking man all his life, rough around the edges but smooth as a pebble on the inside, and he always took time out to appreciate nature's marvels, big and small.

I often wondered what must have been going through his mind as he sat there all alone, but it simply wasn't my place to pry. The man was entitled to his personal musings, despite his wife's contrary opinion.

Without a word, I took a seat next to him on the rock, unwilling to disturb his peaceful tranquillity when the heart of where this man lived and breathed was in such upheaval. He didn't turn to look at me, didn't change the expression on his face. He just stretched out his cupped hand and offered me one of his stones, which I took without hesitation.

I could remember being sent there many times as a child to fetch him for Ma, but I'd faked a lot of those times just so I could be with him. Da had always called me his little duckling and had even walked around in a zigzag to watch me follow his exact path, which I did without fail. I loved my mother, I really did, but I was daddy's little girl. He and Ma would even have to pull fast ones on me so he could get out the door without having me in tow. I'd throw a fit when I finally got wise to it and go in search of him anyway. In fact, there were times when I'd sit on the dock for an entire day just waiting for him to return from his day of lobstering.

My da had been the reason why my love of sports had begun in the first place. Sitting on his knee in his favorite recliner, he'd schooled me on football as if knowing everything about it would make the difference between life and death in a postapocalyptic world. And I even had my very own stool down at Maggie's, Stonington's one and only pub.

The sun reflected off his beard, its direct attention bringing the golds and tangerines of his Irish genes to life.

"Do you remember that time when you bet the boys down at the pub that I could recite the starting lineup for Dallas? It was 1993, I think," I asked.

"Yep. Offense, defense, and special teams," he added with a proud smile. "Took three seasons of us doing that before those dimwits figured out you were a prodigy. We made a lot of money off that old trick. Even more when you could take any player they chose and go through their stats as well." Da laughed and then patted my knee. "I knew then you were destined for greatness someday." He nudged me lightly. "Thanks for never ratting me out to your ma."

"Thanks for giving me half the take," I said with a nudging of my own, to which he laughed again, because you bet your sweet patootie I'd blackmailed him.

My father wrapped his arm around me so I could lay my head on his shoulder, and it was as if time suddenly rewound and I was his little duckling again. Life was so much simpler when I could just follow his lead. Figuring out how to fool Ma and the boys down at Maggie's was one thing, figuring out how to fool Shaw about my feelings for him would be something else entirely.

"What's on your mind, kiddo?"

"Boys," I answered truthfully with a pitiful sigh.

"Ew!" Da said, shoving me away. "Boys are gross and they have cooties!"

I laughed because I couldn't help myself. "Da, stop."

"Why? That's what you used to tell me when you were but a wee thing." He skipped a pebble across the water. "I was sure glad of it then."

"And you're not now?"

He shrugged. "Your mother wants grandchildren. I suppose that might not be such a bad idea."

"Oh, God. She's rubbing off on you," I said, rolling my eyes.

"So tell me about this boy problem," he said, skipping another stone. "Did you and Casey get things worked out?"

I threw my rock as well, but it hit the water with a *kerplunk* instead of skipping. I was so out of practice. "We broke up."

"I didn't realize you'd gotten back together."

"We hadn't. It's just . . . it's complicated." I took another go at the rock skipping and the second attempt was worse than the first.

"Matters of the heart usually are, pumpkin." He looked off into the distance, watching the ripples on top of the water from what was likely a turtle being a busybody beneath the surface. I wondered whom the turtle would be reporting back to on this latest gossip. "You two were brought up together, so people made a lot of assumptions about what that meant for your future. The problem is, just because he was all you'd known, it didn't mean he was all you'd ever know."

Da handed me another stone, nodding for me to try again, which I did. And failed.

"You throw like a girl," he said and laughed. "It's all in the wrist. Like this." He threw his stone and it made five skips before sinking.

"Show-off."

Da laughed again and then sobered. "I don't know if you'll remember it or not, but when you were seven, I brought you down to this exact spot to teach you how to do this." He leaned in—because that was just the sort of thing smart-asses did—and whispered, "You were much better then."

"Whatever," I said, shouldering him.

"Anyway, you looked up at me, completely out of the blue, and told me they have buildings in the cities made out of this rock"—he patted the chunk of granite that had become our favorite spot—"and that you'd like to see them. Threw me off because I couldn't figure out how in the hell you knew what those buildings were made out of, but then again, you were always smart."

I laughed. "I do remember that. Though I don't remember how I learned that, either."

He looked at me then, a story untold lurking behind his eyes. "Do you remember that I asked you if there was anywhere in the world you could go, where would it be?"

I shook my head.

"I do. Never forgot it. Never will. You said anywhere but here." Da got quiet, contemplative. "That was when I knew I'd lost you. That was when I knew I had to make sure you got off this rock."

A prickling of emotion tingled on the tip of my nose. It was always the first indicator that tears would soon follow, no matter how hard I tried to hold them back. "You didn't lose me, Da."

"I know I didn't. You were never mine. I was yours, baby girl."

A rebel tear slid down my cheek. My da was never a sentimental man. He was either all business or full of laughs and chuckles. This was a side of him I'd never seen before. Not when I'd left Stonington for college, and not even when I left college for San Diego.

He smiled, throwing his arm around me once again to give my shoulders a comforting squeeze. "I know I've been a stubborn old man, too afraid to let his baby girl go. And for that, I'm sorry. It's okay to make a home somewhere other than Stonington, Cass. Just like it's okay to love someone other than Casey. If you want to sail off into the sunset with Shaw, do it. Just don't forget your anchor."

And just like that, the tether that had bound me to this place snapped. My father had set me free. Though I didn't feel I could soar just yet.

"I love him, Da. I love Shaw," I confessed. Hearing the words said aloud wasn't such a bad thing. The sky did not darken, the water before us did not turn to blood, demons did not escape from the Gates of Hell, and the end of the world did not happen. And what do you know . . . my lips did not fall off. So why was I still so terrified?

"I know that. But does he?"

Sometimes my father was wiser than I gave him credit for. His question was the answer to mine. Shaw didn't know how I felt about him and I was terrified to clue him in. Rejection sucked. Plain and simple. I wasn't sure I could put myself out there like that only to have Shaw look at me like I was some pitiful little schoolgirl with a crush on a boy band's lead singer.

"I can't tell him."

"Why the hell not?"

"Because I don't want him to think I'm stupid." I sounded really pouty. I knew I did. But a woman in the company of her father, no matter how grown she might think herself to be, no matter where she'd been or what she'd done, always had the right to revert back to the girl who'd cried on his shoulder as a child. Dads just made it all better somehow. Maybe because he was the one man whose love for her would always be unconditional.

"Ah, darlin' . . . The last thing anyone would ever accuse you of being is stupid. You're not. And neither is he. In fact, you might be surprised by what he says back."

I fiddled with the thread that was unraveling on his sleeve. "He'll probably tell me I'm fired. He is my boss now, after all."

"Is that right?" Da's voice registered his shock at the news. "When did that happen?"

"When I lost the Denver Rockford contract to him. He made partner, so he's my boss, technically."

"You lost it? Or gave it up?"

I drew my head back to look at him. "You knew? But how?"

Da chuckled. "Cassidy Rose, you're the most competitive person I know. There's no way someone is going to beat you in something you want, no matter how slick they might be. You gave up that partnership because your ma needed you here. Didn't you?"

"You can't tell her," I said, wagging a finger at him.

"Don't you worry about that. It'll be our little secret," he assured me. "Just like my using our only daughter to win some bets in a pub that daughter had no business being in in the first place."

"Good. We should both get back to the house before dinner gets cold and she sends a search-and-rescue posse out to drag us both back."

"Yeah, you're probably right," he said with a groan as he hopped down from the rock.

I was about to follow, but Da put his big, meaty paws on my waist to help me down. Just like he did when I was a child. And even though I knew it was likely killing his back to do so, I rested my hands on his shoulders and let him. He was my da; my unconditional love, my partner in crime, and the only man I'd ever have wrapped around my little pinky.

All that was left for me to do was to just pull up my big-girl panties and face Shaw as the woman my father had raised me to be today.

CHAPTER 19

Shaw

Anna Whalen could cook her ass off, too. I was going to be so fat when I left Stonington, but fuck it. I'd have Ben schedule some one-on-one sessions with one of the trainers at my gym when I got back, and that would fix the issue. Until then, I was going to enjoy the hell out of the home cooking for as long as I could.

Chicken pie, baked apples, and fried green tomatoes were on the menu, complemented by Abby's sweet iced tea. I was in heaven and would probably need a very long shower and an early bedtime as soon as dinner was over. But the early bedtime would not happen because there was still so much work to be done outside.

Casey and I had been working together well all day without an ounce of animosity. And after our talk? All the tension between us seemed to just melt away. Oh, there'd always be the underlying alpha competition going on, but I respected the man and his rightful placement in Cassidy's life. I got it. They were best friends; always had been, always would be. Not only that, but they were basically family. I didn't want to come between that.

Casey and I had an understanding now. Cassidy didn't know it, and maybe I wouldn't ever tell her, but he'd played the protective role earlier, letting me know in his own words that I'd better treat her right. Or else. I couldn't get upset about the veiled threat because I saw it for what it was, and I was glad she had someone who cared enough to be protective of her in the first place.

He seemed different, and I knew *I* was different. Partly because of my near-death experience the day before, partly because of my unofficial adoption by Casey's own mother—which he seemed to be just fine with—but mostly because I'd suddenly gotten in touch with my feelings for Cassidy and recognized them for what they were. Fucking love, man. It changed people. Sometimes for the better, sometimes for the worse. I was pretty sure the man I was before was the worse part, so it could only get better for me now.

If she didn't crush me once she found out.

This love thing was sort of emasculating now that I thought about it. Maybe I should just keep those feelings to myself.

"Well, it's about time you two decided to join us. Where have you been?" Anna sounded none too pleased with whoever had dared arrive late. As if I didn't already know who was missing at my side.

I looked up to see Cassidy being escorted into the room on Duff's arm like he was walking her down the aisle on her wedding day, a thought I quickly pushed from my mind because no way was marriage ever going to be in her future. At least not if that future included me. Not only wasn't I baby-daddy material, but thanks to the sham of a union between the man and the woman who'd spawned me, I didn't believe in the institution of marriage. Regardless, my heart nearly jumped out of my chest at the sight of her. I knew then that it would be impossible to keep my newfound feelings to myself, because all this mushy stuff inside of me was going to fight its way to the surface in due time anyway. That's how potent it was.

Cassidy's hair was falling loose from its ponytail; she was sweaty and dirty, and absolutely sexy as hell. Damn.

"Ma, don't fuss. We were on our way back, but then Da spotted Jax stuck in a tree, so he insisted we stop to get him down."

"Who's Jax?" Mia asked.

"Mrs. Jones's cat," Casey told her.

"You should've seen him, Ma. Da was quite the hero. You would be proud." Cassidy kissed her father on the cheek after he'd taken his seat.

"I'm always proud of him," Anna said, satisfied by their excuse and going about her task of making her husband a plate. How she managed to get around so well to make dinner from that wheelchair, I'd never know.

Cassidy gave her father a conspiratorial wink when her mother wasn't looking and then she took a seat. Right next to me. But she was lying through her teeth, the fibber. I nearly choked on the laughter I tried to hide with a cough, which Abby noticed but didn't give away. And then what do ya know? Cassidy's hand went right to my thigh, as if it were the most natural thing in the world for her to do.

"Sorry," she mumbled when I stared at her hand. She made to move it, but I covered it with mine to keep it in place.

The heat from her palm penetrated through the thick denim of my jeans and gave me the warm and fuzzies all over. Which, of course, made all that mushy stuff on the inside go berserk. There was nothing sexual about it. Her hand was just there under mine. Where it really fucking belonged.

A ringing came from the foyer—somewhere in the vicinity of the check-in desk, I assumed—and everyone stopped what they were doing to look in that direction like it was a puzzle they were trying to figure out. It was a distinctive type of ring, like that of a rotary phone. Considering how old-fashioned Anna Whalen was, I imagined it was exactly that.

"Well, looks like they got the phone lines back up and running," Thomas said. "Rude for someone to call during dinner, though."

It was an odd thing for him to say considering the Whalen House was a business, but I chalked it up to one more of those things people in Stonington just did not do. Small-town life had its own rules.

When Anna began to wipe her hands on the kitchen towel, Abby stood. "I'll get it, sweetie. You get that plate in front of your husband."

"How's the dock look?" Cassidy asked Casey.

Casey shrugged, swallowing down a mouthful of food before answering. "It's getting there. Shaw and I are going to ride out to my boat tomorrow morning to take a look at her. She's still there, so I'm guessing if there's any damage, it's minimal."

Cassidy turned toward me with a tilt to her head. You'd think I'd grown two. "Look at you being a grown-up," she said as she rubbed my thigh.

Of course I had to roll my eyes at that. "Don't make a big deal out of it, Whalen. I am capable of letting bygones be bygones."

"Shaw?" I looked up when I heard Abby call my name. She was peeking through the doorway to the kitchen with a puzzled expression. "A young man by the name of Ben is on the phone for you."

I hadn't been expecting that, but of course I should've been. There was something about being in Stonington that made you forget the outside world existed. I was a superstar sports agent—correction: partner of Striker Sports Entertainment—and I'd been away from the office for quite some time. Away and smack dab in the heart of a major hurricane's ground zero. And I hadn't thought to contact my assistant to let him know I was okay? I was definitely off my game.

Wiping my mouth with my napkin, I scooted my chair back and excused myself from the dinner table with an apology for the interruption. Before I left, I was sure to plant a chaste kiss on Cassidy's cheek. "I'll let them know you're okay, too," I told her, earning an appreciative smile.

In the foyer, I took a seat behind the desk and picked up the receiver from where it lay. "Ben?"

"Oh, you remember my name?" was his smart comeback.

"Yes, but I could forget to sign your time sheets, if you want," I countered. "What's up?"

"Dude, you gotta get back here."

If I hadn't been partly responsible for his casual approach with me, I'd rip him a new one. "Ben, I'm your boss and a newly appointed partner at the agency for which you work. Don't call me 'dude.' What's going on?"

"Wade's trippin' . . . *sir*," he tacked on the formal title. It was at least a little better, but not by much.

"And what's he *trippin'* about?"

"Colorado's been blowing up his phone because Denver still hasn't reported for training camp."

My blood pressure shot through the roof. "What?! Why not?"

"I wish I could tell you. He's not answering any of my calls."

"Well then why didn't you call me?" That seemed like the sensible thing to do.

"I tried to. Hello? No cell service, remember? Sent you a couple of emails, too, but I'm guessing you haven't checked them."

Damn, he had me there. I'd really dropped the ball on this one.

"I've been trying this landline for the last couple of days, but I'm guessing the phones have been out due to the hurricane, huh? That's the excuse I gave Mr. Price, anyway. Don't know how much longer I can hold him off with that one, though."

I could just picture Wade pacing back and forth in his office, loosening his tie as he did his best to make excuses not only for Denver but for me as well. I was sure there was probably also a whole lot of him yelling orders over the speakerphone and slamming files down on his desk. All of which were probably scaring the shit out of the entire staff.

"Where is Denver?" I asked, exasperated and starting to freak out a little bit myself.

"No clue. I even drove to his house and knocked on the door. No one answered."

Shit. If Denver wasn't already dead, I was going to kill him. He was probably holed up in another Vegas penthouse suite, hiding from the world. Though I'd thought he'd come to terms with the fact that he was gay and was prepared to face coming out to the world about it, a thing like that could be terrifying. I hoped he hadn't decided to make a run for the hills instead.

"All right, look. I'll try to get ahold of him and see what his deal is. In the meantime, I need you to start booking me a flight back home," I told him, hoping like hell that I could even make it off the island and to the airport. The roads were bad enough as it was, add downed trees and power lines to that mix, and they might be completely impassable. Amazingly, the tin can of a car I'd rented had survived the hurricane with minor scratches and dents, but it was in no way the sort of vehicle one took four wheeling.

"I'm on it," he said. "Just don't get too preoccupied to check your email because that's where I'll send your flight details and confirmation."

Ben was pushing it, but I'd let him get away with that one because I'd earned it. I was in crisis mode now, though.

"Assure Wade I'm all over this and will come to see him as soon as I land. You got it?"

"Yep! And hey, boss?"

"Yeah?" I braced for even more bad news, not sure I could take much more.

"I'm really glad you're okay," he said, his voice sincere. I could never stay mad at the guy. "How about Cassidy?"

"Everyone here is fine, Ben. Thanks for asking," I answered, just as sincere. "Now, hop to it. I need to get busy tracking down our diva of a quarterback."

With that, I ended the call. And then put my head in my hands. I had one hell of a headache coming on. Stonington had made me soft.

"Is everything okay?" I heard Cassidy's voice.

I popped my head up to see her, and was really glad she was there because I had no clue what I was going to do about this mess. "No, not really. Denver's gone MIA."

"Oh, crap!" she said, genuinely concerned. "Want me to call his mother?"

Despite my panic mode, I smiled so wide it hurt my cheeks. The woman never ceased to amaze me.

With a sigh of relief, I melted back into the chair. "Will you? It would really help if you can just find out where he is. I'll handle the rest from there."

"Sure, no problem. Let me go grab my cell. I have Delilah's phone number saved in it."

She started to go, but I grabbed her hand and yanked her back to me, planting a kiss on those delicious lips. "Thank you."

Cassidy smiled down at me, that one small act making me feel tons better. "We're on the same team, Shaw," she said with a wink, and then she was on her way.

Damn right we were.

Within moments, Cassidy had gotten Delilah Rockford's phone number and had given her a call. Delilah was all too happy to get in touch with Denver and get on his ass, telling him to expect my call, which he'd better answer. And as luck would have it, the town's Wi-Fi was back up—though sketchy, at best—so I could reach out to Denver by FaceTime. I loved technology. Even a small town like Stonington relied on it in some way, shape, or form to get on with business as usual.

Back in my room, I pulled up the app on my phone and hit Denver's contact information. It rang twice before he answered, but answer he did. I guessed even big, beefy superstar athletes still feared the wrath of their mothers.

"Hey, man! How's it hanging?" he asked with a cheesy smile. He was propped up against some pillows, shirtless, and obviously in bed. I checked the clock and did the calculation on the time difference between the East and West Coasts. It was only two o'clock in the afternoon.

"Denver, what the hell, man? You're supposed to be in Colorado at training camp," I said, knowing the buddy approach would work best with him.

"Yeah, I know. I've been tending to some important *personal* business." He waggled his brows and nodded toward a lump in the shape of a body under the sheets next to him.

"Great. So you're putting your career on the line for a piece of ass?"

"Not just any piece of ass," a familiar voice came from next to him. The lump started to move and then an arm appeared to push back the covers.

"Quinn?" I asked, shocked by what I was seeing.

"Hey, Shaw," he said with a mischievous grin and a finger wave as Denver wrapped his arm around his shoulders.

My eyebrows reached for my hairline. "Holy shit! How long has this been going on?"

Quinn laid his head on Denver's chest and looked up at him. "How long would you say it's been, honey?"

Denver rubbed his arm, lovingly. "I don't know. What day is it?"

"Oh, it doesn't matter," Quinn said, snuggling in closer. "What does matter is that we've been inseparable and having the time of our lives since you two have been gone. Don't shit all over our happiness, Shaw."

"Shit all over your happiness?" I asked, flabbergasted. "The only person shitting on anything here is Denver on the contract of a lifetime that Cassidy and I worked really hard to get for him. I'm glad you two are happy, but, Denver, you can't put your entire career at risk like this."

"Dude, I'm Denver 'Rocket Man' Rockford," he said like that was all that mattered. "The most sought-after quarterback. Remember? Missing a couple of days of training camp isn't going to make me any less fabulous, and Colorado is still going to be kissing my ass."

I ran my fingers through my hair and over my face. "You'll be fined," I told him.

He gave me a cocky grin. "So? I've got plenty of money."

I decided to go after the thing that mattered most to him: his appearance. "You'll look bad. Really bad. And not only will *you* look bad, but *I* will look bad. So will Striker Sports Entertainment . . . the agency where I just made partner because I signed you. Or did you forget about that? Come on, man. Do me a favor here. I'm going to get my ass chewed as it is. If you don't get to training camp, I'm probably going to lose my job."

"Honey, you can't let him get fired. He's not just your agent, he's our friend. Plus, he's my roommate's boy toy. She'll kill me. Do it for me? Please?" Quinn stuck out his bottom lip in a pout.

"But I want to be with you," Denver told him. I had nothing against his sexual preference. Quinn could've been a chick and I'd still think Denver's whining was a comical thing to see from a man with his reputation in the world of football.

"How about if I go to Colorado with you?" Quinn offered, and then added—quite suggestively, "I'll sit in the stands and watch you get all sweaty."

"Okay, fine," Denver conceded. "I want to introduce you to my parents, anyway."

Quinn's face lit up. "Really?"

"Of course, babe." Denver hugged Quinn to him.

This was probably a conversation I didn't need to be a part of, but I was glad to see them both so happy. Especially knowing how much it had hurt Quinn that his previous lover, Daddy, had kept him hidden for so long. He finally had someone who was proud to claim him.

"Wonderful!" I said, relieved I could report to Wade that the fire had been put out. "You'll hop a flight tomorrow?"

"You know how I feel about flying, man." Denver's fear of flying meant he had to pretty much be sedated in order to do so.

"Aw, don't worry, sweetie," Quinn told him. "I'll be there to distract you."

"Perfect. So . . . tomorrow?" I wasn't going to give up until he agreed.

"Yeah, we can do that," Denver said. "Sorry if I got you into trouble, man."

"No worries, Rocket. I'm used to putting out fires," I assured him. "I'll call Colorado and let them know you're on your way."

"And tell Cass her ass is grass for not checking in with me," Quinn said and then giggled. "That rhymed. I'm so clever."

"Will do. You two have fun, but make sure you *get on that plane*," I stressed. With that, I ended the call.

While I had a decent Wi-Fi signal, I checked my email to see if Ben had sent details for my own flight. He had. In two short days. He'd added a note that the airport had shut down operation until then to allow for the storm cleanup. Doable, but then I started to feel a little chick-ish myself. I'd be leaving Cassidy. Not only Cassidy, but also Abby and the whole town of Stonington. It sort of felt like I was abandoning them.

There was no way to avoid it. I had to get back to assume my place as partner with Striker Sports Entertainment, something I'd worked really damn hard for and wasn't willing to give up. For anyone other than Cassidy Whalen. Who, ironically, was the one person who'd wanted to keep me from it in the first place. I shook my head at myself. Fate was a real kick in the pants sometimes.

But I wasn't going to cross that line until I knew how she felt about me. Because if she was just going to laugh in my face about how serious I was about her, no way was I giving up my dream. So it seemed like it was the fourth quarter with seconds remaining on the clock and one play left to be made. Everything was on the line. If Cassidy was my wide receiver, I was her quarterback, and there was nothing left to do but send the damn ball down the field and hope she'd catch it and run it in for the game-winning touchdown.

And it was exactly that thought that led me down the hallway of the second floor until I found myself standing right outside her door.

CHAPTER 20

Cassidy

The knock at my door was expected. Or at the very least, I'd been hoping it would come. Shaw had said he didn't want to be alone anymore, and I was really glad it didn't turn out that all of that talk was about the storm and the trauma of drowning, making it a one-night-only thing or a fleeting moment of desperation.

Showered and smelling less like a tomboy, with legs as smooth as a woman's should be, I checked myself in the mirror one last time—rolling my eyes at how chick-ish I was being—and went to let him in.

When I opened the door, he was standing there, fresh as a daisy as well, dressed in a simple gray T-shirt that hugged his neck in a sexy sort of way and a pair of jeans that did the same thing to his hips. Jesus, he was gorgeous. And quiet.

"Hey," I greeted him with a warm smile in place.

Why did he look so nervous?

"Hey," he echoed, his eyes making a sweep over my body so intimately that I could feel my skin warm as if they'd been his hands. And he still wasn't moving or saying anything. He was beginning to make *me* nervous, even more so than I already was.

"Is something wrong, Shaw?"

Finally meeting my gaze, he smiled. "No. I was just wondering . . . So, um . . . did you want to be alone tonight?"

Oh, thank God, I thought, relief washing over me.

I laughed and shook my head. "Not in the least. In fact, come here. I want to show you something." Taking his hand, I practically yanked him inside and then dragged him across my room to the open window. Stooping, I stepped through and onto the roof, making sure to check my footing. "Careful," I warned Shaw before releasing his hand so he'd have them both free to follow safely without a slip.

Traversing the eave, I made my way toward the pitch, leaning forward to distribute my weight evenly. That was hard enough on its own, but there were also some shingles missing, courtesy of Ayla, that made the foot placement tricky. I'd have to be sure to tell Da about those.

When I looked back over my shoulder, I noticed Shaw was just standing in place. "What are you doing?" I asked.

Good Lord, but that sexy little smirk of his had come out to play. "Admiring the view."

"Well, it's better up here, if you'll stop dillydallying," I said, laughing.

He cocked his head to the side and licked his lips as his attention went straight to my backside. "We're going to have to agree to disagree on that one, Miss Whalen."

"Shaw!" I said, quickly straightening as if that would hide my ass. But the sudden movement succeeded only in making me lose my balance. I caught myself, though, just in time to also catch the fear on Shaw's face when he'd realized the accident that had almost occurred.

"That's it. We're getting down," he said, his tone all business as if he was the boss of me. Again, technically, he was. But in San Diego, not Stonington.

"If you're scared, say you're scared," I taunted with a smirk of my own.

Shaw made that growly sort of sound I'd heard too many times while pleasuring him and it went straight to my girly bits. So much so that I'd started to calculate whether or not we could fuck on the roof of my parents' home and livelihood before deciding that the shingles might not feel very pleasant on a bare rump.

Reaching the roof of the center dormer, my bedroom window, I finally took a seat, letting my legs fall to either side of the ninety-degree pitch, and then I waited for Shaw to join me. I might have delighted in ogling the way the tendons in his forearms flexed with his climb and the way he had to bend over just a bit to equal out his balance, allowing me a breathtaking view of an ass I'd become obsessed with.

When Shaw finally reached me, he took the only seat left, mimicking my position as he also straddled the pitch right behind me. Apparently not satisfied with the distance between us, he moved closer to hug me to his chest, wrapping his arms around my waist. I was glad he did.

"Can't have you falling off," was his excuse. As if he'd needed one.

And then we just sat there.

Casey and I had had the crow's nest for our special place, but this spot was my personal secret. No one had ever been there with me. Until now.

Tilting my head back to let it rest on Shaw's shoulder, I looked up at the sky. The stars were bright and plentiful, a twinkling light show to accentuate the half moon so brilliant and so high above. There was a gentle yet steady breeze blowing in from the bay, balmy thanks to the wind streaming in from the south. I sighed, feeling within my element and allowing the energies of the night to help steel up my nerve.

The sound of crickets was almost deafening, or maybe it only seemed that way in light of the silence between Shaw and me. I'd had so much to say, and now that we were alone, I was at a loss for words. So I said the first thing that came to mind.

"You know, if you don't look down, you can almost pretend Ayla never happened."

Shaw tenderly pulled my hair away from my neck, and then his cheek was at my ear. His warm breath tickled my skin before his soft kiss followed. "Is there anything else you'd like to pretend never happened?"

I closed my eyes, as the feel of his palms to the inside of my thighs was intoxicating and sending me into sensory overload when mixed with our setting and the wicked thing he was doing with his lips to my neck and ear.

"No," I whispered.

"I really love these legging things," he said, his hand inching closer and closer to my center. "Are they warm? Because they feel . . . warm." He swept my center, the pressure from his fingertips finding its mark without error.

I gasped, my back arching and any rational thought evacuating as a flood of "yes, please" rushed to meet his touch. Reaching to hook my hands under his thighs, I held on, loving the thrill of sitting so precariously on the edge of a roof while this man whom I would never get enough of made me feel as if I could soar.

"God, you smell so good." Shaw inhaled deeply, humming his approval on the exhale while he continued to rub me through the leggings.

His tongue was on my neck, a string of openmouthed kisses leaving a hot trail cooled only by the breeze. My body tingled, my flesh pebbling from the sensation. I was lost to him, to his touch, to his mere presence.

What was I going to say to him? I decided it didn't matter.

Well, it did, but it could wait because Shaw's hand was drifting up my abdomen and slipping under the waistband of my pants for some skin-to-skin contact. My muscles contracted, that thing we women did to make our stomachs seem flatter when a man touched us there. And then Shaw was inside my panties, touching and caressing.

Cupping my pussy, he slipped his fingers between the folds to coat them with my wetness. "That's for me?" he asked, curling his fingers back to tease my clit with a slow approach.

I could do nothing but nod. If I thought words had failed me before, it was nothing compared to now. Shaw was well skilled at the art of finger play, like a guitarist masterfully strumming his instrument to make the most beautiful music ever composed. Back and forth, round and round, slow then fast then slow again. His movements were accompanied by varying degrees of pressure applied in a legato fashion. The symphony he created was maddening and unpredictable, but it was harmonic.

His cock was hard against the small of my back. I could feel him ready and in need of release, but his only concern seemed to be giving me mine. He'd have it if his persistent fingers had anything to say about it. And it wouldn't take long.

Shaw's teeth scraped my earlobe, tugging and sucking at it before he moved down to my neck again. I could hear his breaths, feel them against my back with each rise and fall of his chest. He loved this, loved making me see stars behind my eyes even though there were so many to behold if I'd just open them. I did. I opened my eyes and looked up at those stars, dreamed of reaching out to touch them. All while Shaw pushed me closer and closer as if I were weightless and adrift in a never-ending universe.

It was almost impossible to describe an orgasm. But not tonight. Tonight it was like kicking off the surface of that moon and reaching for the brightest star in the galaxy, and then hugging it to me to let it burn in the most blissful sort of satisfaction.

Putting one hand over his and wrapping the other around his head, I turned my face into Shaw's neck as I reached for that proverbial star and held my breath. My orgasm washed over me with a whimpered "Unnmph," which was meant for him and only him to hear.

The death grip I had on his head was likely creating a very uncomfortable bend to his neck, though he didn't seem to mind in the least. In fact, he resituated himself, taking my jaw into his free hand and kissing me fully. He'd stolen my breath, but it wasn't the first time. He could have it. He already had my heart, so the need to breathe was useless anyway.

Shaw pulled back, rubbing his nose back and forth against mine before kissing the tip. "Let's get you inside," he said.

I honestly wasn't sure my legs would be steady enough for the precarious climb back down the roof, but I was sure Shaw would guide me to safety without fail. So I put my trust in him, something I never would've thought I'd do before our time in Stonington, and let him lead the way.

Once we were back inside, Shaw closed the window behind us and then turned to face me. He looked nervous, like something was on his mind he'd yet to say. Or maybe he was still just super horny. I chanced a look down at his crotch, but the erection I was sure had been there before was gone.

"What's wrong?" I asked.

Shaw raked his fingers through his hair. "I think we need to talk."

Uh-oh. Nothing good ever followed those words. So then I got nervous, a thousand scenarios swarming my brain and trying to come up with a counter to the problem I didn't yet know existed. Was this the part where he dumped me? Was the orgasm he'd just given the last he'd bestow?

"Wait," I told him, not quite ready to let him go before he knew how I felt, and really not sure if it would change his mind even if he did. But if I didn't tell him what I needed to tell him, I knew it would take a whole lot of jazzing myself up to get the nerve to do so again.

Shaw started to pace. "This can't wait any longer, Cassidy. I have to go back to San Diego, but I'm not going a damn place until I get this off my chest."

He was leaving. I wasn't sure why that shocked me so much. It wasn't like either of us could stay here forever. But it felt an awful lot like the bubble we'd found ourselves in within the relatively safe confines of this little island was about to pop. As much as I'd liked to think I'd escaped, I'd found myself right back in the Stonington frame of mind, that the outside world didn't exist. It did, and I had no choice but to get back to reality—a reality that was staring me right in the face. "Fine. Say what you've got to say, then."

"Look, there's a whole lot that's gone on in the last few days—the last few weeks, actually—and it's all been happening really fast. So fast I'm having an incredibly hard time keeping up, and I'm all mixed up in the head. Everything I've known, my whole way of life, has changed. I don't know if I'm coming or going, who I am or what I want to be. But what I do know is this thing between us has to change."

He wasn't the only one mixed up in the head, and his chaotic rant wasn't helping the matter. "Just say whatever it is you're trying to say, Shaw."

"I want more, Cassidy." His words were very precise in the way they cut through the air between us.

Understanding dawned on me. The cold, hard truth. "I'm not enough." I let the words hang in the air until they really sank in. "I read you loud and clear."

"Obviously not," he said. "Because I want more of *you*. Like on a permanent basis, more."

I furrowed my brow, not quite sure I understood what he was saying and unwilling to make any assumptions without further clarification, because the last thing I wanted was to look or feel like an even bigger fool if I got it wrong.

Shaw must have read my distress. "My whole way of life has changed . . . because of you. Don't you get it? All I'd ever known was struggle. I'd had to fight my way out of the slums. I'd had to fight to keep a roof over my head and food on my table. I'd had to fight my way into the boardroom. And I'd had to fight to prove I was worthy of being there.

"I'm tired, Cassidy. I'm tired, and I don't want to fight anymore. Not unless I'm fighting to stay by your side. Not unless I'm fighting my way into your heart."

"Don't say that to me, Shaw. Don't say that unless you mean it."

"I do mean it." He stepped to me, cupping my face in his hands and looking me in the eyes. "I love you. I have never loved anyone. And as egotistical as you think I am, the truth is I haven't even loved myself."

I was as frozen as an ice statue, with all the mobility of one, as well. But I didn't feel its arctic chill. No, quite the opposite. Shaw's words had set me aflame with their potency. I was stunned. Maybe even a little confused. Crap, this must have been what going into shock felt like.

Shaw's baby blues turned a rainy-day gray. "Please say something."

Well, there was a novel idea. "I don't know what to say." What the hell was I talking about? Of course I knew what to say! So why were the words refusing to come out?

He released the hold on my face and stepped away. "Oh, God. I'm making a total ass out of myself here." He turned toward the window and then back again, exasperated. "I just told you I love you and you don't know what to say?"

There was a pleading in his eyes, a sort of desperation and vulnerability I'd never seen there before. Like a man dying from a self-inflicted wound to the chest who suddenly changed his mind and wished he could take it back. And I was the only one with the ability to keep his heart from bleeding out all over the place, but I was too terrified to do anything about it.

Did he mean it? Of all the women who had likely passed in and out of his life, why was I more special?

Fed up with my stalling, Shaw shook his head in defeat and turned to walk away. And that simply was not okay with me. In fact, it terrified me even more than applying pressure to that gaping wound.

Closing my eyes and swallowing my pride, I let two syllables slip past my frozen lips and hoped they would be enough. "Shaw, stop."

He did, though he kept his back to me. "Why?"

"Because there are a million things I want to tell you right now, and they're all coming at me at the same time. But I know if you walk out that door, I'll never get the chance to say any of them. Especially the most important thing."

He faced me, everything about him demanding an answer to a question that had not yet been spoken. "Then say it. What are you so afraid of?"

I needed him to understand my fear, even if I didn't understand it myself. "If I do, it changes everything. There's no going back. You understand that?"

"You're the one who doesn't understand." Shaw's shrug and the exasperated shake of his head was the proverbial towel being thrown in. "That Hail Mary I just threw already pushed me past the point of no return, anyway. You got the interception, now run the ball back."

"This isn't a game, Shaw."

"You're right, Cassidy. It isn't. So stop playing with me."

It suddenly occurred to me why I'd been so terrified to tell him what I knew to be in my heart. And it was time he knew it, too.

"Shaw Matthews, you're pretentious, domineering, melodramatic, stubborn, and vain. You break all the rules, think you can sweet-talk your way out of any situation, and most of the time the simplest of human emotions is lost on you."

"Well, don't hold back. Tell me how you really feel."

"You're a risk," I told him.

Shaw's eyes dropped to the floor, and I couldn't stand to see him that way.

So I approached him slowly, lifting his chiseled chin so he'd see the truth written all over my face. "But you're a risk I'll always take. Just don't make me regret it."

That winning smile spread from cheek to cheek as he wrapped his arms around my waist and pulled me against him. "So you like me, huh?"

I grinned. "Maybe just a little."

He quirked a brow. "Oh, just a little?"

Laughter bubbled up and out of me because he was just too damn cute for his own good. He had me . . . heart, body, and soul. "Shut up and kiss me."

"Not until you say it," he baited.

I feigned annoyance. "Fine. I love you. There. Are you happy now?"

"Extremely," he said. "Especially now that I finally understand the true definition of happiness. I owe that to you."

I furrowed my brow at him. "If you're trying to make me girly . . ."

He laughed. "I wouldn't dream of it. I love you just the way you are."

"This is getting entirely too mushy," I told him, only half-joking.

Shaw fisted my hair and pulled it back so that I was forced to crane my neck to look up at him. And then he kissed me hard on the mouth, sucking and biting on my bottom lip and then pushing his thick tongue inside to caress mine with deep, probing strokes of domination. And I let him . . . because he was "the" Shaw Matthews, and he was mine.

When he was done proving his point, he pulled back to look at me, a gaze steeped with desire in his eyes and a very prominent bulge hard against my belly.

"You're right," he said. Releasing the hold on my hair, he was lightning quick when he grabbed the waistband of my pants and shoved them, none too gently, over my hips and ass. "Bend over the goddamn bed, Miss Whalen. I'm going to fuck that pretty little pussy until you come, and then I'm going to fuck your mouth until I do."

Yes, we loved each other. We were both clear on that now. But that didn't mean our sexual dynamic had to change in the least because of it. So I did what I always did. I set my chin in defiance and got my sass on. "You don't get to tell me what to do."

One side of Shaw's mouth lifted into that cocky, albeit sexy, smirk I loved so much. Challenge accepted. He grabbed my hips, turned me around, and put one hand on my back to shove me into the position I'd refused to assume. And then he held me there while he worked his pants loose, never once seeing the satisfied grin on my face as he did so.

With a quick, hard thrust—that very well might have caused some damage to my girlie bits—he entered me. My whole body would've come off the bed if he hadn't been holding me down, but I wasn't complaining. He was mine and I was his, and I wouldn't have it any other way.

Once he'd worked himself completely inside, he leaned over my back, encompassing me until his mouth was at my ear. "My title of partner says differently. And you bet your sweet, delectable ass I'm going to take full advantage of it."

With slow, yet deliberate strokes, he fucked me. Hooking his arms under mine to hold onto my shoulders, he made sure I wasn't going anywhere. Not that I would have even if I could, but I loved his closeness and his labored, grunting breaths at my ear.

Shaw's thrusts were short, his grind on point, and his teeth on the back of my neck on the mark. I came, the pulsing of the walls of my pussy even more pronounced thanks to the very well-endowed thickness of his cock.

"You're welcome," he said, like the egomaniac he was.

Then he unhooked my shoulders to rise into a standing position, grabbing my hips to pound into me harder.

"And that goddamn tattoo is getting removed the second we land back in San Diego," he ordered, apparently none too pleased by the reminder of Casey's name there. "You're fucking mine."

Yes, I was, and I'd happily oblige his request that wasn't really a request. Lots of things would need to be dealt with upon our return to the real world. Though for now, he was dealing with giving me yet another orgasm. His possessiveness was a driving force. I almost hated to admit it to myself because I'd always been such an independent woman, but I didn't mind being submissive to him. In the bedroom alone, of course. Outside the bedroom? Well, that was another story, another storm, and another part of who we were.

When my second orgasm had subsided, Shaw's cock abandoned the confines of my pussy and he maneuvered my body yet again until I was facing him. Stroking himself with one hand, his expression softened. "I love you," he told me in the sweetest tone I'd ever heard him use.

"I love you, too," I answered, not only with my voice but with my eyes, as well. Because I meant it.

"Good. Now suck cock," he ordered, putting his other hand on my shoulder and pushing me down in front of him.

And I loved that, as well.

Sinking to my knees, I let him cup the back of my head and press the head of his cock to my lips. It was sticky and wet with my orgasm, so I stuck out my tongue to taste him, an act that made him groan in approval. Shaw was a visual sort of lover. He liked to watch, and he appreciated the show. So I gave it to him. Swirling my tongue around the head, I closed my eyes and moaned at the taste of myself on him.

"Jesus, that's sexy," he said in that breathy sort of way.

I looked up at him, a sudden rush of wetness coating my still-exposed pussy again when I saw the way his teeth were pulling at his bottom lip. I wanted to bite that lip, so I chanced a little dominating act of my own and yanked at his arm, making him bend over and release his hold as I grabbed his head with both hands and kissed him. I was pretty sure the only reason he'd let me was because he'd wanted to taste me, too, but I'd only just begun before he'd gotten wise to my agenda and tried to pull away again. I was pretty damn proud of myself for managing to hold on long enough to bite into that juicy morsel I'd been craving and forcing him to nearly split his lip with his attempt to pull free.

"Enough," he said, straightening again. He licked the spot, checking for blood and giving me a look of admonishment when he saw the way I delighted in it.

"Yeah? You think you're cute?" he asked, and I nodded. "Take your shirt off," he told me, and I pulled the stupid thing over my head, reaching behind my back to also pop the clasp on my bra and tossing it to the side.

"That's my girl," he said with approval. "Now let's see how cute you look gagging on my cock. Suck me off."

Grabbing the back of my head again, he pushed his cock past my lips and into my mouth. "Wider," he ordered, and I fell in line, letting him stretch the corners of my mouth with his thickness until he could go no farther. And his "Good girl" was my reward.

Though we were both playing our roles, Shaw was careful not to get too rough. He knew my limits, and though he tested them, he never pressed too far.

With a pace that was preferable to him, he thrust in and out of my mouth. I did my best to keep up, and I did a pretty good job of it, too, but there was a whole lot of Shaw to take. He helped with the task, stroking that part of his cock that he couldn't fit into my mouth, watching the whole time.

The veins in his arms were thick with his blood, the tendons taut and moving fluidly beneath the skin with his strokes. Shaw's lips parted as his breathing became labored, and I knew he was close. God, I would've loved to have been able to see those glorious ass muscles flexing as he fucked my mouth, but I would be denied. It didn't matter because I could see his face; his brows furrowed in concentration, his messy hair hanging over his forehead and in need of a trim, and those blue eyes looking down at me like I was the most beautiful, most seductive woman in the world.

And then he made this sound that I lived to hear. A sort of whimper that turned into a grunting growl. His engorged cock swelled even more in my mouth and I braced for the eruption, even though I really didn't want him to come in my mouth. I would've let him because I wanted to please him. But Shaw proved himself once more when he chose to respect my preference on the matter, and instead, he pulled out of my mouth, continuing to work himself until his semen made an appearance, a stuttered spurting that sent the hot, creamy substance all over my bare breasts.

I'd thought the sound he'd made before was sexy, but it was nothing compared to the one he made with his release. I loved it. So much that I didn't even care that he had come all over my tits. I'd give this man anything he ever wanted. And I knew he'd do the same for me.

Life could be rough. Shaw was a walking testament to that. And it was stupid hard to face alone, though we'd both proven we could do it. But why do it alone if we didn't have to? Even a person as independent and capable as the two of us were, needed someone else they could depend on, someone to be their ride-or-die. And I was glad Shaw turned out to be that for me. Because if I was going to face the world with someone at my side, I couldn't think of a more worthy person.

We'd started out as each other's most formidable competitor in business, but had somehow become partners on a personal level. And yes, the personal partnership was a risk, but one well worth taking. Our mentors, Wade Price and Monty Prather, would be proud. Though they really didn't need to know about the coming-on-the-tits thing. Shaw and I would keep that our very dirty little secret.

EPILOGUE

Two months later ...

Mia

Mornings were my most absolute favorite time of the day. Sitting behind my desk with my laptop in front of me and a beautiful view of downtown Stonington and Penobscot Bay, I could watch the new day's sun crest on the horizon while letting my imagination run wild. The move to my new home had been like a dream come true, and the townspeople of Stonington had welcomed me with open arms as one of their own.

And speaking of the townspeople, I was in absolute awe of them. In two months' time, most of the cleanup from Hurricane Ayla had been completed and construction was well under way to restore some of the homes and businesses lost. Tourism had not suffered, and the lobstering industry had not taken much of a hit. Everything seemed to be business as usual. I wasn't sure any other town or major city could've been quite as resilient, but I guess that was just the sort of stuff Maine's islanders were made of.

I'd tried to use their resilience as inspiration for my own career. As the deadline for the manuscript I'd been working on drew nearer, I was in full-on panic mode. The words had been harder to come by and I was running out of story to tell, falling short of the word count I'd been contractually obligated to provide. I was worried. And the more I worried, the more I stressed. The more I stressed, the harder it was to write.

Maybe I should've waited until after the manuscript was complete to move. Maybe I should've been less distracted by my personal life and more concerned with my career. But I was a Pisces, and Pisces were notorious for being overly romantic and dreamy, which was both helping and hurting my career at the same time. Though finally, with more stability now present in my life, I was settled enough to get my head back in the game and the words were flowing a little easier.

I just hoped it wasn't too little too late.

A fresh cup of coffee, mixed with three Splendas and plenty of Cinnabon creamer, magically slid in front of me on my desk.

"Good morning, beautiful," a sleep-laden voice said at my ear.

I smiled without having to see where the voice had come from, but of course I wanted to. All my worries about the deadline melted away the moment I turned to look up at my roommate. Casey. *My* Casey.

His hair was still sticking up all over the place—which might have been compliments of his pillow, but I knew it was because of my own fingers—and his beard was nice and scruffy, just the way I liked it. He was shirtless but had managed to put on his favorite sleep pants—though I would have preferred he hadn't—and still smelled like sex.

"Good morning, gorgeous."

Casey leaned down and kissed me, the sort of kiss that made my toes curl, and then he peered over my shoulder to read what I'd written.

"Wait, I'm pretty sure we did that last night," he said.

"You are correct, sir," I confirmed. "You are my muse after all. I'm still stuck on this one part of the scene, though," I said, scrolling up to show him the gap at the beginning.

He read over the part I'd indicated, as genuinely interested in my career as I was in his. And he was always quick to offer suggestions about the story, though he was a guy, so he'd thrown in the idea of a murder or two. Which was a gruesome twist for a romance novel, but at least he tried.

"Huh. Well, let's see if I can give you some inspiration," he said with a wicked sort of glint to his eye. Over time, he'd caught on to, and had become quite fond of, the more sexy elements of my job. He'd reaped the benefits, after all.

Casey turned my chair to face him as he went to his knees before me and hooked his fingers under the waistband of my panties, giving them a hard tug. I giggled as I lifted my bottom to make the task easier for him. God, but I loved the way this man inspired me.

I wasn't sure where my panties landed once he'd thrown them across the room, but then again, I really didn't care. Casey had me bare before him and had pushed my knees apart so he could kiss the inside of my thighs. And even though I was perfectly aware that it was his mouth suckling at my skin, I closed my eyes and let him take me away to a place inside my head where fictional stories came to life.

I was a lucky, lucky girl, and he was a talented, talented man.

With his hands behind my knees, he yanked me forward until my ass was on the edge of the seat. And then he tasted me.

Casey was never hurried when he ate my pussy. He liked to savor the experience, and I was all too happy to let him. His lips were soft as he lightly kissed my clit, and his tongue was generous between my folds. Two thick fingers eased inside me and he worked them back and forth, slow at first and then quickening once I'd acclimated to the presence and he'd found my G-spot. He was an expert at finding it now. Having been quite traditional when we'd first started making love, I'd convinced him to open up to new experiences, which had led to a whole lot of pleasure not only for us but for my characters, as well.

His thumb found my ass and he slipped it inside, a move that forced me to fist his hair from the all-encompassing pleasure his multiple manipulations gave. His mouth on my clit, his fingers working my pussy, and his thumb's presence in my ass would make short work of my journey toward one hell of an orgasm.

Casey's head moved back and forth between my legs, his hair tickling my thighs while the warmth of his face beckoned them closer. But it was the scruff of his beard that teased me to no end. He knew it, and he used it to his advantage every chance he had.

Suckling my clit, he moaned when I tugged at his hair. It was a warning, one he knew I'd ignore because my punishment would be my reward. His fingers plunged knuckle deep inside me and his mouth became more persistent while his thumb began to move in and out.

"Baby . . . Oh, God . . . Don't stop," I begged, even though I knew he wouldn't.

Harder and faster his fingers and thumb worked. I spread my legs wide, giving him room because it would only benefit me more if he had free rein. Casey did not disappoint. I abandoned all thought of my characters and their story, opening my eyes to watch him as his tongue and lips did unspeakable things to my clit and the muscles in his arms became taut with his insistence. The thumb abandoned my ass, but I was okay with that because it was the only way he could fuck me with his fingers properly, really utilizing their length. And yeah, they were as long as they were thick.

His mouth was the next to go, and he sat back to watch as the end result of all his glorious work came to a head. Casey knew my body like no other. All the signs were present that my orgasm was there, and he loved to watch it coat his fingers. Harder, he pounded into me, his knuckles smacking against my folds and jarring my entire body.

My breathing and heart rate were off the charts, and my abdomen tightened. Baring down, I allowed my orgasm to come flooding forward with a hearty moan that was none too quiet.

Casey watched. Watched and licked his lips. And then just as it ebbed, he pulled his fingers free and gathered his reward in his mouth. Another orgasm hit, and although instinct made me want to close my eyes and arch my back to it, I didn't. Because I was hypnotized by the sight of him between my thighs.

He continued to work me with his mouth until I finally came down. And then with one last soft kiss to my very sensitive clit, he sat back with a smirk.

Getting to his feet, he leaned over and kissed me fully on the mouth so I could taste myself on his lips. "Write that," he whispered into my ear, and then he sauntered out of the room with all the swag and confidence of a man who'd earned the right to.

"I love you!" I called after him.

"I love you, too!"

Cassidy

Having an affair with the boss was not an easy thing to manage. But so far, so good. Shaw and I had kept up our previous bitchiness toward each other while stealing precious moments together behind closed doors. Truthfully, the arguments had fueled our lust for each other even more. Neither of us was the sappy type, and it had been the constant cutthroat attitudes we mutually shared that had landed us in bed with each other in the first place. So it was just like any normal day. Only when Shaw was done bending me over a desk to fuck some manners into me after I'd shown him up in front of the boardroom, he'd cap it off with an "I love you."

We'd spent every night together, except for the few between the time Shaw had had to return to San Diego and when I was able to leave Stonington to join him. Those were tough nights, but I'd thrown myself into helping out Ma and Da as much as I could before they'd practically shoved me out the door and onto a plane to send me back to him. Apparently, I'd been moody without him and driving them up the wall. Go figure. They'd spent years making me feel guilty about not returning home often enough only to tell me I'd overstayed my welcome.

I was glad to get back to my reality, though. And I couldn't wait to get back into Shaw's arms. I'd spent every night curled up next to him in bed. Sometimes his, sometimes mine. We hadn't done anything stupid like move in with each other, but we did keep things like pajamas and toothbrushes at each other's apartments.

Shaw had managed to hang on to his title as partner of Striker Sports Entertainment despite the catastrophe Denver's little disappearance act had nearly caused him. A catastrophe my roommate, Quinn, had been in the center of. I was happy for Quinn. Denver had come out of the closet during a press conference, and despite the derogatory backlash that we'd all expected would happen, he and Quinn and their relationship had survived. It was big news for all of about a month, though eventually it had settled down. I honestly thought Denver would be disappointed when the circus left town, but he was still making headlines with his skills on the field, which kept him in the limelight, so he was satisfied. He was a total attention hound. As was Quinn, which made them the perfect couple.

And speaking of perfect couples . . . Landon and Sasha were still going strong. He treated her like a perfect gentleman should treat a lady, and the only tears she cried now were tears of joy. We honestly expected he'd propose any day now. Landon was one of those undercover romantics, so it wouldn't surprise me in the least.

What I was surprised by was the fact that Chaz had finally gotten over himself and his hang-up about his financial ranking long enough to ask Demi out. The little slut had been so excited, she'd given it up to him on the first date—a fact that Sasha, Quinn, and I reminded her of every chance we got. And she used every chance she got to brag about how good he was in the sack. Good for her.

Monkey Business was still our favorite hangout spot, and it was becoming more and more crowded. Though our table was still safely guarded by our favorite barkeep, Chaz. There was something to be said for preferential treatment. It was our place, our home away from home. So that was where we found ourselves sitting today, just like any other normal day. Only thing was that I hadn't had a cold beer in a really long time. I wasn't sure my stomach could handle it.

I'd been sick for a couple of weeks now. Nothing more than a bit of queasiness that came and went. I'd attributed it to the stress of travel and readjusting to life back in San Diego with a hurried routine, while trying to catch up on all the work I'd missed while away. Things had really been piling up. Not that Allie hadn't done all she could to keep things nice and tidy. Some of my clients simply required one-on-one attention from their agent and weren't satisfied with speaking to anyone other than me. I was okay with that, just really exhausted all the time.

Shaw was at the bar with Landon and Chaz, nursing a frosty mug, and it made my mouth water. Well, I wasn't sure if it was the sight of Shaw or the ale that turned on all the gotta-have-it, but since I couldn't exactly mount Shaw here, I'd decided to go for the amber. With no more than a nod in his direction, Chaz caught the cue and slid one down the bar.

The bottle was ice-cold in my hand, the aroma of the hops teasing my olfactory senses and really making me crave the taste. I'd no sooner raised it to my lips than it was yanked away. My narrowed eyes and a growl took aim at the culprit, Demi.

"Not gonna happen," she said, handing off the bottle to her partner in crime, Sasha, who passed it over to a confused Landon.

Just then, the bell above the door chimed and Quinn came bounding in. He was light on his feet, giving the evil eye to a couple of patrons who'd crossed the beeline path he'd been making toward us.

"I've got it," he said, motioning toward a plain brown paper bag under his arm. "Come on, let's go."

"You guys, this is so stupid," I whined when Demi and Sasha jumped up, prepared to abandon our table.

"It's not stupid. You agreed to do it," Demi reminded me.

I really hated them sometimes.

"Fine," I said with a huff as I got to my feet. "Let's get this over with so you can see how silly you're being."

Like the president of the United States under the protection of the Secret Service, I found myself in the middle of my friends being escorted to the restroom in the back of the building.

Sasha pushed open the glossy wooden door, popped inside, and then stuck her head out again. "Clear," she said.

Demi peered over her shoulder toward the bar and satisfied that our sudden disappearance had gone unnoticed, shoved me inside. Aside from the handicap stall, there was only one other and a shared sink. Which meant it wasn't nearly a big enough space to hold four people with very giant personalities, but we squeezed in regardless.

As though he wasn't satisfied by Sasha's check, Quinn pushed open both stall doors to be sure no one was there. "Here," he said, handing off the brown paper bag to me.

Just then, the bathroom door opened and a tall woman with a shapeless figure popped in. Or at least she tried to.

"Nope! Occupied-o!" Quinn told her, holding the door to keep it from opening any farther while pointing back toward the way from which she'd come.

The woman drew back her head and snarled at him. "You're not even supposed to be in here. This is the ladies' restroom," she told him.

Quinn put a hand on his hip and squared off with her. "Honey, I'm more of a lady than you'll ever be. You ain't fooling nobody with that water bra. Maybe if you waxed those hairy-ass legs," he said, looking her over. "And your lip," he tacked on, snidely.

The woman gasped. "How dare you!"

"How dare I?" Quinn asked, insulted. "How dare *you*? I know fashion trends run in cycles, but you're trying to take us all the way back to the cave. Shame on you, Wilma. Ya better go see what Fred and Betty are up to down at the quarry. 'Cause don't no woman giggle like that unless she's getting tickled *right*," he said with a mocking giggle of his own. Then he gave her a finger wave and shoved the door closed, forcing the woman out and locking it behind her.

Demi high-fived him while Sasha got her giggle-fit on. And then they all turned their attention to me again, with three pairs of raised eyebrows.

My head fell back as I closed my eyes and sighed. They weren't going to let this go. "Okay, fine!" I turned and stomped into the stall, the three of them moving in closer and just standing there, staring at me.

"Do you mind?" I asked, motioning for them to back up so I could close the door. God, they could be so rude.

"This testy attitude of yours is just further proving our suspicion," Demi said through the door.

I silently mimicked her, though she couldn't see my sass, but got on with the task presented before me anyway. If for no other reason than to simply prove them wrong. Pulling the contents from the package, I yanked down my pants and assumed the position. Once I was done, I stood there and waited. And waited.

"Time!" Sasha called.

My hands shook as I picked up the little pink and white stick and read the result.

When I opened the stall door, they were all there, crowding me in and not leaving any room for me to move past. All I could do was stare blankly at my friends as dead silence filled the room.

Quinn was the first to make a move, slowly maneuvering himself to get a look at the stick with his own eyes.

"What's it say?" Demi asked him.

"Rizzo's got a bun in the oven."

Crap.

ACKNOWLEDGMENTS

I've thought about what and whom to include here for, like, a million hours, running through all the regular material and the normal people. And while I'm still going to include those people—because, yeah, they were there for me—I've decided to do it in a way that will really let them and you, the reader, know how much of an impact they truly did have on this book.

In past acknowledgments I've said the book was hard to write, but they were a piece of cake by comparison. *Getting Rough* got *really* rough. And not because of the storyline or the characters being difficult. This one was personal. Very personal. I'll spare you the gory details, but everything that happened to me—that I allowed to happen to me—while writing this book can be summed up because of one reason: I'd forgotten who I am.

There were a lot of invaluable people present in my life who tried their damnedest to get me back on track—Patricia Dechant, Whittney Sherman, Kimberly Rackley, Maureen Morgan, Janell Ramos, Melanie Edwards, Brittnie Day, and Bobbie Butler—and while their efforts made all the difference in the world because they know me better than anyone else, I had to figure things out for myself. Which took a huge chunk of my time and energy as I struggled to find the words to the story I knew I wanted to tell.

Not for one second did I take for granted the opportunity before me, though an author is still a human being capable of having to weather through real-life drama of her own. Things going topsy-turvy in the real world can and will have a direct effect on the work she produces. As such, there are bits and pieces of my soul scattered throughout this book. You'll see it in Cassidy's confusion, Shaw's figuring out what's really important in life, Casey's learning to let go, Mia's escape from reality, and in the storm that wreaked havoc in the lives of innocent people.

My incredibly understanding editor, Shauna Summers, and agent, Alexandra Machinist, had my back like you wouldn't believe. I honestly don't have the words to thank them for being so accommodating and supportive. And a special note: Thank you, Shauna, for giving me the freedom to express myself and trusting me to tell a story that's real.

The "aha!" moment came at a time in my life when I—a romance author—had started to believe fairy-tale romances were only a thing of fiction. Fate introduced me to a man who defied that ideal and changed my mind. Thank you, my Superman, for making me believe in fairy tales again.

My incredibly difficult journey to self-actualization was hard fought, but I came out the victor. So here's to you, Ms. Parker. . . . May you never forget yourself again.

Read on for a sneak peek at the final book in C. L. Parker's
sizzling Monkey Business Trio:

Coming Clean

Available from Piatkus Books.

PROLOGUE

Shaw

"Okay, now. I need you to roll over and get on your hands and knees for me."

Cassidy's eyes popped wide. "On my hands and knees? But why?"

"Because it'll give me a better angle to work with," said the British gentleman whom Cassidy had insisted we use. Though I was seriously considering how much of a gentleman he truly was at this point.

I could do nothing but watch as Cassidy complied with the soft-spoken command, her movements awkward as she shifted around in the small bed, much like a turtle on its back. When she finally assumed the position, the sheet slipped off her hips, falling to barely dangle from her delicate ankles and exposing her ass for all to see. For the first time in my life, I couldn't get hard at the sight of a naked woman's backside, even though it was attached to the woman I loved.

"Cassidy, I want you to listen very carefully. What I'm about to do might be a bit uncomfortable, but I need you to try to relax as much as possible." The deep timber of the Brit's dreamy accent—

per my girl—pulled me out of my trance, and I had to stop myself from launching across the bed and knocking the bloke away from her. Especially when he slipped his large hand between her legs and starting doing God knows what to her vagina.

My vagina.

I heard Cassidy's slight intake of breath, followed by a string of mumbled curses, and my stomach heaved in protest. The lousy cup of stale coffee I had drunk earlier threatened to make a reappearance on the linoleum and my knees started to give. Before I could kiss the floor, a none-too-gentle shove had me seated in a nearby chair with my head between my legs.

"Is everything okay?" Cassidy's voice came from far away, sounding as weak as I felt.

A cool cloth made its way around my neck and the nausea eased somewhat so I could respond. "I'm fine, sweetness."

"Not you, Shaw. The baby. What's going on?"

"There, I've got a pulse," Dr. Edwards, aka Dr. McDreamy said. "Not a bloody good one, either. Get the lot of them in here. Now."

I lifted my head as the door opened and what seemed like a swarm of people scurried into the room like ants at a free-for-all buffet. Controlled chaos reigned over the room as IV bags were hung and nurses scuttled around, grabbing supplies and placing them on the bed. Someone wearing blue-colored scrubs and a surgical mask around her neck stood at the head, pushing medicine into Cassidy's IV. Words like *emergency C-section* and *prolapsed cord* were singled out of the verbal montage coming from different people in the room. I couldn't tell who was saying what.

All the while, Dr. McDreamy still had his arm up my woman's no-no zone and hadn't even broken out in a sweat. Maybe that was because I was wearing it for him.

My eyes darted to the fetal monitor beside the bed. The volume had been turned all the way down, though the heart icon continued to flicker. I had no idea what the flashing numbers meant, but the hurried movements of the staff had panic rising up with the force of a tsunami.

I had never felt so fucking helpless in my life. The room seemed to shrink and my vision blurred around the edges until I couldn't catch my breath. I struggled to hold on to my resolve with each passing second. Shit wasn't going right, and there was absolutely nothing I could do about it except be there for her. *With* her.

"Shaw . . . Oh no! Shaw, something's wrong!" Cassidy's voice acted as my lifeline and pulled me back into the moment. I turned to see the woman who had become my reason for breathing looking panicked and afraid as she was rolled off her knees and onto her back once again. And that scared the shit out of me. Nothing frightened Cassidy Whalen. She was fierce, a force to be reckoned with, unshakable. But the tears swimming in her green eyes confirmed just how fragile she was and how I needed to man up.

Working the boulder-size knot down my throat, I feigned a confidence I in no way possessed and pushed my way between two nurses, ignoring the one giving me the evil eye as I did so. Being careful not to show my own worry in my expression, I gave the hand of the mother of my unborn child a reassuring squeeze. "Everything's going to be okay, sweetness. I promise. I love you."

"I love you, too," she said, and then a tear slipped down her cheek.

Fuck. I'd just made a promise I knew I couldn't keep, seeing as I really had no control over the situation. If anything happened to our child, if anything happened to Cassidy . . . I just couldn't go there. But someone in this room had better damn well make sure I wouldn't have to.

"We need to move, people. The baby is in distress."

"We're going to OR C. Call NICU for standby."

"I'm only thirty-eight weeks. It's too early. Can't you stop it? You were supposed to stop it." Cassidy was frantic, begging for answers from anyone who would give them.

"Shh, sweetie, you need to calm down," one of the nurses with a gentle voice said as she patted Cassidy's arm. "Yes, it's early, but luckily not too early. Your baby should be fine. You've got the best of the best working for you, but we need to take the little one now."

"Should be? Should be fine?" I repeated, hung up on those two little words. *Should be* was not a guarantee, it was an opinion. It might be worth noting to this particular nurse, however caring she might be, that this child's mother and father preferred fact to opinion. I'd just been unscrambling the words in my jumbled-up brain to do so, but I was too late. The "best of the best" were on the move.

"Shaw, don't leave me." Cassidy's hand slipped from mine as I was jostled to the side as if I were of no importance to the woman carrying the baby they were trying so hard to save. But how do you get mad about something like that when it's your baby?

The hospital staff pulled the bed away from the wall, yanked the cord from the monitor and proceeded out the door. I went to follow but an iron grip wrapped around my wrist and held me back.

"I need to go with her." I growled the words and tried to yank out of Nurse Evil Eye's hold.

"And you will," she promised. A scowl was etched on her face, accentuating her features into one long line of disapproval. She slapped a plastic-covered package to my chest. "As soon as you put this on. I'll be waiting just outside the door to escort you when you're ready."

"Okay." I ran my fingers through my hair, not really sure where to start first, but knowing I needed to get my ass in gear.

"Unless you want to miss the birth of your child, I suggest you get a move on," Nurse Evil Eye said, reading my mind. Or maybe she'd just done this a gazillion times during her career and had already known what to expect.

"Right." Dropping the package at my feet, my fingers went straight to the belt of my jeans.

"No, no, no," my escort said, stopping me. "They go over your clothes, genius. Hurry up." And that was all she said before she turned and made a speedy exit, shutting me in the room that had just been bustling with activity only moments before and leaving me all alone.

Alone. I definitely felt the weight of that word, but I didn't have to because I wasn't the only one likely freaking out about all of this. Though she was no doubt surrounded by too many people, Cassidy was the one who was alone. The medical staff— adept as they may be—were strangers. Not the father of her soon-to-be-born child. And that wasn't okay with me.

Holy shit, I was about to be a father. I'd had thirty-eight weeks to prepare for this moment—actually, twenty-eight weeks, considering Cassidy had been eight weeks along when she'd first found out, but had waited another two weeks before telling me—and I was suddenly aware of how unprepared I really was. From the moment I'd heard those two little words—"I'm pregnant"—I'd gone through a whole lifetime of emotions. *My* lifetime.

I'd had the shittiest parents in the world. They couldn't even be called parents as far as I was concerned. Born the only child to a swindler father who was never around and an alcoholic mother who wished she wasn't, I'd been left to fend for myself on the brutally hard streets of Detroit. I'd seen nightmares happen before my very eyes, survived by any means necessary, and my seed donors never knew or even cared to know how I'd done it. I was a burden, plain and simple, just an extra mouth to feed that they never fed, but the government funding sure was a nice bit of icing on their dysfunctional cake.

I was going to be different. I was going to make my child, gender as yet unknown, the center of my world. Everything I did from here on out would be all about making a better life for him or her. Fuck my hang-ups over my own parents. Fuck the flip-flopping between being terrified, anxious, happy, and then terrified again. Failure had never been an option for me, and it sure as shit wouldn't ever be now.

Besides, I had the most determined partner in life that I'd ever known. Cassidy Whalen.

We'd started out as adversaries, and not one single person I'd encountered in my life had been able to give me a run for my money quite the same way Cassidy had. Not even close. We'd gone toe-to-toe for a partnership at the same sports agency where we worked, Cassidy winning, though I'd ended up with the title when she'd turned it down. And what had started out as an underhanded evasive maneuver to throw her off her game and into my bed had only managed to catapult her into my heart instead.

The impossible had been made possible by her doing. She'd tamed me.

I loved her. Really fucking loved her. And I'd never thought the emotion was possible for a man like me who'd done a damn good job of keeping illogical shit like that at bay. If it wasn't driving the bottom line, it didn't deserve my time. Now, because of her presence in my life, I was a regular guy; a domesticated man with a little woman at home and an unofficial family, her family, in Stonington, Maine.

And our family was getting bigger. Christ, moments from now, I'd know if I had a son or a daughter. I'd be someone's daddy . . . provided he or she survived the birth process. My heart hammered hard and fast in my chest with trepidation and anticipation.

Shoving one leg after the other into the scrubs, I grabbed the rest of the blue stuff in the bag and donned it the best I could figure out. I'd just tied the cap on my head when Nurse Evil Eye popped the door open again.

"They're not going to wait on you, sunshine. Let's go." Why couldn't I have gotten the nice one?

Cassidy had a death grip on my hand and it was starting to hurt, but I refused to tell her that. Not after seeing all she had been through for the last few hours. Shortly after three A.M. she had woken up with contractions strong enough to take her breath away. Things seemed to move pretty fast after that and there wasn't time to think about how early the baby was coming, how unprepared I felt, and how scared shitless I was at the thought of being a dad. When Cassidy's water had broken in the car, I'd wished to hell I had said yes to those stupid birthing classes. I was starting to feel light-headed as my breathing picked up and matched laboring Cassidy's erratic pace.

Now sitting on a small swiveling stool in the OR, my fingers were about as numb as the rest of me.

Cassidy tugged at my arm. "Can you see anything? What's happening?"

God, please don't ask me to peek over the blue drape. I don't think my stomach could take it.

"Aren't you, like, supposed to be knocked out or something? Why are you awake?"

Not waiting for a reply, I repeated the question to the doctor beside me, the same one who had given Cassidy medicine through her IV earlier in her room. "Why is she awake?" My leg was doing an imitation of a Mexican jumping bean under the paper scrubs I was given back in the exam room. Armani it was not.

I had since learned that said doctor was the anesthesiologist, and he would be making sure that Cassidy was comfortable during the C-section. Panic bubbled and fizzed inside my gut and I was suddenly unprepared for this moment. The constant beeping from machines coming from something that resembled a prop used on a *Doctor Who* episode wasn't helping. And I had yet to figure out if I should be concerned with all those squiggly lines dancing across a monitor, spiking up and down in an erratic pattern.

"She's fine, Mr. Matthews. And she has an epidural for pain relief. She should be fairly comfortable throughout the procedure."

"Fairly?" First *should be* and now *fairly*. I had the sudden urge to ask everyone present in the room for their credentials. Starting with the anesthesiologist, aka Dr. Feel Good.

"What the hell does that mean?" Cassidy asked as she tried her best to give Dr. Feel Good the stink eye. Which, admittedly, was kind of hard to do when you were strapped down to a table with your insides about to be brought out to play by the medical staff.

Ugh, that visual is so not helping you, Matthews.

"It means you might feel some tugging shortly, Mrs. Matthews, but that's totally normal."

"Ms. Whalen," Cassidy corrected him. "We're not married."

"My apologies," Dr. Feel Good said, with a cut glance in my direction, I might add. "What you shouldn't feel is pain. If you do, let me know."

At that point, Cassidy winced and I leaned in closer, kissing her cheek. Sweat coated her face and neck, her copper hair damp. She looked what she would call a hot mess. But she was my hot mess, and she was about to give birth to my child.

She had never looked more beautiful.

"You okay?" I didn't like the way Cassidy's color seemed to drain from her face.

"Yes . . . it's just . . . a lot of pressure." She managed a weak smile.

Feeling helpless, I pushed her hair back and away from her face, stroking her scalp with the pads of my fingers, offering her some sort of comfort in the only way I knew how. My gaze never left hers and a single thought ran through my mind with utter clarity. This was where I belonged. I had found something essential, something invaluable, and it was mine. Ours. Cassidy and I had created a child; a tiny, living human made up of pieces of ourselves. A connection no one could take away or break. As overwhelming as that was, it also felt so fucking right.

"Get ready to meet your little bundle of joy, folks."

Forgetting how much I didn't want to see Cassidy's insides, I rose from the stool and peered over the drape.

Okay, let's just say what was on the other side was *not* pretty. In fact, I forced my eyes away from things that needed to be unseen and zeroed in on what could only be described as a tiny alien covered in blood and body fluids. I felt a little green behind the gills until I spotted what looked like an impressive package dangling between the smallest legs I have ever seen.

"Holy shit, it's a boy! Look at the size of his cock. . . ." I cleared my throat. "I mean, his penis." Damn, but the little dude took after his dad.

The surgeon quickly cut off my son's dick, and before I could blink, he passed the baby off to someone standing near and holding out a blanket. "Whoa, Doc. I didn't know you did the circumcision so soon. Did you have to cut off *that* much?" My poor son, minus part of his junk, was then whisked away to the corner of the room where a shitload of other people had gathered.

"Um, no. That was the umbilical cord," came the subdued reply from the doctor. "But you were right, Mr. Matthews. Congratulations, you have a son."

The most unbelievable wave of pure warmth and joy spread through every fiber of my being. A son. I had a son. The smile that bolted up my cheeks made my face instantly go numb.

I had a son. . . .

But something was wrong. You could sense it with how quiet the room grew as the staff huddled around some sort of contraption where they had placed my little man. I couldn't see anything. There were too many people. And my throat had shrunk down to the size of a grain of sand, allowing only a wheeze to escape as I stood frozen, unable to breathe.

"What's going on?" Cassidy sobbed, trying to lift her head. The anesthesiologist bent down and tried to console her. Something I should have been doing. But I knew if I turned to her—looked at her—I would lose it.

"Shaw, why isn't he crying?"

God, please let everything be all right. Please cry, little man.

I have never been a religious man. But in that moment, I prayed. Hard. I would have begged and bartered my own soul with the devil himself. Every second that passed without a sound from that corner felt like a thousand minutes. A million lifetimes.

Muddled voices giving explanations I couldn't comprehend bounced around my head. I was drowning. Again.

"Shaw . . . stay with me." The feminine, docile tone pulled at me, as I struggled to keep my head above water. Blindly, I reached out and felt Cassidy's cold fingers grasp my own. Her touch grounded me and gave me the strength I needed.

Finally, after what seemed like an eternity, the most wonderful earsplitting wail filled the operating room.

I collapsed back on the stool like a stone and let loose a long, shaky breath. "He's okay." I squeezed her hand and tried to squelch the lingering fear under my skin. "I mean, he's truly okay? Right?" I asked for confirmation from the doctor, who I couldn't see behind the drape. My palm was sweaty but I refused to let Cassidy's hand go.

"Sounds like he has a strong set of lungs, Mr. Matthews. He just needed a minute to clear out his airway, and it didn't help that the umbilical cord had been wrapped around his neck. That's what was causing all the trouble in the labor room."

Really, I heard nothing past *strong set of lungs*. All the rest was gibberish; medical mumbo jumbo that meant nothing to me. The little bugger hadn't stopped bawling, and a niggling of doubt resurfaced. "All that crying is good, right? He's not in any pain, is he?"

One of the nurses—hell, it was hard to tell with all the blue scrubs, masks, and awful head covers in the place—approached the bed. In her arms was a tiny blanket-wrapped bundle. She arranged the squirming wad of cotton on Cassidy's chest. "Why don't you take a look for yourself," she murmured behind the mask.

I lost the ability to move. I had no words.

Peeking out from his warm cocoon, his pink face scrunched up in midcry, was the most amazing thing I had ever seen.

When I remained frozen and didn't respond, the nurse chuckled and placed my arm behind my son to help keep him in a protective hold before stepping away.

"You have your legacy, Shaw. He's beautiful." Cassidy's softspoken words had the effect of a battering ram, right in the solar plexus.

Shaw Matthews, a rehabilitated selfish asshole extraordinaire, had a legacy. It was hard to tell which of us he looked like in his current state, but there was no denying he had his mommy's ginger curls. A lot of it, too, which I'd been told would explain all the heartburn she'd had. And then he took a chance and slowly opened his eyes to take a glimpse at the world. Baby blue peepers. Just like his papa, who, incidentally, was the first sight he beheld.

"No, he's more than beautiful," I told her, falling in love with the way he blinked his eyes. "He's perfect." My voice cracked, my face hurt from smiling nonstop, and my vision may have blurred a little with unshed tears, but I was too damn happy to give a shit.

I reached out and stroked his cheek with my thumb. *Incredible.* He was soft and warm. And when he turned his head toward my touch, his tiny mouth working in a sucking motion, I was a goner.

"So?" Cassidy said around a dazzling, brilliant smile of her own. "Have you decided which name we're going with?"

We'd opted to wait until the birth of our baby to know the sex, but Cassidy had picked two names for each. Although I'd liked both of the names she'd come up with for a boy, I'd wanted to wait until I met him to decide. One look at him, and I knew.

With a nod, I said my first words to our son. "Welcome to the world, Abe. It can be a cold, cruel bitch, but we've got your back." The words felt thick on my tongue, but were no less true. I would not fail my son like my parents had failed me. I would be there, for everything.

"Always," I swore.

And I fucking meant it.

"Abraham Whalen Matthews." Cassidy's voice caressed each syllable as if embracing them in that motherly tone would cement them in time. I think it did. "We're going to love you forever. You'll see."

As Cassidy leaned forward to kiss his forehead, I did the same to her. She shivered as if an invisible, yet unbreakable, bond between the three of us had formed with our dual action. Real or not, it didn't matter. It was there, and I was going to protect it at all cost.

This was my family.